I0667751

TO TRUST AND PROTECT

A SHIFTER ROMANCE

CLAIMED

CHRISTINA MATTINGLY

To my readers-
This book is for everyone who's ever been broken and didn't let it stop them from creating a new life for themselves.
I hope you find your Owen, I hope your Axel gets the fate they deserve, but mostly I hope you create a life where you feel safe and loved.

You're not alone.
With love,

Christina Mattingly

NOTE TO THE READER

This book is the second in a series.

The story is standalone, but if you want a full picture of life in Pinehurst and the magical world it's set in, I highly recommend starting with Battle Within.

CHAPTER ONE

OWEN

*E*ngine 30, respond, emergency traffic at the intersection of Red River Parkway and Jennings Road in reference to a single-vehicle MVA. Unknown occupants, unknown injuries.

"Engine 30, copy," Owen mumbled automatically into the radio he'd fumbled from his nightstand as soon as the tones had dropped.

Cursing loudly, Owen heard his partner next door doing the same as they rolled out of bed, dressing with nothing but muscle memory as his brain jolted awake. He looked at his watch - just after midnight.

"Gods damn it," Owen grumbled. He'd had a long shift at the Sheriff's department the day before and was looking forward to a night without calls, but of course, the EMS gods had different plans.

"Fuck this shit," John groused as he emerged from his room at the same time.

"When will people learn they can't drive down the highway going forty over in the rain?" John demanded, opening the fridge. "Want anything?"

"Nah, I'm good," Owen said, shaking his head at the stupidity of reckless drivers.

HUMANS ARE STUPID, Finley, his wolf, said grumpily through their mental link as they made their way back into the EMS base

Yeah, they are, Owen agreed as he sank into the chair in the dayroom, tipping his head back in exhaustion.

He glanced across the room and groaned. The bright green numbers on the microwave clock announced it was just past three in the morning. Paramedic John McIntyre stood at the open fridge, texting his mate, who was up with an acute case of pregnancy-induced insomnia.

Owen seriously considered doing his report in the morning, closing his eyes for just a second when tones cued up over the radio again. Owen kept his eyes shut determinedly as if keeping them shut would keep him from getting paged.

EMS respond to 987 Runner's Way, reference a sick person.

"Don't do it," John said warningly to the radio, but dispatch continued.

Fire respond to 987 Runner's Way for a lift assist.

"You've got to be kidding me," John groaned, letting his head fall against the side of the refrigerator door.

"I've got it. You get some sleep," Owen said.

"I'll come - it's Mrs Jenkins," John replied, pocketing his phone.

The EMS crew, Ryder and Blake, emerged from their rooms, bleary-eyed. Blake nodded to Owen and John, who piled into one of the county's pickup trucks and pulled out just after Blake and Ryder left in 301, the county's new ambulance.

The night continued in the same fashion, running Owen and John ragged until the next morning when everything went blissfully quiet, giving everyone a chance to catch up on reports and caffeinate.

Ryder sighed, rubbing his eyes as he looked over his last report, squinting at it with one eye shut before growling out of mental and physical exhaustion.

"Hey, you know if Emma is stopping by before the meeting?" Blake asked on his way through the kitchen. "I was hoping she might bring me an extra shirt."

"She is. I'll ask her," Ryder said, pulling out his phone, and staring at the screen for a moment before remembering the code to unlock it.

"What are they in town for? I assumed they were still testing their... stuff," Owen said, unsure what exactly Ryder's mate and her best friend had been doing at the Lodge where they'd been working on a big project.

"The testing for their project has been accepted by the legal team. Now they just have to get it approved by the local government people," Ryder said as he texted his mate. "So, today's the meeting for that."

"They got a meeting that fast?" Owen asked, eyebrows raising. "Damn, what kind of magic does James do? Just scheduling road repairs is a challenge, not to mention organizing a magic production."

"He's a charisma mage," Blake volunteered.

"Well, that explains that," Owen commented. "That's one way to get things done, I suppose."

"Yeah, a few days ago, James went into everyone's offices with a notice for the meeting with a time and place and a menu for the catered lunch stapled to the outside of their proposal. Now it's happening," Ryder said with a shrug. "Blake, Emma wants to know if you need a shirt or a whole uniform."

"May as well bring the whole spare uniform," Blake said. "If I don't ask for it, I'll need it."

"You think they're using magic to influence the outcome of the meeting?" Owen asked quietly.

Blake and Ryder shared a brief look across the room that confirmed Owen's suspicion that James and Emma were doing exactly that. Owen chuckled to himself. Ryder was normally a stickler for protocol. It made him an excellent training officer, and a great person to work with new paramedics and med students who came to fulfill their education requirements with Pinehurst EMS.

If Ryder stayed silent while his mate used magic to influence government officials for a project, his imprinting on Emma was the only logical reason for his complicit attitude. The Ryder Owen worked with before he'd imprinted never would have let that stand.

Half an hour later, the men were preparing to do the morning's base duties when Emma breezed through the front lobby. She looked stunning in a navy blue dress that hugged her curves and swished tantalizingly around her thighs as she moved.

"Hey baby," Ryder nuzzled Emma's cheek with an affectionate rumble.

"Hi there," Emma said in a low, seductive voice that made even Owen's wolf perk up.

Wooo, Finley thought. *I wish they shared! I bet she's feisty in bed.*

They do, but I don't think Ryder's crazy about it, Owen replied back through their mental connection.

"What are you up to?" Ryder asked.

"James, Connor, and I have a meeting with the chief and a few others. I wanted to come over and say hi to you first," she said, running her fingers through Ryder's hair.

"Mm, I'm glad you did."

Sipping the energy drink Owen had grabbed from his emergency stash, he watched Emma.

"You guys feeling confident about this meeting?" Ryder asked as his mate played with his hair, closing his eyes and growling as she used her nails on his scalp.

"Oh, we'll definitely get approved. There's no question," Emma said confidently, earning a frown from Ryder, who seemed reluctant to open his eyes and interrupt her.

Ah, there he is, Owen thought with a chuckle. *Mr. Rule follower.*

"Why is there no question? I thought the Chief Ranger was dead set against it." Ryder asked.

"Well," Emma grinned guiltily, ducking her head as she pressed her hips against his. But he wasn't going to be distracted, no matter how appealing she was.

I want a mate like that, Finley thought wistfully.

One who gets us in trouble by doing magic she shouldn't? Owen asked.

Well, maybe not that. But how about someone who bakes?

We'd get fat, Owen said, not opposed to the idea.

We could exercise it off with her! Finley suggested.

Fair. I'll start looking for girls who bake.

With hips, and a nice butt for smacking. Assuming she likes that. She should like that since that's one of our things. Add that to the list too! Finley added.

Owen gave his silent agreement and returned his attention to Emma and Ryder. The two of them had gotten off to a rough start, and when they argued, it tended to be volatile. While it did make him happy that Ryder was happy, Owen wasn't watching for his own pleasure. He wanted to make sure Ryder's wolf, Xander, didn't take offense to Emma's provocative outfit or to make sure Ryder's concern about her not following the rules didn't set off Emma's hair-trigger temper.

"What did you do?" Ryder asked his mate quietly.

"I didn't do anything. James may have had a discussion with him," Emma shrugged, a mischievous smile tipping up the corners of her lips.

"Baby," Ryder warned, tilting her chin up with one finger.

"What?" Emma asked with false innocence.

Connor, an intense weather mage who worked with storms and lightning as a specialty, strode in through the same door Emma had just come through, looking sharp in a business black suit jacket, a black shirt, and dark wash jeans. Owen thrust his chin in greeting. Connor raised two fingers in return.

"Don't do anything to get you into trouble," Ryder ordered Emma, not looking up from his mate.

"I'll make sure they don't," Connor said from behind Emma.

"Thank you," Ryder said, pursing his lips at Emma.

Emma spoke before Ryder could lecture her on safety or ethics, which Owen figured she wouldn't have listened to in any case.

"Hey, I have a question. I was wondering if you wanted to go on a hike tomorrow?" She asked, stepping forward so her hips pressed into his.

Owen opened his tablet, starting on one of the reports from last night. If Connor was here, he could probably handle Emma and Ryder better than Owen could, so Owen returned to his work.

"Just a hike, or..."

"Well, I've been so busy, and I was thinking I could spend some time with you before things get really hectic around here. A girl has needs," she reminded him flirtatiously, speaking softly so other humans with normal hearing wouldn't overhear.

Considering most of the station was made of shifters, it was pointless, but the briefest glance at Ryder told Owen that Ryder wasn't thinking about that as his fingers traced up the back of Emma's arm.

"You know, I have an office with a perfectly good desk I haven't bent you over yet," Ryder suggested huskily.

"Ryder, get a hold of yourself." The chief's voice cut through Ryder's sensual promise like a bucket of ice water.

"Morning, chief," Emma laughed, pulling away as Ryder snapped up from the place where he'd reclined, leaning back on the table with her standing between his legs.

"You walking over?" The chief asked Emma.

"Yeah."

"Where's your... young friend?" the chief asked.

"He's waiting outside," Emma supplied.

"I'll see you there in a minute. I have a few questions I want to ask him before we get into this meeting with everyone else," their chief said.

"Definitely, I'll be right there," she promised.

As the chief walked away, she settled herself between Ryder's legs again, thrusting her hips suggestively. Ryder groaned, pulling her against him, and kissed her neck several times before she pulled away.

"I've got to go, but I'll see you tonight. Want us to save you some food?"

"You could save me some food," Owen called from across the kitchen.

James had rented out the Lodge, the only real accommodations in Pinehurst, then hired a few local girls with skills in the kitchen to cook for the video crew. At James' invitation, anyone who worked at the base was welcome to drop by anytime for food. Owen didn't enjoy cooking just for himself, and anything the cook at the Lodge made was usually fancier than what he would make. Who was he to turn down good food he didn't have to make?

"I will!" Emma promised over her shoulder.

"Butt out, Owen," Ryder said without rancor as he winked at Emma. "That would be nice. Have a good time with your guys. Good luck, I love you."

"You love me? Are you sure?" she teased.

"Don't tempt me to make you late for your meeting because you were bent over my desk because you were asking stupid questions," Ryder threatened as she walked away.

"Mm. Sounds promising. Maybe next time. I'll be good."

"Don't be reckless," he half-commanded, half-pleaded.

"I've got my eye on both of them," Connor promised gravely, with a nod to Ryder before he followed Emma out.

"I'm gonna go grab my stuff. Be right back," Blake promised, following them out into the hallway, leaving Ryder and Owen alone.

"So, clearly you two are... good now," Owen said with a nod at the door Emma just exited through. "But, are you good?"

"With regards to..." Ryder grabbed a drink from the fridge, holding up a water bottle to Owen.

Owen nodded, so Ryder tossed him one before grabbing another for himself.

"Everything. Your imprinting, your wolf... problem." Owen said, "It was a rough couple of months, and while Blake's a great partner, I imagine it's not the same talking to your girl's brother."

"It's hard. I still have times when I struggle. When I'm doing a lot and I'm breathing hard my brain... resets somehow because of what she did to heal the bond between Xander and me. It takes me a second to get my head on straight. The imprinting isn't so bad now that Xander and I aren't at each other's throats all the time."

"What's it like, being so in tune with another person?" Owen asked.

Imprinting was rare, so rare it was little more than a footnote in medical textbooks.

"It's like having my soul ripped out and walking around in someone else's body."

"That sounds… romantic," Owen laughed.

Um. That sounds awful. Let's… not do that. Finley said uneasily.

I completely agree. Owen thought back.

"You know that feeling when you first start dating somebody and it's all new and fresh? You wait for every text, smile at every phone call?"

"Yup,"

"It's like that, but every day it's still new. Like, Emma doesn't do anything before coffee. When I bring her coffee in bed, she makes this one particular smile that hits me in the feels, every time. Everything's like that," Ryder said with a little grin.

"That's pretty fucking cool," Owen said.

You're being polite, right? Finley asked, concern filling their mental bond.

Of course, I am. Telling your friend him finding his mate sounds like the worst case of puppy love in a grown man you've ever seen isn't nice. Owen thought back, fighting the urge to roll his eyes.

"It makes it a lot worse when we fight, but there are ups and downs to everything. How are things with you?"

"Not much, really," Owen said. "Just work, mostly. Thinking about selling my mom's house and getting a place of my own, but I don't know. My apartment is fine and without a family, I don't want more space to manage. I guess I'm just keeping things simple until something comes along to change that."

"Well, then it can be your turn next," Ryder said with a laugh.

Tones dropped, calling Ryder's unit over the radio. Clapping

Owen's shoulder as he stood, Ryder chuckled as Owen shook his head.

It was all fun and games to joke about, but Owen wasn't looking for the head-over-heels insta-love affection that imprinting brought. Slow and steady was just fine. Ryder and Emma's courtship had been a whirlwind of drama and angst, but Owen didn't have the energy or the patience for that - he'd stick with traditional courting, whenever he found the right girl.

CHAPTER TWO

CAITLIN

*C*aitlin had just finished a batch of scones. She would need to run to the store to get some flour - maybe she could get home and back before Axel was awake. Pouring her tea into a travel mug, Caitlin walked into the front hall and grabbed her coat off the accordion coat rack, and slipped it over her shoulders. Her eyes traveled over the unfinished wood of the rack, the surface covered with grime after many years of use.

She walked back into the kitchen to add cleaning and painting the rack to her list of projects she wanted to do to make their trailer nicer. None of the projects were big, but each one she completed gave her a sense of satisfaction, and over time, she would make this place nice.

Last week she'd borrowed her mother-in-law's sewing machine to make a set of old curtains into valences in the kitchen and dining room. She took a sip of her tea, glancing around the room. The navy blue fabric covered in small white paisley swirls wasn't her favorite. She never would have purchased the fabric if she'd gone to the store, but it had been free from the church's swap meet and it had thrilled her to use it to make their space nicer.

Looking over the finished valances, she swelled with pride, a little bubble of excitement growing in her.

"What do you think?" She gestured around the room when Axel came in from work. She didn't bother to greet him with a kiss. If she tried to kiss him now, he would rebuff her and make her wait until after he'd showered.

"About what?" he asked, looking around with bland disinterest.

"The valences! I made them!" Caitlin exclaimed.

"What's a valence?" He asked with a frown.

"The short curtains," she answered, her excitement dimming a little at his lack of interest or enthusiasm.

"They're nice," he said with a shrug.

"Do you like them?" she pressed.

She should have known if he didn't care enough to volunteer more information the first time she asked, then pressing him further wouldn't make him say anything she wanted to hear, but she pressed on, looking for any scrap of approval.

"I don't see the point in curtains that don't cover the windows, but if that's how you want to spend your time, that's fine. I thought you wanted to start that bakery thing?" He'd kicked off his boots and walked in before getting a mason jar of water.

Axel drained the jar haphazardly, leaving a trail of water leaking down his beard. Her mate sighed and wiped the liquid off his beard and onto his stained jeans, then set the jar down on the spotless counter. Caitlin suppressed her frustration as she watched as condensation from the jar made a ring of water tinged with black grime from his hands on her clean countertop. Suppressing a sigh, she picked up his boots and placed them on the boot rack that was less than a foot away from where he'd dropped them. He unbuttoned and untucked his work shirt while she wiped up the mess on the counter with a warm, wet cloth.

"Having a pleasant space to work in" she started to explain for the hundredth time, but he wasn't ready to hear her.

"Whatever, Kitty Cat. I just want you to be happy. If you want pointless curtains and that keeps you from complaining, then I'm happy. Just don't complain to me about not having money when you're spending your time on stuff like this. It must have taken forever sewing it all by hand."

"I borrowed your mom's sewing machine," she informed him, wincing when he set down the jar with a loud thud behind her.

She kept her back turned to him while she worked on heating his dinner, closing her eyes and praying that he would just let it go.

"You did what?" he demanded.

"She didn't mind," she tried to explain.

"Great, now she's going to think I can't afford to get you things."

"If the shoe fits," she muttered under her breath.

Not that she minded not having a lot of money, but it didn't feel nice to have to agonize over every purchase and to wonder where she would have to scrimp when she needed to spend money for even the most basic things.

Axel stomped out of the kitchen, slamming the bedroom door behind him. She breathed a sigh of relief. Maybe he would pout while he played a video game and they could avoid a fight. At least for a while, she had some quiet while he showered off the grime that came with being a mechanic. She finished heating his food and set it out with a cold beer on the table, then made herself a cup of tea and sat looking at her mother's old worn cookbook. Maybe tomorrow she'd go to the store and get some supplies. One of the wolf pack ladies had said they'd pay her to make some treats for her holiday party.

It was a little while before her mate emerged from the bedroom, freshly scrubbed, but looking no less irritable.

"Aren't you eating?" he asked, glaring at his lone plate.

"I ate a while ago," she said, not looking up at him.

Would the Snickerdoodle cookies be better, or maybe the brownie cookies? The brownie cookies were fancier, but Caitlin hadn't made them in years. If the recipe was in her mother's book, she knew it would be tasty, but Caitlin wanted these to be excellent, delicious enough to make the women in the pack want more.

She decided to make a small batch of brownie cookies in the morning as a trial, but use the Snickerdoodle recipe if she wasn't satisfied with the results. At least Axel wouldn't complain about having fresh baked goods in the house - probably.

"You couldn't bother to wait for me?" he loomed over her, placing a damp hand on the page of the cookbook while he bent to glare at her.

"You don't wait for me when I'm not here," she pointed out.

"I was working, Caitlin! I wasn't sitting around gossiping with your sister."

Lifting his hand from the cookbook, it came away with a loud rustle and a ripping noise that felt loud in the quiet of her kitchen. Caitlin winced and smoothed out the page before she replied with patience she didn't feel.

"I wasn't sitting around gossiping. I was helping her plan her baby shower."

She'd explained this a dozen times, but he refused to see it. Harriet was having her third baby. She'd asked Caitlin to help her plan the baby shower. Caitlin had texted Axel to tell him she'd be an hour later than she'd planned. She'd come home to a sullen husband who spent the rest of the night on his game system in sullen silence.

"I don't understand what's so complicated about it. She's already got two babies. Doesn't she have enough crap for them? It sounds like she just wants more attention."

"Wanting attention isn't unhealthy. Everyone needs positive attention. It's a basic human need. Besides, it's been nine years since she had the boys. She wants new girl things for little Eliza."

"Typical." he rolled his eyes. "Any excuse to throw a party for herself. I guess some things never change."

"If you're going to be an ass, I'm going to bed."

"Fine."

She'd made herself a cup of strong valerian tea and curled up with a book. When her eyelids grew heavy, she closed the book and switched off the light, burrowing under the blankets. The tea made her groggy, and she had no idea how long it was before she felt his body climbing into bed behind her. He pressed against her with an appreciative groan.

"Let's not fight anymore," he murmured.

"Okay," she said, halfway to the dream world.

"I was looking forward to spending the other evening with you. I was disappointed, and I was hurt that you didn't want to spend it with me."

"It was one night, Axel," Caitlin reminded him.

"It was the only night I've been home in two weeks and you couldn't be bothered to be home," he fumed.

"Yeah, because you've been drinking and playing poker up the street."

"You could come with me, but you won't."

"The smoke makes me feel sick," she said, her words slurring.

"You can just take your allergy medicine," he suggested.

Irritability surged through her, but she couldn't quite work up the physical energy to do more than murmur barely coherent responses.

"Allergy medicine doesn't make cigarette smoke good for your body," she said, rolling onto her back so she could see his face, making a monumental effort to stay conscious as her mouth opened in a jaw-popping yawn.

"I need to network for my business, Caitlin. You know that. What's with you?"

"I drank sleepy tea. Besides, playing cards with the same four guys you grew up with isn't 'networking' - that's hanging out."

"And what the hell would you know about it? You know so much about running a business from what, all your time babysitting?"

"I thought you didn't want to argue," she pointed out.

Gods, she was so tired. She was sleepy, but also weary of his constant belittling. All she wanted to do was sleep. Everything would be better in the morning. He would leave for work and she would have a few hours of peace.

"I'm not the one arguing!"

"Fine. You win. Goodnight." She rolled back over to her side and sighed, letting herself sink into exhaustion.

"I'm sorry, Kitty Cat. I'm just trying to make things better for us, and this is the only way I know how."

She thought of the marketing books she'd gotten for him that had sat unopened until she'd stopped renewing them and returned them to the library after she'd renewed them for the maximum time the library allowed. Those might have had some ideas, but that would have required him to do something new, which would never happen. The thought was the last one she had before sleep took her.

SHE COULDN'T HAVE BEEN sure, but she thought she was awake when she felt Axel's hot body pressing against her, his erection digging into her back painfully.

"Kitty Cat, I'm sorry," he whispered in the darkness.

"S'okay," she mumbled, scooting away from him.

"Please don't be mad at me. You know I can't go to sleep if you're mad at me," he cajoled.

"I'm not mad. I'm sleeping," she mumbled.

Now there was no mistaking it. His erection dug into her back again as he pressed his hips into hers.

"I want to give you everything you want," he was murmuring in her ear, along with other words her brain was too foggy to process.

"Okay," she heard herself say.

"Thank you, Kitty Cat," he pulled on the waistband of her underwear.

"Axel, no," she objected.

"I'll be quick, baby. I just need you."

"No, I'm tired. I want to sleep," she objected.

"Baby, I need this."

She sighed in resignation. She was too tired to fight him and didn't want the days of pouting that would follow if she rejected him.

"No."

She said the word, hoping that this time it would matter. She threw it out like a life raft, even as he pushed one of her legs to the side and slid his fingers over her entrance.

"You're wet for me, baby. I knew you wanted me," he said, voice heavy with relief.

It was easier just to let him have what he wanted, so she didn't resist when he spread her legs, rolling her onto her stomach to give him access.

He climbed between her legs, sighing as he entered her. She squeezed her eyes shut as he took his pleasure with her, finishing with a grunt. She rolled back onto her side as sleep overtook her, his seed slipping out of her as she fought the familiar disgust that she'd given in to him and not held her ground.

CAITLIN OPENED HER EYES. She wasn't in the trailer. She was in Pinehurst, safe in her therapist's office. Olivia was holding out a fidget toy, which Caitlin took with a grateful nod as she reoriented herself in her therapist's office.

"Was that the first time he assaulted you?" Her therapist, Olivia, asked.

"Oh, no. Me saying no was never really an option. He only ever listened when I was screaming or angry. Even then, it was a battle." Caitlin said, twisting the fidget toy in her hand. "But I think that was the first time that I said no and he just flat-out ignored it. I know it's not what I'm supposed to say, but I feel bad bringing it up."

"Alright, let's examine that. What makes you feel bad about bringing it up?" her therapist prompted.

"I mean, but what if he misunderstood? It's not like I fought him off."

"Should you have to fight off your partner?" Olivia asked.

"No, I guess not."

"What should not-consenting look like?"

"Not like that," Caitlin forced a chuckle, trying to diffuse her tension. When Olivia said nothing, Caitlin shrugged. "I guess I don't know, actually."

"Why shouldn't it look like that?" Olivia prompted.

"Because they should listen to my words the first time," Caitlin recited with an irritated head bob. "But what if he thought me opening my legs was me consenting? Was it my fault for giving mixed signals?"

"Giving in to coercion is not the same as consenting," Olivia instructed, her tone gentle.

"How can your partner tell the difference?"

"They shouldn't be coercing you in the first place, Caitlin. If Axel had respected you the first time you said no, or the second, you wouldn't have been put in a situation where you had to choose between upholding your boundaries and giving in to keep things peaceful between the two of you so you could go to sleep."

"Right," Caitlin said, trying to see it that way, even as the familiar guilt nagged at her.

"It is not your fault," Olivia emphasized.

"I'm not sure I believe you. I want to, but it feels like maybe it was my fault," she confessed, her eyes staying focused on the spinning balls of the toy that rotated under the pressure of her fingers.

"Yes, that's normal, and it may feel that way for a while. But trust me when I say that I would be honest if it was your fault, and it is not. My job isn't to help you feel good, it's to help you see the truth," a timer sounded on Olivia's phone. She reached over to turn it off. "Okay, we have fifteen minutes. Is there anything else you'd like to talk about before we wrap up?"

"No," Caitlin said. Reliving memories from her marriage to Axel was plenty for her for the day.

"Alright, so your homework is to say no, stand up for yourself, and/or put five boundaries in place before our next session."

"What? Why? That sounds terrible," Caitlin said, wrinkling her nose.

"It might feel terrible, and as to the why: one of your goals was to learn to feel safe having boundaries. The best way to do it is to practice it in a situation not related to your triggering incidents. Don't overthink it - keep it simple and low-pressure. I'm not talking about changing your life overnight, just practicing saying no to small things."

"I might hate you," Caitlin said without meaning it, standing and grabbing her purse from the couch.

As she walked to the door, she spotted a flyer for a bake sale to benefit the Pinehurst Fire Department. Grateful for an excuse to bake for other people, she took a picture with her phone.

"Do you want to do the bake sale? I'm sure anything you make would sell like crazy."

"That could be fun," Caitlin mused.

"I know the coordinator. Want me to tell her you're bringing something to sell? No pressure," Olivia said. "I just know how much you love to bake, and this way, it isn't sitting around the house for the kids. Plus, it's for a good cause."

Never needing much of a push to bake something, Caitlin agreed.

"I'll tell her you're bringing five hundred of your amazing cookies," Olivia said with a twinkle in her eye.

"Five hundred?!"

Caitlin looked at her in horror, then rolled her eyes when her therapist gave her a cheeky wink, her fingers poised over her cell screen, waiting for the real number she would bring. Caitlin pointed one finger with the hand that was wrapped around her purse strap.

"I'll bring fifteen or twenty batches, something around there. This better count as one of my five boundaries," Caitlin insisted with a laugh.

"Hah, if you like. See you at the bake sale," her therapist replied with a smile.

"Same to you, Olivia. Thanks for today."

CHAPTER THREE

OWEN

*T*he woman had one of those smiles. He didn't know who she was, but it didn't matter. The way her eyes sparkled was... something else. Finley perked up as Owen looked at her, his interest piqued. She was sturdy, with curvy hips that begged to have a man's fingers dug into them. The wavy brown hair from her ponytail wrapped around his fist. Owen had to force himself to look away before his imagination ran away with him.

"Hey, who's that?" Owen elbowed Calen Merrick, a fellow paramedic who was too busy chasing after his own potential mate to give Caitlin a second glance.

"I think her name's Caitlin. She's a friend of Olivia's," Calen replied.

"How are things going with your girl?" Owen asked, his eyes still on the girl who was adjusting the velcro on a wrist brace, wincing as she flexed her fingers.

I like her. Finley declared. *Awoooo, buddy, look at that body. She definitely has a nice booty. I wonder if she bakes, too!*

"She's stubborn," Calen grinned, "Giving me hell and not showing any signs of letting up."

"Has Cheyenne accepted you courting her yet?" Owen asked.

Shifters could declare their intent to court someone, which, if accepted by their intended mate, would give them a year. During that time, it was a sort of trial period to see how the couple got along. Most shifters preferred to take a style of dating more like the humans', but Calen was a biological alpha.

Born with the genes to be alpha of his own pack, he could go off and start his own pack if he wanted, but he preferred to stay as he was, living under the authority of their pack leader, Fire Chief Jason Beckett. Even if Calen didn't choose to exercise his right to start his own pack, the desire to claim a mate was stronger than most shifters.

When he'd met the beautiful Cheyenne, he and his wolf had decided to claim her and prove his worth as her mate, despite her reluctance and outright defiance. Cheyenne was one of the few women born with the alpha female gene, which gave her the pick of just about any male shifter she wanted. The wolf part of a male shifter's biology was too strong to ignore. Cheyenne hadn't taken much of a shine to Calen, so he'd been doing everything he could to impress her, bordering on the ridiculous. The more she pushed back, the more he wanted her.

Owen didn't get it. But then again, he wasn't an alpha. He wanted his women enthusiastic and freely consenting, with no reluctance and no misgivings. Fighting a potential mate for their attention sounded like torture to him personally.

"Man, I don't know how you do it. That would drive me crazy," Owen said.

You're driving me crazy. I wanna go talk to the Caitlin girl! Finley complained.

"Oh, it is. She's still trying to see other guys," Calen said darkly.

"How's that going for her?" Owen asked with a chuckle.

"Not very well. I ran Matt off the other night," Calen grinned at the memory. "I've never seen any wolf run so fast."

"Part-time medic, Matt?" Owen clarified.

"Same guy." Calen agreed. "I don't blame him. He's a decent guy, and pheromones are pheromones. He's a Beta, he can't help it. She's got that alpha female blood."

Calen blew out a breath, clearly enjoying the thought of his hot-blooded woman.

"Yeah. You can only fight biology so much," Owen agreed.

Speaking of fighting it off, stop talking to him and go say hi to her. He's not nearly as pretty as she is! Finley prodded.

"Why don't you quit staring and go say hi before she thinks you're a psycho?" Calen asked.

"What? Who?" Owen asked, tearing his eyes away from the girl.

"Olivia's friend, who you've been staring at since you came over."

"Oh. Well... " Owen said, hesitating.

"Man, just go say hi. Seriously," Calen said with a shove and a laugh.

OWEN MADE his way across the room, nodding politely to the other volunteers who greeted him. Instead of making his way over to the girl, he headed for their mutual friend Olivia. Everyone who was a part of the local EMS, sheriff's department, or fire department knew Olivia.

Working with the fae-blooded therapist was mandatory for all the town's first responders. When shit went down and calls went bad, Olivia was the one who got called in to provide counseling.

In most first responder agencies, a culture of 'I'll be fine,' pervaded, but Olivia's magic encouraged open honesty. Her easy laid-back demeanor made her fun to work with, and it didn't hurt that she was easy on the eyes. If you were going to have to bare your soul to some-one, doing it to a beautiful woman was much less intimidating than to a peer you'd have to sit next to for the next hundred shifts.

"Hey Livi, how are you doin'?" Owen asked, sidling up to her with a friendly smile.

"Just fine. How about you, Owen?" Olivia gifted him with a friendly smile as she arranged several stacks of disposable cups.

"I'm good. Do you know that girl, the brunette with the ponytail?" he asked, pointing to the girl in the dress.

"I do," she said with a knowing smile.

"Is she single?" Owen asked, scuffing the toe of his boot on the concrete floor of the bay.

She better be! Finley thought.

"She is, and she has a thing for fresh squeezed lemonade," she said with a meaningful look at the dispenser filled with lemonade on the table beside her.

"Thanks, doc," Owen said, grabbing a cup.

"Anytime," Olivia said, watching him approach him with interest, but he didn't notice. He only had eyes for the girl.

As he approached, Owen felt nervous sweat break out across his forehead. He could run into a burning building or deal with a shootout with nerves of steel, but the brunette across the room was

Why are you so nervous? Finley asked in his head. *You're making me itchy.*

I can't help it. Have you seen her? Owen took a deep breath.

Oh, I've seen her. She's nice looking, but you've got to calm down. If you look half as crazy as you feel, you're going to scare her off, his wolf advised.

Thanks, that's helpful. Owen retorted, taking a moment to breathe deeply and settle himself before approaching her.

"You look thirsty," he said, holding out the cup of lemonade, and thrusting it into her hands. She barely caught it, some of the yellow liquid spilling over both of their hands. "I'm Owen."

Smooth, Finley snickered.

Do you have any better ideas? Owen snapped sharply.

His wolf's mental voice was laced with amusement when he replied. *No, you're doing just fine. We planned to stay single forever, right?*

"Oh, thanks! I'm Caitlin. Are you here to lift heavy things for me?" she asked hopefully.

"I definitely can be."

Maybe she'll let us lift more than that if you can stop being weird. Finley suggested as he noticed the swirl of her skirt when she turned to set her drink down on the table.

Not. Helping. Owen replied, trying unsuccessfully to swallow the lump in his throat.

"Oh, sorry, I wasn't trying to assume. Olivia was supposed to send someone over for me. I've got a bum wrist," she said, biting her lip.

"I'm here to help out, so you just let me know what you need and I'll make it happen," Owen promised, blocking out the rather crude things Finley wanted to help her out with that also involved biting her lip.

"Really? Anything?" She asked, eyes shining with mischief.

"Oh, for sure," he agreed with an answering flirtatious smile.

I like her. His wolf approved. *And she smells good too!*

"These coolers need to be filled with ice, the blue one on this end, the red one down at the other end..." she directed him. He moved things for her, positioning them just so for her until she was satisfied.

"This looks perfect. I should grab my cookies from the car."

She does bake! Finley exclaimed. *Okay, she's got the things on the list, that means we're gonna take her home if she wants to, right?*

Finley, Owen growled, *shut up.*

"I'll give you a hand," Owen volunteered, eyeing the brace on her wrist.

He followed her out to her car. She began chatting, and Owen noted with some satisfaction that he wasn't the only one with nervous energy. Working hard to keep his eyes up on her face and not on the tantalizing skirt or the amount of leg the shirt left exposed, Owen listened to her.

"Thanks. I feel useless all the time these days. I had to have the kids do most of the work for the cookies." He listened to her recount the stories of their baking adventures in rapt attention.

She's enthusiastic, and she has kids! Finley all but pranced.

Yeah, she seems really sweet. Owen thought as he listened to her talk about the kids, her eyes shining with excitement and pride.

"How old are your kids?" he asked.

"Oh, no, they aren't my kids. They're my sister's. I'm just sort of the stand-in mommy at the moment while she's out of town for work. I'm not attached to anyone. It's just me." She explained, her cheeks coloring a little.

"No mate or boyfriend to help you out?" He asked casually.

The talky doctor said she was single already.

I'm not asking to see if she's single! Owen suppressed the desire to roll his eyes.

You totally were. Finley argued.

"Nope. It's these tubs." She indicated two enormous clear plastic bins sitting in the front and back seats of her car.

"Is this all cookies?" He asked in disbelief, eyes widening.

"Um. They said to expect a big turnout?"

"This might be enough cookies for the whole town," he said. As he shifted the large tub for easier carrying, he inhaled deeply and groaned in appreciation as his stomach rumbled. "But they smell amazing."

"Well, if they don't sell, I'm sure I could leave some at the fire station."

"Oh psh, people leave things there all the time. The deputies would appreciate it a lot more," he assured.

She eyed his Pinehurst deputy's softball t-shirt and chuckled.

"Would they?"

"Mm-hmm. The deputies here are chronically under-appreciated."

The Sheriff, a man with an enormous rounded stomach and a jovial smile, walked by in his uniform, greeting people with a friendly handshake and a booming laugh. Owen added in an undertone, "And underfed, clearly."

Caitlin stifled a laugh, then reluctantly stood by while he arranged the packages of cookies on her table.

"There should be a container at the bottom with a bunch of small cookies?" she asked. After he dug around, she rewarded him with a winning smile that made his chest swell like he'd just completed a task from the gods, not grabbing a bag of cookies.

"Perfect," she said as she set the smaller cookies into a bowl.

"Why are those smaller?" Owen asked, watching her. He didn't think it made a difference how the cookies sat in the bowl, but when she was finished arranging them, she nodded in satisfaction.

"They're samples," she explained.

"That's genius." He said, snatching one and popping it into his mouth. His eyes widened as he chewed the brownie-cookie mixture, which dissolved into an explosion of flavor in his mouth.

"Holy hairballs," he moaned, "This is the best thing I've ever eaten."

"Careful there, Owen, you're gonna make Patrick jealous." Brian Lawson, one of the EMS supervisors, said from beside him. The muscular medic carried a tub, similar to Caitlin's but smaller, on one shoulder.

"I hate to say this, Brian, but she's got Patrick beat by a mile," Owen said, snatching another cookie from the bowl, gesturing to them with enthusiasm.

"Hey! Those are samples. If you want more, buy some," she laughed.

Owen took out his wallet and counted the cash in his wallet, throwing it all down on her table.

"Forty-nine cookies, please."

"That's an insane amount of cookies," she said, not touching the money, eyes wide.

"Not these cookies, it isn't," he said, chewing his stolen sample.

"They can't be that good," Patrick objected, shifting the container he was carrying to grab one from the bowl.

"Sorry, I'm Brian. This is my husband, Patrick. He feels strongly about baked goods," Brian explained as his mate chewed slowly.

"Hold the baking pan. These are amazing," Patrick said, looking at Caitlin in awe. "I have to have your recipe."

"The recipe is part of the auction," she said helpfully, smiling with a look of pleased amusement.

"Hold these," Patrick said, shoving a box of his own baked goods into Owen's arms and striding purposefully over to the auction table.

Owen barely got a hold of the bin before it crashed to the floor.

"Sorry, he's... dedicated to his craft. Where are we setting up?" Brian asked, shaking his head with an indulgent smile as his partner made his way over to the auction table.

"Each vendor gets their own table." Caitlin said, "But they aren't assigned."

"I guess I'll set up here, then," Brian and Owen went to set up Patrick's baked goods while Caitlin packaged up Owen's cookies.

"Where do you want these?" She asked, gesturing to the several grocery bags full of cookies.

"I'll put them in my truck so none of these fuckers touch them," he said, opening another cookie after he grabbed the bags, eying a passing firefighter like he suspected he would try to tackle him and steal his snack.

"So, you're a firefighter too?" she asked Brian as he set down his tubs.

"I'm a medic," he corrected, "Although a lot of the EMS guys are also firefighters. I don't think we've met before. I'm Brian Lawson. The baked goods enthusiast is my mate."

Brian towered over her. Caitlin wasn't small. Owen estimated she was five-foot-four, but both of the Lawsons were behemoths with bulky frames, built like they'd been sired by a brick house.

"Are you new to town?" Brian asked.

"No, I live on the other side of Red River with my sister."

"What brought you here? Let me guess: you have a thing for fire-fighters? If you're looking to catch a mate, those cookies are the way to go," Brian said with a grin and a wink.

I wonder if we should buy them all, Finley worried.

And who needs to calm down now? Owen shot back as he walked away toward his truck with his cookies.

"No, nothing like that. I heard about it through Olivia," she said, looking pleased with the compliment.

"Ah yeah, Livi. She's awesome." Brian agreed as he arranged small loaves of bread on the table beside hers.

"She is," Caitlin agreed. "Can I help?"

"No, you rest that hand. Do you bake for a living?" Brian asked.

"That's the dream, but right now, I limit myself to bake sales and feeding my nieces and nephews. I'm staying with them while my sister is working out of town."

"Ah, kids are the best," Owen heard Brian say before their conversation was swallowed into the sounds of the bake sale, while Owen took his cookies to his truck.

"Hey, Owen, can I grab you for a second?" Ryder's Emma asked, bumping his shoulder affectionately.

"Sure thing. Emma, this is Caitlin. You've got to try one of these," he said, grabbing a sample cookie and handing it to Emma, who took it with interest.

"Oh wow, these are good," she said, eyes alight with pleasure.

"What's good?" James leaned over her shoulder, his unshaven cheek brushing hers.

One muscular forearm reached around Emma's arm to grab her wrist, bringing her cookie to his mouth, claiming the last bite, gently taking one of her fingers in his mouth briefly with a wicked gleam.

"James! That was mine!" Emma objected, but James just raised his eyebrows with a charming grin that faded into pleased astonishment.

"This is the best thing I've eaten in this country," James declared with a thick Scottish brogue, reaching for the sample bowl.

"They're amazing," Owen agreed, pleased to see how Caitlin flushed with pleasure.

"Those are samples! Pay her if you want more," Emma said with a laugh, swatting James's hand.

"You know I don't carry cash," James frowned.

"They can take your cards over at the register, but there's a five-dollar minimum, so you can look at the other tables," Caitlin explained, but James waved her explanation away.

"Oh, no. I don't need to." James said. "We'll take twenty."

"Okay, sure thing," Caitlin said as she started to package up the cookies.

Ryder came up to Emma's other side not occupied by James and kissed her on the cheek.

"Hello, beautiful mate of mine," Ryder greeted.

James nodded to the medic while Caitlin watched the three of them, faces filled with open curiosity. Owen enjoyed the confusion she tried to hide, seeing the interaction, clearly trying to figure out who was with whom. She studied James' face with concentration for a few long seconds.

Why is she looking at him like that? Finley asked.

Probably because he's good-looking, filthy rich, internationally famous, and his magic makes him irresistible when he wants to be. Owen said, unbothered, but watching her closely. She didn't seem aroused, merely speculative as she bagged up his cookies.

"You look really familiar," she finally said as she handed James his bag of cookies over the table.

"Do you know the song The Mountain Calls?" Emma asked before James could respond.

"Yeah!" Caitlin's eyes lit up, snapping her fingers and pointing at James in recognition. James nodded in acknowledgment, mouth full of cookie.

"That's his," Emma said, elbowing James familiarly while Ryder stepped a half-step closer and put his hand familiarly around Emma's hips, drawing her closer.

She leaned into the embrace, laying her head against Ryder while he planted a kiss on top of her hair. Owen didn't miss the brief, wistful expression on her face when Caitlin noticed, but she covered it up with a bright smile a moment later.

"Guilty as charged," James said once he'd swallowed. Reaching into the bag to retrieve a cookie, James handed one to Ryder, unbothered by the man's show of affection toward Emma. "Try this."

"I didn't realize you were so..." Owen watched her struggle to find the words. Watching her look at James in awe, a slight streak of jealousy slithered its way into Owen's thoughts.

I sort of hate that she's looking at him like that. And before you say anything, yes, I realize that's ridiculous. Owen thought.

His wolf's reply was not the mocking he'd expected, but soothing. *Relax, he's famous, right? So this is normal, right? It's not like they're exchanging numbers for meeting up for sex.*

"Gluttonous is the word she's looking for," Emma supplied, her eyes twinkling.

"Oh wow," Ryder said, speaking around a mouthful of cookie as he grabbed another medic who was walking by the shirt without removing his arm from his mate, "John, you've got to try these."

"Do you have a card?" James asked Caitlin, who shook her head.

"I don't. This is just a hobby."

"Well, I'm gonna need more of these. If you're looking to make some money at it, I'd love to buy some."

"Oh, sure. I love baking."

"I need a... lot. Let's say two or three hundred a week for the next three weeks?" James said, looking at Emma for confirmation.

Ryder's mate just laughed and shook her head. Caitlin was at a complete loss for words, didn't say anything, just stared, her mouth opening a few times.

"Text me your price and I'll send it to you." James pulled out his phone and Caitlin gave him her number. He immediately sent a text with his name and the number of cookies he wanted before they moved on, skipping over the other tables to check out.

Oh, well, so much for not giving out her number. Maybe we should get her number, too. Finley suggested as they watched the exchange.

"Who needs two hundred cookies a week?" Caitlin whispered as James walked away to no one in particular.

"They've got a bunch of people staying at the Lodge for a video they're filming," Owen informed her.

"The Lodge. That sounds familiar, but I'm not sure I know where that is."

He wondered what had brought her to Pinehurst, but didn't want to pry. She knew Olivia, which could mean she was a patient or just a friend. Either way, he wanted to get to know her more.

"It's on Highway 40 on the way back to Red River. You drove right past it to get here." Brian explained.

"Oh yeah, I've seen the signs. That's- wow. How cool. I've never had an order that big," she confessed, pressing her lips together, and rubbing the glitter lip gloss in a gesture that made Owen wonder what she would taste like if he kissed her.

"Well, I'd say your dream is coming sooner rather than later," Owen said with a smile.

"I don't know how I'll make it back here," she said, her forehead pulled down in a frown.

"We could have a unit pick them up. We're up there all the time if you're anywhere near Mountain Regional," Brian offered. Owen gave him a look and piped up with his own offer.

"Yeah, I'm working Thursday. If you can have them ready then I'll let you know when we're coming up to Mountain Regional and meet up and grab them."

"Okay, that would be awesome," she said, her face lightening with relief.

"Hey, I tell you what, if you don't have plans after this, let me take you to lunch and we'll talk about the specifics," Owen suggested.

Caitlin blushed but agreed. His wolf let out an unrestrained howl of pleasure. Brian looked at him with a knowing grin. Owen just shrugged. Yes, he was coming on strong, but he didn't care. He liked this girl, more than he had any other local girl he'd met. Besides, as Finley pointed out, she did have a *very* fine ass, and the girl could bake. The situation definitely warranted getting to know her better.

CHAPTER FOUR

CAITLIN

*O*nce word got around, Caitlin's table was sold out in minutes. She found herself inundated with offers to buy her recipe, or begging her to make more for the knitting club or other local Pinehurst clubs and events. The Fire Chief even ordered a batch for the next EMS training day. She'd never been so pleased to be overwhelmed.

When the bake sale was finished, Owen helped her clean up her table and carried her empty totes to the car before walking her down to the quaint diner, where he pulled out a chair for her from one of the tables in the middle of the room.

She'd loved how interested he was in getting to know her, but she wasn't really sure what to talk about. Caitlin had spent so much time wrapped up in life with Axel that she found it hard to talk about herself without mentioning him, which she didn't want to do. She had an amazingly handsome and nice man sitting across the table from her, flirting innocently. The last thing she wanted to bring up was her ex, but it was beginning to feel inevitable.

"What's the happiest you've ever been?" she asked, hoping to turn the conversation back to him for a bit. In her experience, men loved to talk about themselves, so if she could keep him going, maybe she wouldn't have to reveal what a flat, boring person she'd become during her years living with Axel.

"The first time I shifted," Owen answered. "It was like I'd found the other part of myself I'd always known was there, but couldn't access. I felt complete. How about you?" He asked, looking genuinely interested in her answer.

"The happiest I thought I was... it wasn't real. So, I'm hoping that I'll have something that I can look back on one day that's my happiest moment that's way better than the old one." She explained, feeling awkward, not wanting to overshare and make her lunch awkward. Still, it hurt to feel like she couldn't talk about someone who had been such a large part of her life, no matter how dysfunctional things had been.

"How can a feeling not be real?"

"I was with someone, but it was a lie. He lied about... important, foundational things in our relationship. It tainted everything after that," she said with a shrug, "But that's the past and I'm making a new, better life now."

"I'm sorry. You deserve better," Owen said with feeling.

"You don't know me. I could be a terrible person. Maybe I don't deserve better. Maybe I'm a serial killer?" Caitlin joked, catching the view of someone she thought she recognized in the window, but they were gone too quickly.

She shook her head to clear it of that feeling of being watched. Despite Olivia's reassurances, Caitlin still found herself watching for Axel, even though she had no reason to think he'd look for her here. She repeated the mantra in her head that Olivia had given her. I am in a safe place. Returning her attention to the handsome man in front of her, he was smiling charmingly.

"I'm an excellent judge of character," Owen informed her with a confident smile. "You're not a serial killer. Serial killers don't get passionate about cookies the way you do."

"Maybe that's just what I want you to think," she said, some of her tension easing as she raised a teasing eyebrow at him.

She wasn't in a place to date, but just for a few more minutes she could pretend to be the person who could go out to lunch with a nice man and be the kind of girl he was looking for: someone whole and not a shattered shell of a human barely holding herself together. She could flirt a little and enjoy the company of a nice man like a normal human being, even if it wasn't real.

"It's hard to tell with everyone here, but from what I can tell, you don't smell like a serial killer."

She hesitated for a moment, then held out her wrist for him to sniff. He took her hand in his gently, inhaling deeply.

"Not a serial killer," he confirmed, holding her hand for a fraction of a second, then placing it gently on the table, swallowing hard.

Caitlin had always been very sexual. Even though the last time with Axel had been terrible, she wanted sex, needed it. Her pulse quickened at the thought of the man in front of her pressing her into the bed, saying filthy things to her while he...

"Do you want to get out of here?" he asked, interrupting her fantasy.

"What?" her brain stopped, all the good feelings in her brain coming to a screeching halt as she panicked at the idea of being alone with him.

The fantasy of sex wasn't the same as a real flesh-and-blood male shifter made of pure muscle towering over her without the security of being around other people. Her chest tightened and the room spun. He looked confused, but she couldn't find the words to explain.

"Do you want to get out of here? I know this great trail that has an amazing overlook, and it's not a long walk," he clarified.

"I—can't. I mean, no, thank you. I have somewhere to be, and I shouldn't have stayed this long," she said, standing up from the table in a rush, bumping into the person seated at another table behind her.

"Are you okay? I'm sorry, I know you don't know me. Now you probably think I'm the serial killer," Owen joked, standing as well, pulling out his wallet. "If you give me a second, I'll walk you back to your car."

"Oh, no it's fine, thank you so much for lunch," she backed away with what she hoped was a calm smile as she felt herself unraveling. Based on the look of concern on his face, she was doing a terrible job of hiding her panic, but there wasn't anything she could do about that.

"Are you sure?"

"Yeah, totally. Thanks, this was fun." She said, fleeing and praying he didn't follow as panic gripped her. By some stroke of luck, Olivia was walking through the parking lot as Caitlin walked to her car.

"Hey, what's going on?" her therapist asked after taking one look at Caitlin's ashen face.

"I don't feel safe. But I want to. I really do want to," Caitlin said as her therapist drew her shaking body into a hug.

"Come on, let's go sit in my office for a bit," Olivia said. Caitlin followed her, keeping her eyes on the ground as she walked at Olivia's side, swiping at the tears that were flowing freely down her cheeks.

CHAPTER FIVE

AXEL

"*D*urren Auto," Axel Durren answered, nodding as the teenager who'd delivered the parts he'd ordered left out the door with a cheerful chime of the doorbell.

"Axel, it's Garth,"

"Hey, that piece of shit foreign car acting up again?" Axel asked with a laugh, reaching for the mouse to his computer.

"No, man, the car's fine. I wanted you to know I saw Caitlin." Axel's thoughts ground to a halt.

He hadn't seen heads or tails of her since the slippery minx had run off, taking the contents of their safe and the best parts of his life with her.

"Where are you?" Axel asked.

"I'm in Red River. She was at a diner in a little town a ways from here —Pinehurst. I figured you'd want to know."

"She looks okay?" Part of him wanted her to be doing well, the other part of him wanted her to be pining for him, as sick at their separation as he was.

"She looked good…" Axel's friend replied. Axel could hear the hesitation in his voice.

"Garth, spit it out,"

"She was eating with a guy. He might have been a deputy, but I'm not sure. They looked pretty cozy. I took a picture, so you could see. Maybe that wasn't right, but if it were my girl, I'd want to know," his friend said cautiously.

"Fuck. What's the name of the town again?" Axel asked, his blood running cold at the memory of her leaving him.

That would explain why she'd left if she'd met someone else. He'd never pegged his Kitty Cat as a cheater, but he also never would have thought she'd been unhappy enough to leave him without a word. Sure, they'd had their problems, but they'd never struggled to work things out before.

"Pinehurst. I'm sorry, man."

"Thanks for the heads up. Gotta go, I have a customer." Axel said as an elderly woman toddled up to the counter.

Axel's hands shook as he rang up the old woman.

"Are you sure it's only $100? That man in town said it was at least a four-hundred dollar repair?" she asked in a frail voice.

He hadn't charged her for labor because he knew her financial situation was tight, but not wanting to shame her, he just shook his head.

"That's why you come to me first next time, Miss Gertrude," he said kindly.

His brother came out of the back of the shop, wiping his hands in a futile effort to get some of the grime off his hands.

"What's next, boss?" Timmy asked.

"You still think you can handle this place on your own?" Axel didn't look up as he looked up the town of Pinehurst.

His phone dinged with a picture message. He pulled up the picture that showed a glimpse of Caitlin's profile, and the face of the dead man who was smiling at Axel's mate with a flirtatious look that made Axel's blood pressure spike as he pulled up the Pinehurst Sheriff's page, clicking on the handy page where he scrolled until he found the face that matched the picture.

"Nice to meet you, Deputy Owen Kessler," Axel murmured. "Welcome to hell."

CHAPTER SIX

CAITLIN

SIX WEEKS BEFORE

"*I* was joking, and everyone knew it!" Axel shouted. Caitlin crossed her arms over her chest, standing her ground. "Besides, I apologized, what's the big deal?"

"Axel, you spent the whole conversation invalidating her feelings. That's *not* an apology," She explained impatiently.

"You weren't there, Caitlin. You don't know what I said."

"I do. She told me, and you're not arguing with it. You're saying I don't understand, and I'm trying to explain why I'm angry with how you treated my sister if you would quit arguing and listening for two minutes!"

"You weren't there!" He said slowly like he was talking to someone of lesser intelligence.

"I don't want to do this anymore," she said, uncrossing her arms and going to the kitchen to wash the dirty dishes.

"Do what, exactly?" he asked, following her.

"This," she gestured between them. "You and me. I'm tired of feeling like I need to defend how you treat me to my family and worrying about what you'll say or do when I'm not around that I'll have to fix later. I'm tired of feeling trapped and always frustrated and not knowing when this kind of shit will happen! I'm worth more than this."

"So, what, Cat? I'm not worthy of a relationship now? You think you're better than me?"

"I'm not better than you, but I do deserve better than what you are giving me," she retorted.

"What the hell is that supposed to mean?"

"I mean I deserve better than someone who lied to get me to bond with them, Axel!" She shouted, finally losing her grip on her temper.

"Oh, that again, seriously? How many times do I have to say I'm sorry?"

"It wasn't like a little white lie that you can just say you're sorry for and move on. You told me you *imprinted* on me! You told me your wolf would die if you couldn't have me!" She bit back angry tears.

"You weren't convinced I was serious about you," he shouted back, "When all I ever did was treat you decent!"

"Oh, so lying to me was your solution?" Caitlin demanded, turning the water on in the sink to start washing dishes, squirting too much detergent into the sink in her anger.

"It worked, didn't it?" He asked, "We ended up together, just like we both wanted."

"Oh my gods, you're such a selfish ass that you don't see how you lying has basically broken all trust between us, do you?" She asked hotly, grabbing the green sponge shaped like a smiley face her mother had given her the day before when they'd come for a visit.

"Well if you're so unhappy, then why don't you do something about it instead of complaining all the time? Put up or shut up, Kitty Cat."

"You know what? Fine. I'll just go if you're going to treat me like this." She said, throwing the soapy sponge on the counter. His fist flew out of nowhere, sending her body careening into the refrigerator before she blacked out.

. . .

CAITLIN HAD COME to in their bed with Axel's arm slung over her waist, his breathing slow and even as she slept peacefully. He'd hit her. Actually hit her with his fist. There were a lot of things she'd been able to justify, things she'd explained away and things people wouldn't understand if she'd told them, but there was no explaining this away.

A punch to the face wasn't something you could just do to someone you love. For the first time, Caitlin decided to obey exactly what her husband wanted, without any reservations. She was done complaining and waiting for things to change. It was time to put up or shut up.

She made it to the hallway without disturbing him, going to the bathroom on the other side of the house so she could turn on the light without disturbing him. Grabbing her cell phone on the way she made it to the bathroom and stood for a moment in the darkness in the windowless little room, dreading what she would see in the mirror when she flicked the light on.

Caitlin would have locked the door if the lock worked, but he'd replaced all the door handles with ones that didn't lock after she'd locked herself inside their bedroom once when he wouldn't give her space. Afterward, he'd said he couldn't handle when she 'froze him out' and felt like it was unhealthy for there to be locked doors between them. She hadn't entirely agreed, but he'd changed out the door handles the next time she'd gone out.

Flipping the switch, the fluorescent light hummed and flickered a few times before its light was steady, bathing her in an unflattering yellowish light. She stood looking at herself, the purpling mark on her cheek and gash on her forehead had been wiped, but not cleaned well. Dried blood covered her face from the cut across her jaw.

Before she could stop herself, she raised her phone and took a picture, then placed her phone on the counter and grabbed a washcloth, cleaning herself as best she could. She took another picture when she was cleaned up.

Her head hurt, so she decided to go back to bed. Turning off the light, the silence in the house was deafening. She was too tired and her head hurt too much to make any plans, but she was done with this.

"Kitty Cat?" Axel came out of the bedroom wearing a white t-shirt and boxers. He stopped her halfway down the hallway, planting his left hand on the wall beside her head. His right hand raised up her chin while he inspected her face. "Don't ever talk about leaving me, baby. You know it makes me crazy. My wolf and I, we really can't live without you."

She felt his arm go around her, his lips on hers as he kissed her. He began kissing her tenderly all over, moving across her cheek and down to her neck.

"Don't ever leave me, Kitty Cat. I need you. I'm sorry, I just couldn't stand it. You know it really does make me crazy to think about living without you. Don't leave me," he murmured, repeating variations of the plea over and over until she finally murmured something in agreement.

"My head hurts, I really should go to bed," Caitlin finally said, her voice sounding like it came from somewhere far off.

He nodded and took her hand, taking her to the bedroom tenderly, like it was their honeymoon, not like he'd just assaulted her. She shivered when he put his arm around her.

"You cold, Kitty Cat?" he asked solicitously, then pulled the fuzzy blanket that lived at the foot of the bed up over her, tucking her in with great care, "There you go. I love you."

THE NEXT MORNING she didn't get out of bed to make him breakfast like she usually did. He came over to her side of the bed to kiss her, brushing back her hair from her face to place a gentle kiss on her cheek. She didn't know if he meant to kiss the bruise forming there as an apology or if he simply chose to ignore it but his lips on her made her wince. Then she had the horrible thought that maybe he'd kissed her there on purpose, like some sort of punishment, or a warning not to do it again. Caitlin pushed that thought away and got out of bed.

The day passed in a daze, ignoring her older sister's calls and the things she'd planned to do that day. She had to be smart about what she packed or he would notice, so she decided to 'organize' each room so she could hide the things that were missing.

For the next three days, she cleaned and organized every inch of the single-wide trailer, even going as far as to dust and label things. Absurdly, she thought maybe it would help him stay organized and maybe not be so frustrated after she left. She knew it wasn't true, but she had to feel like she wasn't just abandoning her mate, the one she'd promised herself to for life.

She'd gone to bed early and risen after Axel was gone for work, avoiding him. He either didn't notice or didn't care. A sick part of her wanted him to see the distance in her eyes, to fix it. The rational side of her brain told her that it was better for her to leave, that it was safer for her. She listened to the logical side, promising herself that one day she would be whole again, so she didn't have to fight her own brain and fight her instincts to make good decisions for herself. One day, she would be able to trust her feelings again, but it wasn't today. Today she had to be smart.

Caitlin didn't call her little sister until the day before she planned to leave.

"Hey - what's up?" Charlotte answered.

Before Caitlin could change her mind, she sent the photos she'd taken the night he'd hit her to Charlotte's phone.

"I need you to look at something, but don't let the kids see it."

"Ooh, this sounds exciting," her sister said. "One second. Brooklyn! Come stir this for mommy for a second. Okay, Cait, I'm back. Are you taking dirty pictures for- oh gods." Her sister, always the type to come up with lists and plans in stressful situations, started talking at once, "Oh my god. What happened? Were you attacked?"

"Axel happened," Caitlin said, her eyes filling with tears she blinked back. "It was a few days ago."

"*Days* ago? What the fuck, Caitlin! Why didn't you call me? I'm coming to get you right now."

"No, don't. I need to leave, and I don't want the kids here, or you.

No one knows where you live, so I can come to you without anyone knowing about it."

When Charlotte had packed up and left town after a blow-up with her parents, Charlotte had cut off all ties with everyone but Caitlin, even going so far as to change her last name. The fight had been so bad, Caitlin hadn't even told Axel they'd talked. He was close to her parents, he never would have gotten it. At the time it had felt deceptive, now she was grateful for it.

"I don't like this," Charlotte said.

"I've been packing when Axel's at work, I'm planning on leaving tomorrow night. I can stay with you, right?"

"Of course," Charlotte said. "I'll send you my address. Is a text fine? Do you have enough gas money?"

"Yeah, I just need a place to go," Caitlin said, looking at the valences she'd sewn with a pang of regret.

She'd worked so hard to make this place nice, to make it a home. She'd worked on this trailer almost as much as she'd worked to repair her sham of a relationship. Caitlin walked to the cabinet and took another heavy dose of medicine for the headache she'd had for days.

"Okay, well come here and we'll figure everything out together. I love you. When are you leaving?"

"Before he gets up Saturday. He usually drinks and stays up late Friday, so it'll be easy," Caitlin assured her sister with confidence she didn't feel.

"If I don't hear from you by 8, I'm calling the cops."

"Deal," Caitlin said. If something went wrong and Axel caught her, she'd be grateful for someone to come save her.

AT 6:11 THAT EVENING, she'd heard him open the door that led to the side yard. She steeled herself and forced herself to try to relieve some of the tension she carried, relaxing the tension that was gathering in knots in her shoulders. Axel had been working late and going in early

since their fight. She'd been going to bed early and rising after he left, to avoid talking to him.

That night she'd made roast, letting it get dry on purpose. When he came in and saw that she'd made his favorite meal he nodded and visibly relaxed. Caging her in the corner with one arm on either side of her as she cut the roast, he nuzzled her hair. She tried to fight the impulse to shy away.

"I thought you'd still be mad after the other night. I was wondering if I should even bother coming home, or if I should just stay and work late," he said in his soft seductive tone that made her skin crawl.

"No, I'm not mad," she lied softly, trying to seem meek, accommodating even.

He liked it when she was submissive and gave into whatever he wanted. The only thing that mattered was getting away from him, out of this house and to somewhere she could be safe, and she would do anything to make it happen. One little lie was nothing compared to the many other things she'd done in the last few days that all felt like a series of betrayals of the trust they'd once shared.

Earlier that afternoon she'd cleared out the money from their safe and packed one of his handguns in her purse and then she'd taken the time to take the slides out of his pistols and removed the cylinder from his revolver, and removed the firing pin from his rifles. All the while, she hummed the country song they'd danced to at their bonding ceremony. She'd packed enough things to get her started in a new place, all of the clothing that would normally be tucked away in the drawers was now safely in the trunk of her car.

"You want to join me in the shower?" He asked, lifting the skirt of the short dress she'd worn specifically to entice him.

The idea of having sex with him turned her stomach, but she'd do it if she had to to help him fall asleep tonight.

"Honey, you're going to smudge my dress," she said, edging further into the corner away from his hands.

She didn't bother to point out that he always fussed at her for kissing him or trying to touch him after work. Clearly, when he wanted sex, that rule didn't apply. She shoved her hurt deep down, adding it to the things she couldn't unpack until she was somewhere safe.

"Sorry, Kitty Cat," he said quietly, letting the flowery fabric drop from his hands.

"After you take your shower, I was thinking we could eat in the living room and put on a movie we don't want to watch." She said coquettishly, glancing over her shoulder flirtatiously, then back down at the roast she was slicing so he didn't see her lack of genuine enthusiasm.

"Hmm, is that right?" he pressed his grime-covered work clothes against her back.

"Dress!" she objected.

"Alright, I'm going to go clean up before I lose my self-control and take you right here."

"No sex until you shower and eat!" she chided jokingly.

He froze, his body tensing. Leaning down so he spoke in her ear, he spoke softly, his voice heavy with sensual promise that felt like a threat.

"That's fine, Kitty Cat. I plan to enjoy every inch of you tonight." He kissed her hair, missing the shiver that ran through her as he walked down the hall, whistling the same country song she'd been packing to hours before.

When she heard the plastic curtains clank as he got into the shower she took the powder of the pills she'd carefully crushed into a fine powder and stirred to dissolve it into a small shot glass of beer she poured out, making sure it was dissolved before grabbing a funnel to pour the beer back into the bottle. When Axel came back out, he was dressed in flannel pajama pants and a worn t-shirt.

"You did something," he said.

"Hm?" Her heart rate increased.

What had he noticed? She hadn't taken her things from the bathroom, that would have been too noticeable.

"You moved stuff around in the bathroom and the bedroom," he said, fingering her braid. "It looks nice, Kitty Cat."

"Do you like it?"

"Yeah, but you know what I really like? This braid. I think it'll be a nice leash for you later."

"I made a roast for you," she said sweetly, handing him the beer.

"Oh, thanks. Someone trying to make up for the other night?" He asked, taking a sip of his beer. She decided she wasn't a good enough liar to address that question without getting emotional, so she switched topics.

"I'm sorry it turned out a little on the dry side," she said, biting her lip and letting her genuine anxiety about her plan show through.

"No worries babe, nothing an extra beer can't fix. Come on, make our plates and we'll eat in the living room."

He turned on a game, consumed his food quietly, occasionally yelling at the players or the refs, and then set down his plate on the coffee table.

"Come here, slut."

Immediately she came to kneel at his feet, her eyes lowered submissively like he liked.

She'd never enjoyed *nice* dirty talk, but tonight it felt different. Instead of making her heart race with anticipation and excitement, his tone sent a thrill of fear through her body, making the hairs on the back of her arms stand and goosebumps appear on her skin.

There had been plenty of times when he'd taken it too far during rough sex, but he'd always apologized and said he hadn't meant to hurt her. She'd believed him, time and again, never thinking that the person she trusted with her body and soul would have the capacity to harm her on purpose.

Now that she knew better, and could acknowledge that he wasn't someone who would never go out of his way to hurt her, this didn't feel like a fun sexy game. Letting Axel put his hands on her and have any control of her body felt like playing Russian roulette. How badly would he hurt her? How far would he take this?

She felt like when he'd punched her, he'd shattered something between them, some barrier that kept her safe.

"You've been a bad girl, but you're going to make it up to me tonight, aren't you?" He grabbed her braid and yanked, forcing her chin up so she looked him in the eye.

"Yes."

He yanked her hair so hard, her eyes watered, "Yes what, my bad girl?"

"Yes, sir," she said meekly.

She just had to get through this, then she could leave. She just had to give him what he wanted, then he would be too tired to feel the drugs kick in that would allow her to leave and give her a head start before he came after her.

He dragged her by her hair over his lap, flipping the thin material of her dress up. Pulling down her panties, he kneaded her bottom.

"You've been a bad girl, Kitty Cat. You were disrespectful, threatening to leave just to get a rise out of me. Even when we disagree, I expect you to show me respect. Right?" The fear turned her stomach into knots, but she responded.

"Yes, sir."

"So you're going to get a spanking, then I'm going to use your holes. You're not going to get to cum tonight, you're just here for my pleasure. You're going to earn my forgiveness."

Her palms started to sweat, her pulse racing like a racehorse thundering down the track.

"How many swats, sir?"

"Until I think you understand the severity of what you did. You pushed me so hard, you made me lash out and hit you. That can't happen again."

Caitlin nodded, trying to swallow, but not quite able to do so.

"Come here, Kitty Cat," he instructed, patting his knee as he released her braid.

With shaky legs, she stood and arranged herself over his lap. He locked her into place with his other leg, his leg crossing over hers with a strength that she used to find comforting. Their size difference, and how much bigger and stronger Axel was than her, had always made her feel deliciously small. Having a partner who could hold her down or throw her around and not struggle because of her curvy figure had always made her feel deliciously small.

Instead of his grip on her giving her reassurance of his ability to protect her from anything, now she felt the muscles of his powerful thighs and felt a small part of herself shrivel, knowing that he was going to hurt her, and there was nothing she could do to escape it. Dread filled her as the first swat came down hard across her bottom, Axel's palm firm and unyielding. Blow after blow rained down on her flesh, which heated beneath his palm.

Eventually, she found a place inside of her mind where the pain didn't matter. It still hurt, but it didn't matter. It took him a few swats to realize, but when he did, the blows stopped.

"Oh no, you stay out of your head, Kitty Cat," Axel said, pushing her up off his lap. "Get up, put your hands on the couch."

"Axel, please, I'm sorry-" she whispered, crawling backwards away from him as he walked out of the living room, toward their bedroom. He stopped at the doorway, eyes gleaming with danger that made her want to run and hide.

"If you're not where I told you to be when I get back, I'll beat you until you can't walk tomorrow," he promised, sounding excited at the prospect.

Her bottom was already hot from his spanking, but not unbearable. She scrambled to be in position for him, her hands sinking into the couch cushions as she waited, her knees almost giving out as she wanted to sink to the floor and disappear.

"Ah, so my bad girl can obey," he observed when he returned.

Out of the corner of her eye, she saw him swinging his heavy leather belt lightly. When he brushed the leather of the belt she'd bought for him against her hot skin, she flinched.

He placed one hand on the small of her back. She couldn't see, but she imagined he was pausing to admire his handiwork. She took a steadying breath, waiting for the pain to start again.

When she heard the belt whistle through the air and felt it break like fire against her skin, she let out a loud cry. He chuckled as she started to sob. The pain was just starting, and it wasn't the reason for her tears. Time and again he hit her, the soft pliable leather swinging through the air before lighting her bottom and thighs on fire in long red welts.

As he beat her with stripe after punishing stripe, she sobbed for the loss of their relationship, the secret way she was going to have to leave, and the innocence and trust she'd given to him that he'd abused. Each time the leather connected with her flesh stripped her further of coherent thought.

"Please, please stop!" she cried, "Please, I'm sorry."

The words tumbled out of her in an incoherent jumble, trying desperately to scramble for the magic word to make it all stop, but the onslaught of white-hot pain stole her words and shrank her world to a place past logic until nothing existed but the pain. Then, all at once, it stopped. When he didn't resume, she stayed in position, shaking. When he kicked her legs further apart, she started sobbing anew.

"Fuck, you're so wet baby," he said, rubbing his tip against her.

He slid inside of her in one hard thrust. She sobbed again as his skin came into contact with hers, sending fresh waves of white hot, panic-inducing pain through her body. He held her hips, fucking her hard so she was helpless against him. He pulled her tight against him as he came inside of her, filling her with tiny little thrusts and grunts. He'd been surprisingly, and mercifully, brief in taking his pleasure. She closed her eyes in a thankful prayer even as she still shook with sobs.

"Fuck, that felt nice, Kitty Cat," He murmured, sliding out, then back inside of her a few times, then paused to ask her. "Are you sorry?"

"Yes, I'm so sorry," she said through her hiccups. At least that wasn't a lie.

"See? I don't believe you yet." He withdrew. "But, I believe you *think* you mean it now, Kitty Cat. Don't worry, I'll make sure you mean it before the sun comes up."

"The sun?" she asked in confusion.

"It's the full moon. I'm going to fuck this little body all night and show you just how it feels to be disrespected."

Cold dread filled her. The full moon meant that he really could spend the whole night fucking her, over and over without giving her any relief. She doubted that the sedative she gave him would be enough to counteract his shifter's drive to mate under the full moon.

She cursed herself, feeling defeated as she realized that her plan for submitting to him was going to be much, much worse than she imagined. This train of thought stopped abruptly as she felt his tip pressing against her, but not where he'd just been fucking her.

"Red. Red!" she said as he pressed his tip to her other hole.

He spit into his hand and slid his saliva over her other hole with a laugh.

"Oh no, there's no safe wording out of a punishment, kitten. You can scream and cry all you like, but I'm going to fuck this pretty ass of yours. I'm going to ruin you, Kitty Cat."

At 6:09 in the morning, she climbed into her car, wincing and sucking her breath in through her teeth as her thighs and butt pressed into the cold leather. He'd passed out before the sun was fully up, but that hadn't mattered. More than one place on her skin his fluids had dried on her skin. She hadn't taken the time to shower, despite how badly she wanted to. The best she could do was to grab the sponge from the sink, barely turn it on so the tap dripped silently, and use that to clean the worst that she could off her face.

Despite the burning pain from everything that touched her skin on the lower half of her body she waited until 6:11 to leave. He'd come home at eleven minutes after six the night before, she needed to leave him at the same time the next morning. She knew it wasn't rational, and was perfectly aware that it made absolutely no sense whatsoever, but when the digital screen flicked without a sound, she knew it was time to leave.

She couldn't control everything, but she could control that. She sent a quick text to Charlotte to let her know she was on the way, started the car, and rolled slowly down the gravel driveway toward the rising sun that lightened the sky.

She'd driven down the route she'd pre-planned, bought a prepaid cell phone so she could turn off her phone, and then headed to a used car lot where she'd traded her car for cash. She'd walked next door and used that cash to buy another small car and drove until she was too tired to drive anymore.

It wasn't until she pulled into Charlotte's apartment that she allowed herself to break down. In her sister's arms, she cried until she was too tired to cry anymore.

She was free, but it didn't feel like freedom. She would never be free of what he'd done to her.

CHAPTER SEVEN

OWEN

"*W*e're doing what, now?" Owen's EMT Aiden Matthews asked, looking at Owen in confusion.

"Picking up cookies. It's for Emma," Owen explained, trying to master his patience. Aiden was annoying on the best of days.

It wasn't *exactly* for Emma, but all of the shifters unilaterally accepted that as the girl Ryder imprinted on, if Emma wanted it done, it was happening. Mate bonds were sacred, and imprinting was so uncommon that everyone was going out of their way to make sure things with Emma and Ryder were smooth. Delivering cookies was no big deal if it meant Emma and James were happy, allowing the training officer to focus and concentrate at work.

Plus, the last thing Owen wanted was to explain to his EMT how he felt about Caitlin, considering they'd just met and it felt a little premature. Aiden had a big mouth, he was annoying as a thorn in the pad of your paw, and with all the imprinting jokes going around, Owen didn't need that shit.

"Okay," Aiden shrugged in the passenger seat, clicking away on his tablet.

Owen sat in the parking lot until he saw her little blue beat-up piece of junk car pull in.

If we claimed her, the first thing we'd do is take that thing away and get her a new car. That thing looks about as safe as the din of a rabid bear, Finley thought critically.

Owen agreed but stopped Aiden when he moved to get out of the truck.

"I've got this," Owen said.

"I can help- oh." He grinned when he saw Caitlin, turning to wink at Owen, snickering. "I gotcha. I'll leave you to help her with her... *cookies.*"

"Shut up," Owen said as he got out of the truck, straightening his shirt before coming around to the side of the rig she was parked on.

"Hi," she greeted shyly.

"Hey," he was trying to find the words to say when she beat him to it.

"I'm so sorry about the other day at lunch. I really did appreciate you asking to take me on a walk, it was nice. I just...freaked out," she explained. Before he could respond, she continued, her face flushed, "It wasn't you. I just got out of a really bad relationship and I'm a bit broken. More than a bit, actually. Sorry, I'm rambling. I do that when I'm nervous. But, I do appreciate you asking me and I'm sorry if I made it weird-"

"Caitlin." Owen said, taking a step toward her, wanting to hug her, but thought better of it and hovered near her, just within reach, "It's fine."

"Oh," she let out a big breath, looking grateful.

"I'm sorry that what I said at lunch upset you," he said sincerely.

Ask their name, then we can offer our condolences on their death. Finley thought with dark promise.

"It's... well, thank you," she said, and he hated how her eyes darted to his hands and she took a slight step back like she was afraid of him.

"How's your wrist?" He asked, wanting to know what had happened to her, but respecting the fact that she didn't want to talk about it.

"It's doing okay. Still healing."

"Okay, well I'll do all the lifting then," Owen smiled.

As if we'd let her do it anyway. You should ask her out again! Finley piped up.

Oh yeah, because that went so well last time. Owen thought back.

Invite her to something in public, not a private thing. If somebody broke her, she won't trust us yet. Finley advised.

"So, there's a chili cook-off next weekend, if you'd like to come. It's open to anyone in the community." He started loading tubs of cookies on the stretcher in the back of the unit, not looking at her.

"I'm not much of a chili maker."

"You can come enjoy then," Owen suggested.

"I think I'd like that. Thank you."

"I'll text you the details," he promised, shoving his hands in his pockets.

He wanted to touch her, not sexually, although Finley was enthusiastic about that idea. Owen just wanted to feel her soft skin against his, to let her curl up against him and know that being with him was a safe place and she was safe now from whatever hurt her in the past.

He hated when people around him didn't feel safe and cared for. It was what made him love his jobs. As a deputy, he helped keep the community safer, and as a medic people knew they could count on him to take care of them when they needed it.

"Thanks. And, thanks for being so cool about my freaking out and acting like a complete spaz." She smiled self-consciously. "I'm not a freak, I promise. Well, that isn't true, but I do know how to function in social situations."

"We all have stuff." Owen shrugged. "You don't have to apologize for not being the version of yourself you want to be right now, we all have things we're working on. If there's anything I can do, or not do, to help you, just let me know?"

Owen's radio keyed up as tones dropped. Automatically, he held up a finger and turned his head to listen to the radio, but the call was for another unit.

"Well, that's my cue to get back in county," Owen said with regret.

"Thank you for coming to get the cookies," Caitlin said.

"No problem," Owen replied, trying to think of something else to say.

Compliment her! Girls like that. Finley insisted. *Tell her her hair looks nice.*

"Oh, here, I made these for you and your partner." She said, leaning into her car and pulling out a plastic container of cookies. "As a thank you for delivering the order."

"Oh hell yeah. Thanks!" Owen grinned.

Awoooo! Somebody should wife her up, like the humans say. And by somebody, I mean us! Finley exclaimed.

Will you chill for two seconds? Owen demanded.

"You're welcome," she said, and Owen had to give Finley a mental growl so he wouldn't enumerate all the ways he'd like to thank her.

Owen nodded, opened her car door like a gentleman, and shut it behind her as Finley continued to suggest the many ungentlemanly things they could do to her. nodding as he opened his cookies and popped one in his mouth before climbing in.

"Yeah!" Aiden said, reaching for one.

Owen snarled. "Touch one and you'll lose that hand."

"Oh come on. She said they were for both of us," Aiden whined.

"You were listening?"

"Yeah. You need to work on your game," his companion commented, eying the cookies with longing.

"Girls want to play games, a woman wants honesty and trustworthiness. That," he nodded and waved as Caitlin drove away, "that's a woman. Life lesson to learn early: you don't play games with a real woman, Aiden. "

"Okay, old timer." Aiden said with one eye still on the cookies.

THE LODGE WAS BUSTLING with activity when they pulled the rig in. Owen walked inside, leaving Aiden to unload the cookies and carry them into the kitchen while he sought out Emma to give her the receipt Caitlin had printed. Kate, a petite blonde fae girl who usually worked at Olivia's front desk, looked vastly out of place in her office casual wear and smiled in welcome from behind the Lodge's welcome desk.

"Morning Owen!" She greeted cheerfully.

"Morning Kate, how's it going?" He said.

"Got something for me?" She asked, indicating the paper in his hand.

"Um, James ordered some cookies and we're bringing them, I have a receipt."

"I'll take it. Do you need help carrying them in?"

"Nah, my partner's got it," Owen grinned.

"Okay. Are you applying while you're here?" She asked, reaching for a stack of papers.

"Applying?" He asked.

"The security and medic jobs?" Kate prompted.

"Owen!" Emma said, walking out in short pajama bottoms and a crop top t-shirt that fell just below her breasts.

She gave him a friendly hug, which he returned a little uneasily. He wasn't actually uncomfortable with her but didn't want Ryder's wolf taking issue with Owen touching his mate with so little clothing on. Owen barely knew Caitlin, but the idea of someone else touching her made him and Finley bristle with the desire to hurt someone. He didn't need Ryder starting a brawl with him because Owen hugged his mate and accidentally touched her bare midriff.

"Hey," he replied, a movement catching his attention.

Connor was walking down the hall behind Emma.

"Morning," Connor greeted, then headed for the dining area, looking half-awake.

"Are you here to apply? Please tell me you are," She said, bouncing a little on her toes, then pausing as she noticed both he and Aiden were there in full uniform and both sporting radios. "Wait, is someone hurt?"

"I'm here delivering the cookies James wanted," Owen explained.

"Oh, good! He's been talking about them since we left the bake sale." She laughed. "But seriously, you should apply. You're one of the guys Ryder said to get."

"I'm already working a lot," Owen began.

"Please?" She asked, eyes big, "The pay is good, and the food is spectacular. You basically stand around and make sure no one gets hurt, which no one will because we aren't idiots."

"Um," Owen said, edging away from Emma.

He didn't have a strong need for lots of money, he didn't need a lot and as long as his bills were paid, he was happy. But working with mages and taking an easy assignment did sound nice.

"Owen," James came out of the living space shirtless, putting an arm around Emma's waist. "Good to see you, man. You applying?"

"I'm trying to convince him," Emma said mischievously.

"You should do it. We have a lot of fun up here, and it's a cake walk."

"I really don't know," Owen hedged.

They were always stretched thin at the sheriff's office, and getting the time off might be difficult on such short notice. The last thing he wanted to do was screw over someone for a gig he didn't need.

James said a number, eyebrows raised. When Owen didn't understand, James said, "You'll work for two weeks and get paid that amount."

"That's more than I make in six months," Owen said. "Why is it so much?"

"Because the client wants the best of the best," Emma's eyes sparkled, "Which means... you'll apply, yes?"

Owen was reluctant, but felt his doubts washing away as he considered.

"The mayor said he'll give the guys who are accepted time off, no questions asked," Emma said with a hopeful smile. The girl behind the desk appeared at Owen's elbow with a paper application, a clipboard and a pen.

"What the hell are you wearing?" Ryder walked up as he was filling out the paperwork, his eyes trained on Emma.

Thankful he'd already put several feet between himself and Emma, Owen took another step sideways.

"Pajamas," Emma replied, huffing at him.

"You look like a sex doll. Go put some clothes on," Ryder growled.

"I look like a woman who is free to wear whatever she wants. Just because a woman reveals her body doesn't mean she's asking for sex. Owen didn't think I was looking for sex from him, did you?"

Owen stepped further away and made a great show of not looking up from the application Kate had just placed in his hands. "Nope, definitely not."

"Baby," Ryder said low in Emma's ear, "Put some clothes on or I'll drag you upstairs and tie you to the bed."

"I just wanted coffee," Emma said.

"Fine. I'll get your coffee, then you are going back upstairs to get dressed, right?" Ryder said, sliding his hands along her naked torso.

"If you want me to," she said teasingly before Ryder grunted and headed toward the kitchen.

Owen breathed easier as the tension in the room diffused and he was left with Emma, James and a preoccupied Kate.

"Gods. What is he gonna do in a few months when it's summer? I'm not going to be dressing like a nun just because he and Xander think showing my body off is a crime." Emma grouched.

"I don't know." James laughed, "But I do like that shirt,"

"He pisses me off," Emma fumed.

"Think about it this way, the more riled up about your clothes he is, the hotter the sex is," James pointed out.

"Well," Emma hedged, "you're not wrong."

"Alright, one coffee for you," Ryder returned, handing a cup to Emma, and another to James.

Owen turned when he felt the tension rise in the room, Ryder staring at the hand James had wrapped around Emma's waist, resting on her bare skin. James didn't move, staring Ryder down evenly.

"Come on, baby," Ryder said evenly, "I'll walk with you upstairs."

"Don't you have work?" She challenged.

"It can wait," Ryder said, not moving.

James only slid his hand away when Emma moved to walk back down the hallway toward the stairs that led to the upstairs rooms, her voice quietly arguing with Ryder as they walked. Owen finished his application, collected Aiden from the kitchen where he was flirting with the young woman who was in charge of feeding the crew, and headed back to the EMS base.

Ryder and Xander are so... extra these days. Finley observed.

Owen agreed, but didn't respond as they got a call that sent them to a barn where a local teen, apparently a friend of Aiden's, had given herself a nasty slice from an exposed nail while filming a video for their band.

CHAPTER EIGHT

CAITLIN

*C*aitlin was sure that she wouldn't fall for another guy so soon after Axel, but within a week she and Owen had attended the chili cook off together. Then somehow, she wasn't quite sure how it started, they were texting all the time and talking on the phone late into the night. It brought back memories of her teenage years, when things had been simple and uncomplicated.

"Can we talk about something else today?" Caitlin asked as soon as she was settled on the couch in Olivia's office.

"Of course, this is your session. What do you want to talk about?"

"I'm conflicted. So, I've been texting Owen, right? And we've been talking all the time." Olivia listened as Caitlin gushed enthusiastically. "But here's the problem: I feel like I'm dying inside."

"In what way?"

"Sex. And I feel like maybe it's wrong to want sex this bad this early? But seriously, if I don't get some sex I might spontaneously combust." Caitlin confessed.

"Why is wanting sex a problem?"

"Because you can't just rush into sex when you just broke up. That's gross."

"Let's look at it another way. You're both consenting adults, you both have needs, and you enjoy each other's company. Assuming the attraction is mutual, and it certainly appears to be, what's wrong with enjoying mutually satisfying physical pleasure?"

"Are you saying I can go out and have sex?"

"You can do whatever you want. I'm suggesting there are more open minded ways to deal with your situation besides judging yourself for what's biologically normal. Also, considering all you've been through, I would say it can be a good thing that you're able to even consider it."

"I just don't know how much to tell him. I don't want to trauma dump all over him, but he should know, right? I mean - what do you say? 'Oh hi, I feel like this might be going in a direction that leads to sex, which I desperately want to do, but also I'm really fucked up because my ex was an abusive prick?' Isn't exactly the most alluring pickup line."

"You don't have to share everything. He knows you have trauma, if you do decide that sex is something you want to pursue then have a discussion about your limits just like you would with any other partner."

"Um. I've never really done that. I've only ever done things with Axel and that was…different."

"Okay, let's talk about how that conversation should go," Olivia said.

Thankful for the guidance, Caitlin absorbed everything Olivia said, asking lots of questions. Olivia even went so far as to send her a few links to articles that went into detail discussing the topic.

"So, it's okay if I have sex?" Caitlin asked, unsure.

"Oh, it's definitely okay if you have sex. In fact, as long as you're being safe, I think it could be good for you to experience consensual sex with a partner who respects your boundaries and wants to meet your needs. My professional opinion: sex would be beneficial for you."

"And your unofficial opinion?" Caitlin asked, "If I were your girlfriend, what would you say?"

"I'd tell you to go get laid," Olivia replied, closing her notebook. "I think I've given you plenty to do for homework, you have a good weekend."

"Thanks. I'm… excited. And also terrified." Caitlin said, excitement bubbling up inside of her, making her walk with a little more spring in her step on her way out to the car.

Now she just had to pluck up the courage to actually talk to Owen about it.

CHAPTER NINE

OWEN

Owen was sitting at one of the high-top tables at The Bar on Main. It was a typical bustling Friday night.

CAITLIN

I was mated to a bad man.

Was mated? Owen mulled that over. It took a lot to break a mated bond, but it could be done.

"So, there they are, thirteen first responders standing around in their little circle of hope, waiting for us to show up." Cutler, one of the older medics, was saying, "And one jumps forward and asks, *What can we do?* Like he's a fucking idiot."

"What did you tell him?" Emma asked from beside Owen.

"I told him I needed him to get out of the way and to take his buddies with him," Cutler said, eager to share the story with such an eager audience.

"You didn't!" Emma exclaimed.

"Yeah I did, so we…." Owen's phone buzzed again, distracting him from the conversation.

CAITLIN

I left him pretty recently. You seem like a great guy, I guess I'm just saying… I'm not in a place for a relationship.

You seem like the kind of guy who would be good to a girl, so believe me when I say I'm not trying to play games.

OWEN

I'm here, and I don't have to be anything you don't want me to be. If you only want a friend, then that's how it'll be.

CAITLIN

I don't think I can just be friends with you, though.

OWEN

I don't know where that leaves things.

Caitlin

Neither do I.

"WE LOADED him into the truck, met the life flight and he ended up losing the leg," Cutler finished.

"Oh, that's awful," Emma said, her face clouding.

"You should tell her about the call with the twins," Ryder suggested as he draped an arm around his mate.

"Okay, so we got paged out to this house for a sick person, a seventeen-year-old male. We come in, he's white as a sheet, laying on the couch and holding the right side of his abdomen."

"Ooh! Appendicitis?" Emma guessed eagerly.

"Very good, yes. That's what we thought. So we take his vitals, heart rate and temperature are a little elevated, but nothing wild. BP is really low. We start loading them and the mother is asking us a million questions about what we think it could be. You can tell she's one of those patients' moms who put their symptoms into one of those online doctor things. So, we finally get him loaded, we're fifteen minutes out and the kid's phone rings. He answers it, and it's the mother telling us to turn around, that the other son is getting worse and he needs us to take him."

"The other son? What other son?"

"That's what we said. So, apparently, the kid we've got in the truck isn't the sick one. He's the only one who's got insurance, and they've got that twin thing where they feel each other's pain. So they wanted us to diagnose him and send him home so they could get whatever medicine they needed prescribed and give it to the sick one."

"No!"

"Dead serious. So, dispatch sends another truck, picks up the actual sick brother, and the kid in my truck starts screaming, trying to come off the stretcher, completely out of his mind with the pain."

"What did you do?"

"We treated him like we would any other patient."

"When we got to the ER, they rushed him into surgery, the same thing for the brother. Turns out, they both had burst appendixes."

"What are the chances of that happening?" Emma asked, incredulous.

"Insane."

OWEN

I'm not sure what to say, but I'm here.

CAITLIN

Sorry.

OWEN

There's nothing to apologize for, I'm really glad you said something to me. So, what are you up to?

SHE SENT an alluring picture of herself, tucked up on the couch, what looked like a mountain of whipped cream sitting on a plate next to her. He subtly took a picture of himself and sent it back.

> **OWEN**
> Are you eating a pile of whipped cream?

> **CAITLIN**
> Yes, but also, there is a scone underneath.

> **OWEN**
> That sounds delicious.

"Owen, did you just send a selfie?" Aiden asked incredulously.

"Shut up, pup," Owen responded gruffly.

They weren't on shift now, and Owen didn't have the patience for his shit. He already had Finley giving increasingly lewd suggestions as to what they could do with Caitlin and a bottle of whipped cream in his head, the patrons from the bar making noise all around him, and he was trying to figure out what in the world she was trying to say.

She didn't want to be just friends, but she had just gotten out of a relationship and didn't want to hop into another. Owen respected that, he just didn't know what that meant for him.

"Is that for cookie chick?" Aiden guessed.

Owen shot him a dirty look and was about to tell him where he could stick his thoughts on the matter when Emma spoke.

"Ooh, is this for Caitlin?" Emma asked, eyes lighting up in excitement.

"Yeah," Owen confirmed.

Ryder raised his eyes from his drink to Emma's face.

"How do *you* know who Owen is texting?" Ryder asked with a slight edge.

"I know things." She replied loftily.

When she'd dropped by the base to see Ryder one evening last week, Owen had been standing outside, on the phone with Caitlin. Emma had given him two thumbs up and proceeded inside, then showed up the next day with coffee, wanting to know how it had gone with "his mystery girl." Ever since, Emma had been hounding him for updates, thrilled that he might have found someone.

CAITLIN

If you didn't live so far, I'd say come over and have some.

OWEN

I'd jump in the truck right now if you wanted me to come, but it's okay if you want the night to yourself.

CAITLIN

Gah. I hate how complicated being an adult is.

OWEN

Meh, it doesn't have to be.

CAITLIN

It is, though.

OWEN

Why?

CAITLIN

I'm so horny I feel like I'm going to combust, but also... I wasn't kidding when I said I'm really broken.

OWEN

You need someone who will be good to you and take you, broken parts and all.

CAITLIN

That's why it's complicated.

OWEN

I don't understand.

CAITLIN

I like it to hurt. I like being called filthy names and being treated... badly in the bedroom.

"Switch me spots," Emma instructed Ryder, getting out of her spot. He rolled his eyes but complied. Emma raised her eyebrows at Owen, who held his phone out. Emma took the phone and typed out something, handing his phone back to him with a satisfied nod.

"I can't send her that." Owen objected.

"Well, it's true, isn't it? Also, she wants you to." Emma assured, "She's asking without asking."

> **OWEN**
>
> If you're trying to ask me if I will treat you badly in only the ways you enjoy, and then treat you like a queen the rest of the time, the answer is yes. I like to make my sexual partners feel good, end of story.

"Here, drink this." Emma said, grabbing her newly refilled water, the glass leaving a trail of condensation on the bar top table as she slid over to him, grinning conspiratorially as she said confidently, "She's about to invite you over."

"I don't think so, she has-" Owen started to say, but his phone pinged again and they both turned to look at his screen.

> **CAITLIN**
>
> Do you want some scones?

Emma whooped as Owen reached for the water, swallowing it in several large gulps. He reached for his wallet, but Emma shooed him.

"We've got this. Have fun and enjoy your *scones!*" Emma said with a wink as Owen grabbed his jacket from the back of his chair and headed for the door.

OWEN MET her at a little motel on the edge of Red River. It wasn't the nicest place, but it was clean and serviceable.

"Hi," she said shyly, meeting him at the door of her room.

"Hi yourself." He could smell the arousal-tinged fear rolling off her, so he didn't come in, hovering, his arm resting on the side of the doorway.

"Have you eaten dinner?" He asked.

Finley was practically prancing in Owen's head. *Ooh, yeah we should feed her. I like it when she eats! Are we having scones now, or are we waiting till after dinner?*

"I had scones," she informed him with a laugh.

"Come on, I'll feed you some proper dinner and we can talk," Owen said, stepping back and tilting his head toward the parking lot where his truck was parked.

"Oh. I thought..." She looked at the interior of the hotel room.

He could see her pulse increasing in her neck. He wanted her, and she obviously wanted him, but he wanted her to be able to enjoy it and right now she was wound so tight she was like a coil ready to spring at the slightest disturbance.

"I would love to have sex with you, but first, we need to discuss limits and second, if you pass out I want to know it's because the orgasms were just too good to handle, not from lack of food. Also, you're looking at me like I'm the animal control officer here to lock you up. You need to bring your stress levels back about six levels so you can enjoy it *if* we do anything."

She agreed and grabbed her purse. He took her to a noisy steakhouse where he stepped aside to let her into the booth, then slid across from her. They made small talk until the appetizers came. With the food in front of her giving her something to focus on besides her nerves, she looked more at ease.

I really like- Finley started to talk, but Owen was having none of it.

Finley, I swear to the moon if you distract me right now I'm going to go on a vegetarian diet for a month, Owen threatened.

What a horrible thing to say! Finley objected. *I was just saying-*

What she has to say is important. If you want us to be able to enjoy her and not break her, shut up and let me talk to her without your running commentary.

"So, what do you enjoy in the bedroom?" He asked and she began to describe the things she enjoyed while he listened attentively to everything, asking clarifying questions. When she'd finished that, their food came.

"You're *always* submissive?" He asked as Finley fell silent and they started in on her food.

"Always," she confirmed.

"What are your limits?" He asked as he cut into his steak.

"I don't like *hard* hair pulling, and I only enjoy moderate face slapping. Not hard."

"What about verbal limits?"

"Don't call me a bad girl," She said quietly, her posture shifting as she seemed to shrink.

Who would call her a bad girl? Finley demanded, incensed on her behalf.

"What do you want me to call you?" Owen asked, carefully keeping his mind on his food, not on the question he wanted to ask, like the name of the person who had made her feel small, and if they were still alive.

"I like..." she flushed deeply as the waiter came to refill their waters.

When he walked away, Owen looked at her expectantly, waiting for her answer.

"Whore, cum slut, and slut in general is my favorite," she blushed cherry red and Owen worked to keep his face neutral.

Finley gave a growl of approval but didn't talk.

They discussed safe words and then made small talk until dinner was over. She was increasingly nervous as he drove her back to the motel, fidgeting with her hands. When they made it to the door of the hotel room, he stopped her with a hand on her arm.

"Caitlin, I know you have needs. I would be honored and thrilled to take care of you in whatever way feels safest to you, or I can leave right now if you aren't completely comfortable and safe."

"You drove all this way to have sex," she said quietly, biting her lip again.

"Actually, I drove here for *scones*, not sex," he reminded her with a cheeky grin.

"That was just a bullshit excuse," she rolled her eyes.

He made a face, trying to peer around her into the dark interior of her room.

"Are you telling me you didn't bring any scones?"

Wait. She wasn't kidding about the scones, was she? I mean, sexing is nice too! Finley thought. *But also, her baking is heaven.*

"I did," she admitted.

"Okay then. We're good. Seriously... it's okay to be nervous, but I don't want you to be so scared so you can't enjoy whatever happens."

"Come on in," she invited, stepping back for him to enter.

When he came in, she walked to the plastic container where a small pile of scones sat. She got a plate out of the kitchenette and plated one, some of her insecurity gone as she arranged the baked goods just so. He watched her bend over, tracing the lines of her body with his eyes as she retrieved the whipped cream.

"Whipped cream?" she asked.

"However you think it's best."

"Well, these are sweet, they're meant to be enjoyed with whipped cream or icing." She explained, her entire body tensing again as she turned around.

She looks like a cornered rabbit. Finley said with a whine.

She's nervous. Owen thought back.

I think the word you're looking for is terrified. Finley supplied.

Owen watched Caitlin carefully, taking the plate she offered and setting it on the desk. Leaning back against it, he gently took her hand in his.

"Do you need a hug?" he asked.

"A hug?" she repeated.

"You look like you need one," Owen said.

"Yeah, actually." She was stiff in his arms, but he held her against his chest and she eventually melted into his body.

Ten donuts says she cries. She looks like she needs a good cry. Finley observed.

Yup. Owen thought, resigned to the prospect. He readjusted and she tried to pull away but he held her tight.

"No, you're fine. We can do this as long as you need." He assured her. "We could do this all night and it would be just fine if it was what you needed."

"I want to do other things too." She whispered against his chest, so softly he thanked his shifter senses for being extra-sensitive.

"We can," Owen agreed.

I know what I said, but I don't think sexing her is a good idea. She needs to curl up under the blankets and be held. Finley said, grumbling.

She wants sex, Fin. She's got some damage. She's allowed to be scared and horny at the same time. Chill out. Owen responded. *Besides, it's not like we're not going to cuddle her afterward.*

"What's wrong?"

"My wolf has… feelings on the subject of us doing other things."

"Does he?" She pulled away, eyes wide.

Why did you have to drag me into it? Finley demanded.

"He thinks maybe you need cuddling instead of other things."

"We can do both, right?"

"That's the thought. But, before we do anything else, I need to shower off this last shift."

He touched her cheek softly before she pulled away completely, then headed to the small bathroom, turned on the hot water ,and stripped out of his shirt. After a short debate with Finley, Owen stuck his head out of the bathroom door.

"Would you like to join me?"

"I would love to." The hotel room lights weren't the best, but the way her eyes dilated as she looked at him shirtless was unmistakable.

Oh. Finley said. *She* does *want to do things!*

Yeah, she does. Owen agreed with smug satisfaction.

He stripped slowly and gave her a chance to look at him while he pretended not to notice before he climbed into the shower. When she pulled aside the curtain and climbed in, he took her hand to make sure she stepped over the lip of the bathtub safely.

"Ouch!" She exclaimed.

"What? Is it too hot?" Owen asked, moving to shield her from the water.

"Only if I want my skin intact." She laughed.

"Really? I'll turn it down. Hang on." He tilted the shower head away and adjusted the water. "How's that?"

"It's- okay." She said, making a face. He turned it down more and she sighed in relief.

If your plan was to impress her with your size, this isn't going to go how you envisioned. Finley grumbled.

Well, I didn't know she liked her showers as warm as glacial runoff. Owen countered.

They washed themselves in companionable silence until she turned to rinse the shampoo from her hair and Owen had his first chance to look at her body openly.

She was tall. Owen was six foot four and was accustomed to towering over women, she was average height for a woman, and solidly built. Her olive skin was a stark contrast to the entirely white bathroom. Her hair, normally pulled back into a bun or a braid, cascaded down her back. But that wasn't where his eyes were. He'd only made it down as far as her hips when he couldn't tear his eyes away. She was curvy, with hips that just begged to be grabbed. His mouth went dry as she swayed ever so slightly from side to side as she rinsed her hair.

I really hope she doesn't get scared and she wants to do more than cuddling. Finley said.

We'll see. I think she's leaning toward yes. Let's give her a preview, shall we? Owen grabbed the small bottle of soap and spoke close to her ear.

"Do you want some help with your back and shoulders?"

"Oh, sure," she said, with just a hint of tension.

As he used his hands and the soap to work her muscles, she relaxed into him, right against his less-than-subtle erection.

"I'm sorry," she started to apologize, but he gently moved her back with a single finger on each shoulder, barely putting pressure to let her know she was free to step back and enjoy the contact, or refuse as she wanted.

"Don't be."

When he ran out of soap they stood like that for a little bit until she finally said she was finished. He got out, grabbed them both towels, and extended a hand to her to ensure she didn't slip as she stepped over the edge of the tub.

"Hey." He said softly while she toweled her hair. "Should I get dressed? Or.."

She shook her head, but Owen didn't move.

"I'm going to need to hear you say it."

"No, don't get dressed."

"Alright, I'll see you out there." He took a chance and kissed the back of her hair chastely before heading out, closing the door behind him to give her privacy and a moment to collect her thoughts.

CHAPTER TEN

CAITLIN

*O*wen was... something else. Before he touched her, he reviewed her limits and asked if she had any other preferences. She was shocked at how considerate he was, and how cautious he was with her, but the real test would be when they were actually doing things. Caitlin breathed out and leaned into it.

Owen wasn't Axel.

She was safe. This *was safe.* Not only was this safe, but hopefully she was about to have some mind-blowing sex.

"This is entirely in your control," Owen informed her softly. "You tell me how you want to do this."

"I want it - hard and rough." The admission made her body heat with desire.

"Alright," Owen said, nodding with a small satisfied smile, "You, tell me if it's too much, okay?"

"I will,"

"Good girl," he said, something in his eyes shifting. The color maybe? She didn't care, she just wanted to enjoy this.

He sat on the edge of the bed and beckoned her forward.

"You want me to treat you badly?" He asked, his voice tender and at odds with the words while his eyes roved her body, his hands resting on her hips. "You want me to fuck you so hard you can't think straight?"

"Yes, please," she breathed.

"Good. I'm going to use you like my own little cum slut. My own personal fuck toy." She had given him the words over dinner, but hearing him say them sent a shiver through her.

"Get on your knees," Owen said, grabbing her nipple and pinching just enough that she whimpered as she lowered herself to her knees in front of him.

He spread his legs and ordered her to suck him, groaning as she took him in her mouth, his hand going to the back of her head.

"That's a good girl," he said hoarsely as she worked up and down his shaft, working up to taking him deeper. "Fuck, you're good at this. You look all innocent with your skirts and your sweaters, but underneath the good girl look you're just a little slut, aren't you?"

She made a noise as she continued to suck on him eagerly, her head bobbing.

"Fuck, the idea of me forcing my cock down your throat had you so hot in the restaurant I bet every man in the place could smell your arousal." He gripped her hair, pushing her down slightly on his cock, controlling her speed and the depth of how he penetrated her mouth, alternating between fast hard strokes and long, slow movements where she sucked eagerly and used her tongue to explore him. Owen cursed softly as he used her mouth and Caitlin reveled in his noises, the moans and growls he made as he took his pleasure.

He let her suck him off until he was so close to exploding his entire body trembled with suppressed need. Pulling her off his cock, coated with her saliva, he commanded her to open her mouth, spitting in it.

"Nasty little cum slut. I can't wait to fuck your tight little pussy. I might even let you cum if you do a good job. Stand up," Owen said to her in a low voice.

He reached out and pinched her nipple hard, pulling her forward into a rough kiss. She whimpered and kissed him back eagerly.

"Is this what you wanted, whore?" he asked, watching her carefully.

"Yes," she breathed.

"You want me to bend you over and use your pussy now?"

"Yes, please. Use my body for your pleasure," she begged.

Her core throbbed with steady pulses of desire. Shifting her weight slightly as he pinched her, Caitlin could feel the slick proof of her arousal. She needed this, needed to be used and degraded, needed to feel simultaneously safe and worthless all at once.

"Then get in position," he ordered, releasing her nipple.

She scrambled to obey as Owen watched her, tracking her every move like a predator. Grabbing a condom out of the pack he'd grabbed on the way into town, she turned her head to watch him open it and carefully roll it down before positioning himself behind her.

"I love seeing you on your knees for me, ready to take anything I give you," he said, his voice ragged. "One of these days I'm going to eat this pussy so I can swallow all of your juices, but tonight I'm just going to use you."

He guided himself inside of her and if she hadn't been trying not to cum from that alone she would have been embarrassed by the noises she made from just him entering her.

"Shut up," he snapped, and her walls gripped his cock at his words.

"Get a pillow, I don't want to hear your fucking mouth again," he ordered.

As soon as she had her face buried in a pillow, her ass high in the air for him he started moving inside of her, easing in and out, her moans muffled into the pillow as he fucked her slowly. She made all the noise she wanted, his long shaft penetrating her slowly. Her thigh muscles trembled as she felt a powerful orgasm building.

His fingers dug into the soft flesh of her hips, pulling him deep inside of her with a single brutal thrust repeated over and over until her breathing became ragged, little beads of sweat popping up on her back.

"Please, please," she said, turning her head to the side so he could hear her.

"Please what, slut?"

"Please don't stop."

"I'm not stopping, you stupid cunt. I haven't finished yet, and I'm not stopping till I do so shut up, in fact," he grabbed the back of her neck and leaned forward, pushing her face into the pillow, making it difficult for her to breathe.

He redoubled his efforts, keeping a hold of her neck as he railed her. It wasn't long before she was crying out, her walls squeezing him so tight he had to let go of her neck to grab her hips as he fought to stay inside. She could breathe, but not enough, and the restriction made her a little lightheaded, adding to her pleasure.

"Damn," he said, but didn't stop.

He continued fucking her hard until she was coming again. This time he slowed and watched as she rocked on her knees, using his body for her pleasure. When she slowed he flipped her over onto her side and took her, his face tense as he fucked her into another screaming wave of pleasure.

"What a good slut, coming all over my cock and I haven't even touched your clit yet." He eased out of her and pushed her leg so she was on her back with him kneeling between her legs.

"No, I'm so sensitive-" she began, he paused, eyes clouded with a moment of uncertainty.

"Your safe word is red." He reminded her, his hand moving slowly to her clit.

When she didn't stop him, he spread her wide and used his thumb to push over her sensitive nub, sending a jolt of pleasure through her body that made her hips shoot off the bed.

"It's too much!" She insisted.

"Cum sluts don't decide what's too much," he said, continuing to play with her while his other hand pushed her hips to the bed.

"Oh, fuck," she said, the familiar tingling beginning in her spine.

"That's more like it, baby," he coached, "Take what I give you, and thank me for it."

Her mouth opened in a silent cry as her pleasure built while his thumb did slow circles over her sensitive clit, then suddenly his hand holding her hips down disappeared. She felt his tip at her entrance and he shoved roughly inside of her as a sharp slap landed across her inner thigh.

The slight taste of pain sent her over the edge, crying out as she gripped the sheets. Owen cried out with her, slamming into her, grunting as he came hard.

IT TOOK several minutes for her to come back down from the high of her final orgasm, her breath finally returning to a normal pace. She turned to Owen who lay on his side, watching her with a self-satisfied expression.

"You are perfect," he said sincerely, laying one hand on her soft stomach.

"You were- wow," she said.

Much to her embarrassment, she felt tears fill her eyes.

"Hey," Owen said gently, scooting toward her, gently taking her shoulder in his hand so she turned to face him in the bed.

"Oh my gods, I'm so sorry-"

"Hush, now," he said, holding her against his chest despite her protests, "You had a big release, and you were scared on top of that. There's nothing wrong with crying. I'm here, and I'm not going anywhere. You were so good, and it's okay to cry."

He crooned to her, speaking softly as he held her until she was calm again, only leaving to get her a tissue before placing his arms back around her.

"Better?" He asked.

"Better," she agreed, hesitating for a moment before tucking herself against his chest and whispering a faint thank you.

She'd fully intended to stay awake, to send him home and to process her feelings after he left but she felt safe in his arms, safer than she had even with Axel when things were good. Was it too fast to feel this way? Probably, but she was going to embrace it and see where it went.

CHAPTER ELEVEN

OWEN

*A*fter she'd fallen asleep in his arms at the motel, Owen knew he was sunk for sure. As she'd thanked him, her eyes closing sleepily as she nuzzled against his chest, Owen was sure he wanted to keep her around for a lot more than friendship.

He took his cues from her, letting her initiate when it came to sex, but in every other way, he treated her like he would any female he was courting. He understood that she was fresh off a relationship and she wanted to take things slowly, and he was prepared to wait for as long as it took.

I don't understand humans. She likes us! Why doesn't she think we're more than friends? What if she's being 'friends' with other people and sexing them? Finley asked, his irritation mingling with Owen's and trying to threaten Owen's good mood.

Fin, bud, she's got some trauma. She doesn't feel safe. Besides, when would she sleep around? She's texting us constantly. Owen reasoned.

You should have a talk with her. Finley suggested.

About what? We talk all the time. Owen asked as he clocked out at the Sheriff's department.

About being exclusive! I don't want her sexing other people. Or making them fancy baked stuff. I don't like it. Finley growled.

She wants to take it slow, and we're honoring that. Owen reminded his wolf. *Also, she's allowed to bake other people things. It makes her happy.*

She didn't want you to take it slow when she made you late for work. Finley reminded him smugly, thinking of when his alarm had gone off at the hotel. He'd silenced it quickly, but she'd rolled over and used her hands to do things that Owen didn't care to relive right now. The last thing he needed was to have a full hard on in the middle of the Justice Center offices.

"Hey man, you okay?" His partner Tyler asked.

"Yeah, Fin's got some feelings about Caitlin, we're just working through it."

"Alright, just checking in. See you at the base?" Recently, Tyler had started working as an EMT part-time, often on Owen's shifts. They already worked well together, so when Ryder was occupied with another student, Tyler was usually put on a truck with Owen and John as their ride-along.

"Nope, I'm heading up to see Caitlin, actually," Owen admitted.

"Oh, good for you, man," Tyler said, tucking his backpack over his shoulder. "Have some extra fun for me, I'll probably be stuck with Moony Eyes and Blake."

"Ryder isn't so bad if you catch him on a good night," Owen said with a chuckle.

Moony eyes. That's funny. Finley barked a laugh.

"If," Tyler said, pointing to Owen. "I'll catch you on the flip side."

Owen's shift was over, but he had time to kill before he left for Caitlin's sister's apartment. It had been almost a month since she'd met up with him at the motel, she'd finally invited him over to her sister's apartment while the kids were there. Owen was nervous and excited, unable to sit still. He wanted to bring the kids something, but toys seemed like a stupid thing to bring, and he didn't know what they were into.

In the past month, they'd met after her appointments with Olivia for lunch, or he would drive up when the kids were at their bio dad's for the weekend, but he hadn't pressed for more or tried to pin down what they were. The sex was intense, and although she seemed hesitant to talk about her past much, Owen was trying his damndest to be patient, even if Finley and his own instincts were demanding that he take it further.

After a run in the park, he came up with an idea, jogging over to the EMS base, heading straight into Medic One's office, where Patrick was sitting in his leather chair.

"Hey, did you need something?" Patrick looked up from his computer when Owen appeared at his door.

"Yeah, I need keys for 20," Owen said.

"Sure, they're hanging up," Patrick went back to his work.

Owen grabbed the keys for the big engine and heard Ryder's voice coming from the day room.

"Ryder, gimme a hand?" Owen asked, poking his head into the day room.

"Whatcha need?" Ryder asked, stooping to put a chicken in the oven.

"I need help with 20," Owen said.

Ryder straightened and frowned, but Owen didn't explain, walking out to the bay and opening the big bay door.

"What are we doing?" Ryder asked, looking around the bay.

When Ryder's phone dinged, he immediately checked it, and then put it back in his pocket. Owen smiled a little, knowing that out of everyone who would understand what he wanted to do, Ryder was one who wouldn't make fun of him for wanting to impress his girl.

While it was true that shifters would go above and beyond in the process of courting a potential mate, that didn't save you from the ridicule that would follow. Gossip was the lifeblood of a small town, more so in the small base that housed the firefighters and paramedics, and Owen didn't particularly want to make a big deal out of his new not-relationship, especially while she seemed on the fence.

There was enough shared history between Ryder and Owen that Owen knew Ryder wouldn't mind doing this for him and would keep it to himself. Ryder had said and done his own fair share of embarrassing things during his courtship of Emma that taking a cheesy video in the engine wouldn't be a blip on his screen.

"Here, hold this. I need a video for Caitlin's nieces and nephew," Owen instructed.

Ryder nodded and wordlessly took the phone, walking over to the bay opening. When Owen pulled out of the bay Ryder gave him a thumbs up, Owen turned on the lights and gave an enthusiastic thumbs-up with his best winning smile. He'd just gotten out of the cab to check the video when Fire Chief Jason Beckett pulled up in his pickup, walking over.

"What are we doing, boys?" he asked.

"Owen's got some nieces and a nephew he needs to impress," Ryder explained.

Owen cut him a sideways look, but Ryder just shrugged. So much for discretion. The chief nodded and looked at Owen, considering him for a moment before speaking.

"Pull around the block and we'll get you coming with lights and sirens. That's way more impressive." Owen nodded eagerly, pulling around as instructed.

The chief instructed Ryder to go stand in the middle of the road on the double-yellow line. Owen waited until the few cars had cleared, then barreled down the road, lights and sirens going full-tilt. Owen parked the engine back in its spot in the bay and Ryder handed over the phone with a smile, checking his phone again.

"So, you're going up to Red River to meet the kids tonight?" Ryder asked.

"Yep, I'm taking a shower then heading out. Thanks for this," he said, holding up his phone.

"No problem. So, you're meeting the kids. That's a big step, things must be serious," Ryder acknowledged, opening the conversation if Owen wanted to share, but not pressing him.

"I'm not entirely sure where she stands, but I'm pretty serious," Owen said, his chest tight at the idea.

Maybe the kids will love us so much, she'll realize we're good! Finley suggested.

Ryder seemed to be thinking along the same thought. He closed the bay door and they walked back out into the foyer.

"If she's letting you meet the kids, she's serious about you. Or, at least she's willing to be serious. You need anything else?"

"Nah, I'm good," Owen said.

"Good luck," Ryder said, heading back inside the base.

SHE WAS LIVING with her sister's children in a little apartment on the far side of Red River. The sister, Charlotte, worked as an emergency relief coordinator with the government. When Charlotte and her husband had split recently, she had transferred to a desk job with more steady hours. Before the transfer could be approved, a disaster struck. Caitlin had just arrived, intending to stay for an extended visit, so she'd stayed with the kids.

She hadn't said much about her past, just that she'd had a bad relationship and she wasn't ready to talk about it. Owen respected it and was giving her space, trying his damndest not to push her. From the few things she'd said about her ex in passing, Owen was inclined to think he was the sort of man who didn't deserve any woman, and if the reactions Caitlin had sometimes were any indication of the damage he'd done, Owen hoped he was six feet under, but she hadn't volunteered that information and he wasn't pushing her. Owen stewed about it for the entire drive up to Red River to see her, finally pulling his truck into a parking space with a confused look around.

She'd described the apartment building, and the neighborhood, as small but quiet. When he pulled up, he had to work to keep himself from snarling as his wolf's hackles raised. It was quiet but less in the quaint and peaceful sense than the kind of place where conscious parents didn't let their children play outside because they were worried about drive-bys.

She lives here? Finley's mental voice was tight with the same concern that filled Owen.

Apparently. Owen grimaced.

We should take her home to live with us. She would be safe with us. His wolf growled.

What would she do with the kids?

We like kids! Finley insisted, sharing a mental image of Caitlin, pregnant on the wrap-around porch of the house his mother had left him that was standing empty, with several more little kids running around in the yard. The mental image was nice, but Owen shook his head.

They aren't her kids. She can't just - never mind. The answer's no. Besides, we're taking things slow. Owen reminded Finley.

The good news is if you want to get loud and kinky with her, no one will care. Finley pointed out.

Why's that? Owen asked, straightening his shirt before grabbing the bouquet of flowers he'd grabbed for Caitlin on his way out of town out of the passenger seat.

This is the kind of neighborhood where you could be gunning someone down in the street and if it wasn't happening to them, nobody would come sniffing around. Owen grunted in grim amusement.

He knocked on the door of apartment 19. She opened the door with a bright smile that made his chest swell. It had been a long shift. He was bone tired, but seeing her made his whole body react.

"Hi," Caitlin greeted almost shyly.

She opened the door and stepped behind it to let him in. The space was tidy and neatly kept, but Owen bit back irritation at the idea of the woman he was courting, or friends or whatever they were, living in a space that was so poorly maintained. The dated yellowing floor had several cracks, one of which was covered with strips of worn duct tape. The fronts of the cabinets had strips of veneered wood from the panels missing, Owen wondered if the kids ever got splinters from them, and noted that the silicone around the sink was peeling away.

"Hi yourself," he greeted.

He didn't know what the expectations were around the kids, so he greeted her politely with a chaste hug. Their lack of more intimate physical contact didn't keep him and Finley from noticing how her thin t-shirt showed the outline of her bra. A small little girl with stick-straight blonde hair stood in the kitchen, her thumb loosely in her mouth, large light gray eyes regarding Owen warily. Owen smiled over Caitlin's shoulder. Caitlin noticed his look and turned away to introduce them.

"This is Maya. Maya, fingers out of your mouth honey. This is my friend Owen, the one who's coming for a sleepover?" Maya nodded, Owen squatted down and gave her a friendly smile.

"Hi, I'm Owen, I hear you like trucks. I drive a fire truck at work sometimes. Want to see?" The beads in her braids rattled as she nodded. "I think you'll like this."

Owen and Finley were pleased - the kids were delightful. It took them a bit to warm up to Owen, but he'd expected that. Once he'd shown all three the video of him 'being a hero' as little six-year-old Brayden had put it, the children seemed assured that he was someone to be trusted and the evening proceeded without a hitch. Not too long after his arrival, Caitlin issued a general call for everyone to start their evening pre-bedtime routines.

"Is there anything I can do to help?" He asked as the kids all went about their various tasks.

Maya called for Caitlin and she assured him he could just relax as she hurried from the room.

"We're fine, we do this every day. I'll be back out in a few. The remote's on the arm of the couch if you want to watch something."

He couldn't just sit there while she put the kids to bed so he washed the dishes and set them in the black plastic drying rack that sat in the left side of the sink, then wiped down the counters and put away the leftovers from dinner in the fridge. He'd been finished for a few minutes when she emerged. She looked around the kitchen and let out a grateful sigh.

"You didn't have to do that," she said, walking over to him and allowing him to fold his arms around her.

She was soft and she smelled like a strangely comforting mix of that evening's delicious lasagna, her laundry soap, and her own unique scent.

"Aunt Caitlin?" Brooklyn, a ten-year-old who was a carbon copy of her younger sister, straight blonde hair pulled to one side with a dramatic side part, spoke from the doorway of the kitchen.

"What's up, Brooklyn?"

"Can I listen to an audiobook?"

"Yeah, pick one you and Maya both agree on," Caitlin agreed.

"Okay. If I need you..." Brooklyn's eyes cut to Owen significantly.

"I'm not going anywhere," Caitlin laughed. "Just knock if you need me."

"Okay, I didn't know if you needed privacy or, whatever," the girl looked embarrassed.

"You plan on having the door locked?" he teased quietly when they were alone.

"Of course."

"Are you going to take advantage of me?" he pitched his voice even lower, in a playfully shocked tone, putting one hand to his chest in mock surprise.

"No, but I'm hoping very much you'll be taking advantage of me," she said in an equally low voice. "The bedroom's at the end of the hall - straight back, I just need to turn the lights off and such."

"Oh, now you're ordering me to go to your bedroom?" He asked, quirking an eyebrow.

"If you want to fuck me," she said with a nonchalant shrug.

I vote we go to the bedroom! Finley said.

"As you wish," Owen said with a wink, making his way down the hall.

CHAPTER TWELVE

AXEL

For a deputy, this guy was pretty oblivious, Axel thought as he drove in his brother's pickup. Axel had taken a little time to get the things he'd need to relocate for a bit. He wanted Caitlin back, but he had to do it right. He would have to convince her to come home, he'd done it before, but she'd never gone to such lengths before.

He adjusted in the seat, hardening at the memory of when she'd run out in the middle of a rainstorm after a fight. Her soaking white t-shirt and leggings had clung to her body. He'd allowed her to run until she was spent, tracking her at a distance until she was spent, then taking her right there in the mud. She'd liked that, allowing him to take his pleasure and walking back to the house with him hand in hand.

That was definitely what he missed most about having her home. Seeing her willful defiance fade into quiet, fearful submission as he punished her, her clingy brokenness after he was finished, that was what he'd lived for. Then she'd been gone.

Perhaps he'd gone a bit far, but so had she, surely she would see that. She would have to see it his way or he would make her see. They were mated, and wolves mated for life. You didn't leave your mate because of one little fight, and he wasn't going home without her.

The deputy pulled past as he pulled his expensive fancy truck into the parking lot of a rundown apartment complex. Axel parked on the street, watching in the rearview as Owen entered the apartment on the second floor. Axel had his first glimpse of her he'd had since she left and had to fight the impulse to go in. He stayed out in his truck all night, but the fucker didn't leave. Axel noted the address, then went to his hotel to get an hour of sleep before he resumed observing his girl to see when he could approach her alone.

CHAPTER THIRTEEN

CAITLIN

*D*aylight was streaming in the windows when Caitlin heard the bedroom door creak open, a mass of tangled blonde hair poking its way in, followed by a pair of sleepy, but unsure eyes. Caitlin beckoned Maya with the crook of her finger.

"Did you go potty?" She whispered. The little girl shook her head. Caitlin tilted her head towards the bedroom door.

Having performed her pre-snuggling requirement, Maya returned to the bedside.

"Can I get up in your bed?" Her niece asked in a whisper.

After gaining permission, she used the stool that lived by the side of the bed for just that purpose, her niece climbed up and scooted under the blankets Caitlin lifted for her, sliding up to her like a heat-seeking missile. Caitlin held her finger to her lips, pointing over her shoulder. Maya looked with curiosity, then her eyes grew wide as she nodded solemnly when she saw Owen.

A few minutes later, her ginger-haired nephew, who would proudly announce to anyone who would listen that he could read better than any kid in his class, shambled sleepily, pulling back the covers without comment. Caitlin and Maya both scooted across the bed to make room for him.

Caitlin's bottom brushed against Owen who made a sleepy satisfied rumble, turning over and sliding his arm around her.

Maya's eyes grew wide, then had a fit of giggles, covering her mouth.

"Brayden, look." She poked her brother who eyed the arm with a considerable amount of wariness, and very little amusement.

"Good morning my sweethearts," Caitlin whispered softly. "Did you sleep well?"

"Yes," Maya whispered, but Brayden just nodded.

"Did you have nice dreams?"

"They were great!" Maya whispered, a little louder.

"I don't remember." Brayden wrapped an arm around his little sister, saying in a whisper "Oh, look, a Maya sandwich."

"Don't eat me!" Maya objected, giggling as she wiggled between them.

Caitlin pretended to eat Maya, growling a little.

"Ooh, tasty!" Caitlin exclaimed with hushed enthusiasm.

"I'm hungry," Maya said plaintively.

"I'll get her a banana. Come on Maya."

After a rumble from the other side of the bed, Owen's head popped up around Caitlin's, nuzzling her neck with a noise of inquiry, his hand moving to Caitlin's breast, cupping it. Maya frowned for a moment, then laid her hand on top of his in a gesture of inclusion.

"Auntie sandwich!" She cried in delight, pretending to eat the hand on top of her aunt, startling its owner into full alertness.

"Morning," he looked over Caitlin's shoulder, "...everybody,"

Brayden was surprised into fearful silence and put his arm protectively around Maya.

"I heard that you have pancakes here *every* Sunday, is that true?" Owen asked, moving his hand away from Caitlin's breast to her waist.

"For our family," Brayden said cautiously.

"You can come if Aunt Caitlin says," Maya informed him.

"Hm. Aunt Caitlin, can I eat pancakes with you all?" Owen asked innocently as he pressed against her bottom in a subtle and provocative movement.

"Yes, you may," Caitlin said solemnly, moving back against him with equal subtlety.

"Okay! Time to get started!" Maya exclaimed.

Brayden observed his aunt with anxious amber eyes.

"B, you need to talk?"

Brayden nodded, his gaze cutting over to Owen fearfully.

"I'm going to use the restroom," Owen announced, kissing Caitlin on the back of the head before making himself scarce.

"Hey buddy, come here," Caitlin said.

"I don't like that he's here," Brayden said. "Daddy won't like it."

"Yeah. But remember what we talked about? Daddy is in charge of what happens at daddy's house, and mommy and I are in charge of what happens here. Mostly mommy. Your daddy doesn't get to decide what's okay at our house. Owen is very nice to me, and I like having him around. I promise I wouldn't bring a friend here if he wasn't nice."

"Uncle Axel wasn't very nice, I heard mommy say so," Brayden said, "She said he hurt you in places you can't see. Where did he hurt you?"

"Axel hurt my heart," she said quietly, with a glance at the bathroom door, where she hoped Owen wasn't listening.

"Oh."

"But, you know what? Every time I get a hug or a kiss I feel a little better. You know what else?" She hugged Brayden tight to her chest to give her a moment to compose herself.

"What?"

"Mister Owen isn't just a firefighter, he's also a *deputy*," Caitlin informed him with a sparkle in her eye and raised eyebrows.

"Oh." Brayden's eyes lit up with excitement.

"He said if you wanted to, he'd let you come see all the trucks and their equipment at the station, even the ambulances!"

"Can you come?" Brayden asked, eyes going round with worry.

It made Caitlin's heart squeeze to see how much anxiety he had for a six year old, but she hoped that having a man like Owen around, even if it wasn't forever, would help him learn what kind of good men were out there, and they weren't all like the men that Caitlin and Charlotte had picked as mates.

"Yeah. I wanna see them too!" Caitlin answered.

"That does sound like fun," Brayden replied wistfully.

"If you want to do it, you just ask him, Owen would love to take you." Caitlin pointed out.

"Will you ask?"

"Nope. You know the rules. We communicate directly with people." It was hard to teach children to be assertive when one of the parents wasn't big on listening, but it was all the sisters knew to do - to train them as best as they could during the time they had them with them and make the best of a bad situation.

"Yeah. Okay." Brayden looked glum, but she could see his little mind whirring.

He snuggled up against her shoulder, burrowing into her.

"Morning," Brooklyn walked in with long blonde hair a tangled mess that closely resembled a dirty blonde bird's nest. She sat on the foot of the bed, making an inquiring face and gesture at her brother directed towards Caitlin.

"He just needed some love," Caitlin explained, holding her hand out in greeting.

At ten, Brooklyn was at the age where she sometimes believed she was too big for 'little kid things' like good morning snuggles, but many times still wanted them, so Caitlin left it up to her to initiate what she wanted. Brooklyn took the hand and squeezed it, then let it go.

"Do you want to start on the pancakes with me?" Brooklyn inquired of the bundle plastered to Caitlin, "I'll let you get out the sprinkles this morning!"

"I want to pick out five sprinkles!" Maya exclaimed from the doorway.

"I want to get out some!" Brayden's head popped up and they all trooped out in search of sprinkles.

"Close the door, I'll be out in a few!" Caitlin called.

Brooklyn gave a thumbs up over her shoulder and pulled the door shut with a thud on her way out. After the bedroom door shut, the bathroom door opened and Owen walked out, shaking his head.

"Makes me so mad when they look at me like that. That fucker deserves- well." Owen bit his tongue, "No kid should have to look at every new stranger like they have a reason to be scared. I hate it."

"Yeah." Caitlin agreed. She briefly thought that she was grateful she hadn't ever gotten pregnant, so there was a child who could learn to be afraid of people because of how their father treated them.

"What can I do for you this morning?" Owen asked, breaking through her thoughts.

"You can come back here for a minute." She grinned, "There's something I need help with."

He was across the room pinning her wrists to the bed in a moment, rubbing his nose back and forth across hers in what would have been an innocent gesture if he hadn't laid half on top of her, pressing against her in a lewd manner.

"What do you guys call it again?" Owen asked.

"Nosey-nosey." She supplied. Caitlin had done it to Owen several times after their trysts, and Owen thought it was so cute he started doing it back to her.

"Mm. I like that. Was *that* what you wanted, or do you want me to lock the door?"

"I definitely need the door locked."

"Hm. And are you in a nice mood, or...?" She shook her head, blushing a little.

Owen ordered her not to move, got up to lock the door, and returned to the foot of the bed where he dropped his sweats, revealing a growing erection.

He gave a growl of appreciation before crawling over her and rolling her over onto her stomach. Spreading her legs and caressing her bottom before giving it a single resounding smack. He paused to roll a condom on, then he was on top of her, sliding inside of her from behind, his body weight holding her in place. She gasped as he roughly shoved his cock inside of her.

"God, for such a slut your pussy feels good," he pitched his voice low so only she could hear, in case one of the kids came back. "You know what? I don't think you've earned my cock in your pussy this morning. I'm gonna fuck your glorious ass and watch your cheeks clap around my cock as I use you."

Reaching into the nightstand he grabbed the lube, covering himself liberally, then lifting her hips so she was ass up in the air with her chest pressed into the pillow. He eased one finger of his right hand inside of her easily, then added another covered in lube. When he had three fingers seated easily, he withdrew them and positioned his tip at her other hole. Slowly he pushed himself inside of her. She whined with need as he eased inside of her, slow and deep.

"Fuck, your ass is so tight. I don't give a shit if you cum or not, but I don't want to hear you whining that it's too rough. Got it, slut? You're just here to be my cum dumpster when I'm hard." He pumped in and out of her savagely, making Caitlin whimper with each thrust.

Using his left hand he reached around and put his fingers in her mouth, using her jaw as leverage to fuck her harder.

"Please, please..." her hands splayed on the bed sheets.

"Shut up, fuck toy," he growled roughly, pressing hard on the back of her neck, driving her face into the pillow he redoubled his efforts.

She could breathe, but not quite enough, the sensation of breathlessness in combination with his dirty talk and the sex was too much. An orgasm crashed over her, her screams muffled in the pillow.

Releasing her neck, he slowed down, taking long slow strokes in and out.

"Turn over, fuck toy." When she didn't move fast enough he slapped her ass, she rolled across the bed, eyes bright, face flushed as her chest heaved. Straddling her torso, he grabbed her hands and held them to either side of her breasts "Stay there. Don't fucking move. I think today you don't deserve my cum inside of you."

He rolled off the condom and stroked himself aggressively, then with a grunt he came, sending thick ropes onto her torso, his free hand gripping one of her thighs tight as he spilled his seed over her. They didn't linger, immediately getting up to clean up and see to the kids and breakfast.

He watched her clean herself off in the bathroom as he saw to himself, making her blush. She wondered what he was thinking. Did he enjoy it as much as she had? Was he happy with her? Before he left to get redressed, he came to stand behind her.

"You are perfect, you know that? Your body, and everything else about you. Thank you for sharing this with me."

"Well, I didn't exactly do it selflessly. I got off too, very thoroughly." She laughed as she cleaned herself up.

"I didn't mean the sex, Caitlin." He said, catching her eyes in the mirror, "I meant all of it. The kids, letting me into your space, into your life. I love every minute of it, and I'm honored to have your trust."

She couldn't speak, just nodding. He made his way back out of the bedroom he announced congenially.

"Now, let's go make some pancakes. You do know how to work up a guy's appetite."

OUT IN THE KITCHEN, there was happy music playing, but almost no noise in the kitchen, none of the voices or chatter that was the usual hubbub of the house. Caitlin rounded the corner, her heart sinking. David was there in her kitchen, arms crossed.

"No wonder you guys look so glum. Your Auntie Caitlin decided to have a lazy morning?" He looked her over with disgust.

"Aunt Caitlin is not sleeping. She is snuggling Orange." Maya insisted.

"Maya, his name is Owen. O-w-e-n." Brooklyn drew out his name patiently.

"Or-ange!" Maya said, nodding with all the confidence of a toddler who knows in their heart of hearts they have said it perfectly.

Brayden sat at the dining room table, coloring quietly. Brooklyn went back to flipping pancakes, Maya ran over to Caitlin, who scooped her up into her arms.

"What are you doing here, David?" Caitlin asked.

"Coming to see my kids on pancake day." He spotted Owen,

straightened, and looked hard at Caitlin. "Really? Having strange men over with my kids in the house?"

"Owen isn't a stranger, he's a friend." Brooklyn piped up from her spot at the stove. "He's going to take Brayden to see the firetrucks and the ambulances soon!"

"I don't think we've met." Owen offered his hand, and David looked at it with contempt, not moving. "I'm David, the kids' dad."

"Owen, Caitlin's man," Owen replied evenly then turned to Caitlin, "Can I have the squirt?"

Maya grinned and launched herself into his arms when he came near, leaving Caitlin face-to-face with a furious David.

"Orange, will you help me with those sprinkles?" Maya asked.

"Sure thing. Which bowl is yours?" Owen asked.

"That one!" Maya exclaimed.

David's face flushed a deep purple, "What the hell, Caitlin? Bringing some random guy here for a hook-up with the kids home?"

"That one is looking good," Owen was saying loudly.

Caitlin lowered her voice, trying to keep the strain from it as she stood toe to toe with the man who was several inches taller than her.

"What we do here is mine and Charlotte's business. Besides, you didn't give me any notice you were coming or I would have told you we had company if you were going to make an issue out of it, but you decided to be an ass and just show up."

"Mom says we're only allowed to have three kinds of sprinkles," Brooklyn informed Owen, with all the borrowed authority of an oldest sibling enforcing the rules.

"Is that the rule, just three kinds?" Owen confirmed with Maya.

"Yes," The little girl admitted, cutting a dirty look at Brooklyn.

"Whose fault is that? I have to work so much overtime to keep up with your sister's damn child support that I don't have time to do anything else, my shift got canceled and I wanted to see them," David said with much less effort to keep his voice low.

"Well look at my bowl, it doesn't have any. I wish I had somebody to pick out some sprinkles for me." Owen said with exaggerated wistfulness and a glance over his shoulder at Caitlin, a wary eye on David.

"I don't want to argue," Caitlin said, holding her hands up in a gesture of surrender.

"I'm not staying if he is," David said.

As if that would be a problem, Caitlin thought.

"You know where the door is," she answered, moving around him to check on the pancakes and Brooklyn.

"You know what? I'm not leaving. I'm going to spend time with my son," David stomped over in his dirty boots, making strained conversation with Brayden while everyone else finished up their parts of making the pancakes.

CHAPTER FOURTEEN

OWEN

*B*reakfast was awkward and strained until the kids' dad finally got bored and claimed there was a work emergency, checking his phone that hadn't buzzed once, the screen blank of any notifications. After he left, Caitlin excused herself. Owen watched her go, jaw tense. The guy was a real ass, and the way he'd spoken to Caitlin and the children had set him and Finley on edge.

Finley had distinct feelings about how they could handle the matter if they followed him outside.

"Somebody should go hug her," Brooklyn observed, giving Owen a significant look.

"You think so?" He didn't want to intrude, but he did want to see that she was alright. She'd been shaken and upset by David's appearance, even though she'd handled it well enough.

"She usually cries after daddy grouches at her. It makes her sad." Brooklyn informed him.

"Okay, then. Unless you think she'd rather have one from you?"

"No, you can do it. I've done it lots of times before."

Caitlin was sitting on her bed, her face buried in her hands with several tissues crumbled in her grip. The sight made Owen want to follow David out and give him a lesson in what happens when you disrespect a lady, but he restrained himself. That wouldn't help anyone, least of all Caitlin.

"I'm so sorry," she said, looking up when he sat on the bed next to her.

"Hey, you don't need to apologize." Owen turned to wrap his arms around her.

"He was so rude, and in front of the kids. I hate that I can't make it stop. I'm sorry, It must be so exhausting to deal with drama at work all day and come here for sex and then have to deal with this." She cried, her words cutting him to the quick. Is that seriously what she thought? Hadn't she been listening earlier when he'd told her he was here for everything, the whole experience?

"I did not come here for sex." Owen corrected a little more sharply than he'd intended. "I came here to spend time with you and those amazing kids out there. I came here for pancake breakfast and memories. The sex is nice, but it's not the point. Nothing is ruined. I knew you had David hanging around, it wasn't some dirty little secret crawling out of the woodwork to surprise me. I do want to know why the kids let him in though. I don't like that."

"They wouldn't let him in," Caitlin sat up, blowing her nose into her tissues.

"He doesn't have a key, right?" Owen asked, concerned and alarmed at the idea.

"The lock doesn't work." She admitted. Owen's pulse drummed in his ears. That man could just waltz in any time he pleased - hell, anyone could. But surely she didn't mean they had no lock on the front door at all, not in this neighborhood.

"Which one doesn't work?" he asked.

"Either of them. My friend across the hall said it got slammed one too many times, the landlord is just too cheap to replace it. He said it's 'on his list of things to do' which he always says when something isn't going to get done."

"Alright. Well, that's getting fixed today." He wrapped his arms around her, simply holding her until she was calm again.

"Come on, you. Your pancakes are going to be 'ruining,' as Maya says," Caitlin finally said, putting on a bright smile that didn't quite reach her eyes.

You know - Finley started to suggest.

Fin, not now, okay? I probably agree with whatever you're about to say about that piece of shit, but right now I want to focus on having fun with Caitlin and the kids.

As long as we're on the same page and we agree he deserves... well. Bad things. Finley conceded.

Absolutely. Owen agreed.

AFTER EVERYONE HAD EATEN their fill of pancakes Owen pulled out his phone while everyone tidied up from breakfast and pulled up the Pinehurst first responders group chat.

OWEN

Hey, is anybody free to help replace a door? Caitlin's sister's scumbag ex walks into their apartment anytime because her door doesn't lock. I don't want to leave until it's fixed. It's a bit of a haul.

TYLER

...seriously?

I'll bring a door, but I don't have my tools. Send me the dimensions.

CALEN

I can bring my tools.

OWEN

When you get here, the kids are a bit skittish.

JOHN

There's three of them, right?

OWEN

Yup. One boy and two girls.

JOHN

Okay. We got this.

OWEN

The boy has a hero worship thing about firemen and EMS, I guess they saw a lot of them when they were at their last place.

TYLER

I'll come in my shirt and hat.

JOHN

Me too. I'll grab some of the volunteer Fire guys, we just finished up.

CHAPTER FIFTEEN

CAITLIN

A few hours later a swarm of firemen and medics descended on the house. They brought over food for lunch, cold sodas, and big smiles for the kids. After introductions, Brayden was inducted into the work crew. The men outfitted him with enthusiasm, handing him a somewhat big fire station crew shirt and hat, completing his ensemble with a tool belt, hard hat, and the promise of his very own soda in a glass bottle to drink with the grown-up men when they were done.

"Look at him," Caitlin said with tears in her eyes, taking a video for Charlotte on her phone as Brayden helped install a new front door for them. When one of Owen's deputy friends walked by, she touched his arm gently, saying, "Thank you for including him."

"It's our pleasure, ma'am. How are your window locks? All working?" Calen asked.

"Um," her cheeks flamed.

"These old apartment buildings can have some bad hardware," he replied smoothly. "I have some out in the truck, leftover from another project. I could put them in here if you like. It'll just take a few minutes."

"Sure, that'd be great," she said, but before she could say more Owen called her name.

When she crossed the room, Owen was standing there with a man she thought she recognized from the base. He was stockier than Owen, with long sandy blonde hair perpetually pulled back in a pair of sunglasses or a baseball cap.

"Brooklyn asked if we could put a lock on her door. She said she wanted it in case David came back, and if he wanted to yell at them, she could get Maya and Brayden away and he couldn't follow," Owen spoke quietly.

Caitlin's stomach clenched and it felt like her blood had turned to sludge in her veins. She and Charlotte had done their best to make the children feel safe, but Caitlin had only been here for a little while. How bad had things been before Caitlin was here? How much had the kids heard and seen when Charlotte and David were together? Visions of what Axel had done to her flashed through like a movie playing in front of her vision. What memories did the children have? Caitlin couldn't fix everything, but she could give the kids doors that locked so they felt safe.

"Give it to her," she whispered, filled with shame.

"Tyler," Owen said to the other man, but he was already walking away, a thumb's up.

"On it." Tyler called over one shoulder, then louder, "I'm looking for a helper to install a lock on a door - anybody available to help me with that?"

"I'm available!" Brayden's enthusiastic cry came from somewhere else inside.

"I'm available too!" Maya cried as their little feet ran down the hallway.

Owen gave her a quick forehead kiss and a reassuring squeeze of her elbow before going off to keep helping.

When the repairs and upgrades were finished, Caitlin was in awe. A door with a deadbolt, all working window locks, and other little things that hadn't been taken care of by the landlord. They'd even fixed the leaking bathtub, installed the new shower head one of the

TO TRUST AND PROTECT

men had spotted under the cabinet when he was fixing the slow-draining bathroom sink, and they'd even gone so far as to tighten all the hardware on their previously wobbly kitchen chairs, which now were sound and stable. She didn't know what else they'd done in the kitchen, but they'd told everyone not to touch the sink for twenty-four hours and assured Caitlin they'd leave enough paper plates and food so she didn't have to worry about dishes or cooking during that time.

"I don't know how to thank you all," she said, tears swimming in her eyes.

"We happened to be close by, Tyler had the door just sitting around, and I had the hardware for the windows. It was really no trouble." John said with a smile as he replaced the window locks.

She'd seen them run out to the hardware store after counting the broken window locks, but she let it go. There was no way they could afford the extra right now and she wouldn't have had any idea how to replace window locks even if she could afford them.

She watched Owen with the kids and his friends. They all seemed like the kind of men you'd want in your corner, the types of men who would literally give you the shirt off their backs she thought as she watched Calen reach in his car and pull out a stack of t-shirts and hand them to Brayden, explaining that he couldn't only wear the fire-fighter shirts, he had to wear the deputy shirts too.

These were exactly the kind of people that she wanted to be her people, and even though it was too much too soon, she was thinking that Owen seemed to be the kind of man she wanted in her life.

CHAPTER SIXTEEN

OWEN

aitlin looked pensive, but he could see her breathing easier. He didn't want to go, but he could go back home knowing they were at least behind a locked door now and her sister's ex couldn't just waltz in whenever he damn well pleased.

"Mister Owen?" Brayden asked formally when they'd started to wind down after the work was done, breaking out the sodas and lunch.

"Yeah?" Owen asked, squatting down so he was on the boy's level.

"Aunt Caitlin said maybe you would take me to see some ambulances if I wanted to?" The boy's face showed hope and anxiety that made Owen want to bring him in for a hug. The way Brayden stood, trying to hold his bottle like the big-handed men did and hooking one thumb through his belt loops like Calen was doing absentmindedly while he sent a text to Cheyenne, Owen thought maybe he needed to be treated like one of the men.

"I can do that. You can even do equipment checks with us and help us test the lights and sirens," Owen promised. "That's one of the first things we have the volunteers do, isn't that right, Calen?"

"That's right," Calen said, glancing up from his phone.

"For the fire trucks *and* the ambulances?" His eyes grew wide as he wiggled with excitement.

"Oh yeah. Want me to tell you the first lesson we teach the firefighters?" Owen asked, lowering his voice.

Brayden's face lit up, and he shuffled closer. "We firemen call it the engine, or the apparatus. We don't usually call the big truck a fire truck. The little trucks, those are trucks. The big one is the engine."

"Oh. Is it okay if I call it that too?" Brayden whispered.

"Sure. You're part of the crew now." He touched the brim of Brayden's Pinehurst Fire & EMS hat. "I'll get with your aunt and we'll make it happen, alright buddy?"

"I don't like it when people call me that. My dad calls me that."

"I gotcha. I don't want to intrude on something special between you and your dad, I won't do that again," Owen said, standing.

"No, I mean I don't like it and he calls me it anyway. I hate it," Owen and a few of the other men exchanged unamused glances that went unseen by the little boy.

"Is there something else you would like to be called?" Owen asked, but Brayden's only answer was a shrug.

"Well, it'll just be Brayden for now. Maybe we can find you a better nickname," Owen suggested.

"I don't understand why people use nicknames. Why can't we just call people their own names?" Brayden asked, his tone petulant as he leaned against the bricks and propped one booted foot up on the brick, mimicking Calen before turning back to Owen.

"Nicknames are a way of telling somebody you have a special bond with them or a special feeling about them that you'd like to share. It's sort of like a secret code."

"Oh."

"When I was little, my dad called me little man," Brian volunteered.

Brayden looked up at Brian, whose hulking frame more than filled a doorway and who had several inches of height on Owen, and nodded, but his eyes were clouded with doubt, and then his expression changed.

"Do you have a special nickname for my Aunt Caitlin?" The men within earshot grinned or chuckled, and Owen bit back a smile.

He did have several names for Caitlin, most of which were appropriate for the moment.

"I do, I have a few for her actually."

"What are they?"

"Well, one of them is," he leaned in, cupping his hand to the boy's ear, whispering. "But that one is secret."

"We never keep secrets from Mommy and Aunt Caitlin!" Brayden corrected.

"No, it's a secret we share *with* her," Owen agreed, "and of course, you can always tell your Mommy everything we do and talk about. We don't keep secrets from Mommy and Aunt Caitlin, that's a good rule."

"So, I can call her that too?" Brayden asked eagerly.

"Definitely,"

Brayden hopped off the bench, making his way over to his aunt. Climbing up on the picnic table bench she was feeding Maya on, he kissed her on the cheek and said loudly,

"You know, I love you *Cupcake!*" Then proudly returned to his spot next to Owen amidst laughter and fist-bumps from the men.

"She likes it. It made her laugh," Brayden said with a satisfied smile.

"Good. Nicknames should make you feel good. If you don't like them though, I'll just call you Brayden."

"Thanks,"

"Now, how about another soda?"

"THANK YOU, so much. I really appreciate this so much. Are you sure I can't pay you anything?" Caitlin asked as the guys headed out.

"No. The guys wouldn't take money from you, this is just what we do." Brian said before telling the kids goodbye.

"Why do we need a locking door?" Brayden asked when everyone but Owen had gone.

"That way only the people you want to can come in when you want them to."

ONCE ALL THE kids were tucked in, Owen lounged with Caitlin curled up under his arm on the couch.

"I didn't realize how much anxiety I had about that door until it was fixed," she said quietly.

"Do you feel better now?" He asked.

She traced a pattern on the couch for a moment before answering, her nail trailing over the raised white lines.

"I do. Thank you. It really means a lot to me," she said, smiling up at him.

"Gotta keep you and those babies safe."

Little footsteps padded down the hallway. Caitlin sighed, "What is it, Brayden?"

"I wanted to tell Mister Owen something."

"Okay, then it's off to bed."

"What's up, Brayden?" Owen asked, careful not to use a nickname.

"You can call me pal if you want to," Brayden nodded, then reached in for a hug.

Owen moved his arm from around Caitlin to pick the boy up, hugging him fiercely in return.

"Okay, I'll do that," Owen said, holding the boy against his chest until he let go.

After Brayden left, leaving the two of them alone again Owen cleared his throat, kissing Caitlin on the top of her head as he pulled her back under his arm.

"Damn. Right in the feels." His throat was tight, so he cleared it again. "Wanna watch a movie?"

"We can if you want to," she said, not sounding terribly enthusiastic.

"I'm down for whatever sounds good to you. I can go home, and give you some peace and quiet."

"No, stay, please." Moving onto his lap, she kissed up his neck, pausing when she got to his ear to whisper, "You were so good to me and the kids, I was hoping you'd let me thank you properly."

"You don't need to thank me. You don't have to pay it back when someone treats you well." He gently reminded her.

She huffed, then rolled her eyes. "Fine. I want you to take me to the bedroom, fuck me until I can't move, hurt me, and call me filthy terrible things."

"Well, that I'm happy to do."

CHAPTER SEVENTEEN

OWEN

*A*s Owen drove home, he fought a growing sense of unease. The fact that Caitlin and those kids lived in that crappy little apartment in one of the least desirable neighborhoods of Red River filled him with unease. The front door being fixed might keep Charlotte's ex from walking in uninvited, but it wouldn't keep him from being there to visit the kids. He didn't know what it was, but something had changed between them over the weekend. He wasn't sure he could identify it, but it felt like an invisible thread was connecting them and every movement in the opposite direction felt wrong, almost sickening.

Caitlin could come live with us. Finley suggested.

She would want a place big enough for the kids to visit. Owen thought in reply, thinking of their little one-bedroom apartment.

The place was small and neat, but not nearly big enough for three kids to run and play. Their downstairs neighbor wouldn't appreciate the thundering of little feet overhead either.

Oh, right. Finley let their thoughts go quiet.

Owen drove in silence as he and his wolf's thoughts both turned to the same place, a grand Victorian-style home on the edge of town where they'd only visited once or twice a month since Owen's mother had gifted it to him. He checked on the state of the grounds, made sure no one else had been there, and that nothing in the interior needed attention and left. As he drove, Owen mentally walked through each of the rooms. The dining room with an enormous custom-built table and chairs designed to impress.

"Built by the same cabinetmaker who built chairs for the governor's house," his mother used to tell everyone who walked in. They would be struck by the size and craftsmanship, or the unnecessary extravagant show of wealth that was completely out of place in the small, poor town of Pinehurst.

A vision that drew him out of bitter memories from his childhood struck him. Caitlin dragging a friend through to the dining room saying the same words his mother had countless times to her many neighbors. Somehow, when Caitlin said them they wouldn't sound pompous. Her eyes would widen with appreciation and excitement, not an overinflated sense of ego. She would still appreciate the finer details better than Owen ever would.

He thought of the study with its built-in floor-to-ceiling bookshelves with their intricate hand-carved scrollwork. One of the first things he'd done when he'd take possession of the house was to donate the entire collection of his mother's rare books to the Library Society of Pinehurst, wanting to remove all traces of his mother's ego from the house, so long as it didn't require much of his time and energy. Now he could see Caitlin on the step ladder, one hand grazing the spine of a book thoughtfully as she considered her next selection, her toes wiggling as she thought, humming quietly.

Owen had always hated the kitchen especially. His mother remodeled it three different times before she'd said it was right. He'd never seen her prepare anything other than a drink on the expansive labradorite countertops. She'd been so proud of the double ovens, as if she'd ever baked anything in her life. Owen wondered if his mother had even known how to use them. Caitlin would not only know, but she would appreciate the space to spread out her baking.

He could see the kitchen counters covered in a sea of baked goods, see their friends gathered for meals, their entire lives growing as he drove. By the time he'd reached the town limits, he had their life planned out.

I bet we could make it really nice for her. Finley agreed, following Owen's train of thought.

Yeah we could. What do you think? Owen asked in return.

I think she's ours and it's about time we had a place to share with her, Finley said with a finality Owen didn't question because they both shared it.

Whatever the connection was between Owen and Caitlin, it wasn't just friendship, and it wasn't going away.

Let's make it happen. Owen thought to his wolf, who gave a happy yip.

Owen didn't even bother stopping in at his apartment. He pulled into the house, phased so Finley could go for a quick run around the perimeter of the property to burn off energy, then got redressed. Entering the house he turned on all the lights so light illuminated every dusty corner, opened all the windows to let fresh air in, and got to work cleaning. He worked all evening and well into the night without stopping. Every time he would sit down to rest he would observe something else he thought she would appreciate and made a move to take care of it.

Time lost all meaning as he worked, sleeping when he had to, then popping back up to get more work done, only stopping to see if Caitlin had texted. He was over this 'friends' business, he and Finley were going to make this neglected house into a home fit for a queen when they'd tell Caitlin they had a nice place for her to live and ask her to move in with them.

"Knock knock," Patrick Lawson called out from the bottom floor.

"I'm upstairs!" Owen called.

"Thank the gods," Patrick pulled out his phone and sent a quick text letting the shift members know he'd found Owen.

"Hey - come give me a hand!" Owen called.

"Hey, what happened to coming to work- holy hell. What are you doing?"

"Grab that end," Owen was shirtless, glistening in a layer of sweat mixed with layers of dust and grime, holding up the end of a long flat board with two flat metal hooks on the end. "We need to slide it up and hook it into the post at the foot of the bed. Doing them with one person is a bitch,"

"Did you know you're supposed to be working?" Patrick asked, grabbing the end of the board and doing as indicated.

"Oh, yeah I don't have time for that," Owen said, sliding the beam down so it slid into place.

"You don't have time to work?" Patrick repeated slowly, looking at Owen closely to see if he was kidding.

"I've got to get the house ready for Caitlin," Owen explained matter-of-factly without a trace of humor.

"You can't work because you've got to get this house ready for Caitlin?" Patrick confirmed, still puzzled.

"Is there an echo in here?" Owen asked irritably. "Here, don't just stand there asking stupid questions. Help me with this last beam."

"Is this some kind of joke?" Patrick asked.

"Why would I joke about this? Besides, who would I be busting my ass to make this place nice for- you?" Now Owen was looking at Patrick like he was the one who was crazy.

"Owen, have you been drinking?" Owen thought about it.

The last few days were a blur, but he certainly didn't feel drunk. Run down maybe, but definitely not drunk. When they finished sliding the beam into place, Patrick stepped back from the four-poster bed.

"This is beautiful craftsmanship," he admitted, looking at the carvings.

"Mm-hmm. I think she'll like it," Owen said, wistfully.

Patrick pulled out his phone and sent a quick text, then slipped it back into his pocket. Owen's stomach rumbled loud enough that Patrick heard it across the room.

"Have you eaten?"

"I had some food before I got here,"

"When was that?"

"I left Caitlin's early yesterday so she could get the kids ready for the week and have some time with just them there," Owen informed his supervisor absentmindedly.

"When was that?"

"Yesterday."

"You left her house on *what day*, was it Sunday?"

"Yeah," Owen replied, chewing his bottom lip as he looked at the bed and considered what color bed sheets Caitlin would like best.

"Owen, that was three days ago," Patrick said, wiping his hand down his face, and shaking his head.

"Oh. Well, time flies when you're - hmm. I wonder if Jared would deliver some books here if I asked him. I think Caitlin will be sad if she comes in and the bookshelves are empty. Or do you think she'd prefer to pick them out?"

"How would I know?" Patrick asked with a shrug.

"You're gay. Aren't you gays supposed to know the things we straight guys don't know? That's why every girl has her gay guy friend," Owen mused, frowning.

"Book choices aren't included in the gay friend handbook they issue us when we get our gay card," Patrick laughed, but Owen wasn't laughing.

"Let's get some water. Show me what else you've done with the place," Patrick suggested.

"Good idea."

They chatted about the many changes Owen needed to make until another voice came from the doorway, signaling the arrival of Patrick's backup.

"Anybody home?" Chief Beckett called from the front door.

"Straight back chief, we're in the kitchen," Owen called.

"How's it going, boys?"

"You've been mated for a long time!" Owen pointed his glass of water at the chief, "I need your opinion."

"Alright," Chief Beckett shared a brief look with Patrick, who widened his eyes in a 'told you he was crazy' way.

"If you moved Miss Linda into a house, would she want the books to already be there, or would she want to get them herself?"

"I always let Miss Linda make all decisions when it comes to the house. I just pay the credit card bill," the chief shrugged. "Your girlfriend moving in with you?"

"Oh well, I don't know actually. I hope so because I've been putting in some work to make this place nice for her."

"Mm-hmm," The chief said, pursing his lips, "Owen, come here son. Look at me."

The chief stood before him and looked deep into his eyes. Owen stepped back but didn't break eye contact, staring back with a hint of impatience as the old Alpha's wolf looked out at Owen, probing into his and Finley's mind.

"You look hungry. Let's go into town and get you some food." the chief suggested.

"I don't have time," Owen objected.

"I have an idea. I bet if we explain to Miss Linda that you have a girl coming over, she'd get some of the ladies to make this place spic and span in no time."

"Oh. That's a good idea. Let's do that. You don't think she'll mind?"

"No, son, she won't mind," the chief assured, clapping him on the back, grimacing when his hand came back sweaty.

"Owen?" Patrick said.

"What?" Owen demanded impatiently.

"You may want to get a shirt on,"

"Oh. Right." Owen said, wandering off in search of his shirt.

"You said if anyone was acting strange to give you a call," Patrick said, gesturing to Owen's retreating back. "This is pretty strange. About as strange as I've seen. This is easily as weird as when Ryder imprinted on Emma."

"What did he say when you showed up?"

"He told me he didn't have time to come to work. It is possible he's imprinted too? Owen doesn't just fuck off when it's time to go to work," Patrick said, shaking his head.

"Oh, he's definitely imprinted." The chief laughed quietly to himself. "What are the odds? Two shifters in the same town, same pack, that work in the same place."

The chief clicked his tongue and took a toothpick out of his pocket, popping it in his mouth and chewing it as he considered it.

"Okay. I think I'll take him off the schedule for the next week or two," Patrick said.

"Yeah, set him up for family leave so he gets paid for the shifts he's going to miss. He won't care now, but he might once the dust has settled."

"Will do," Patrick said.

"And go find him, the moon only knows what he's found for himself to do instead of wandering around half-naked like a loon."

MISS LINDA CAME through and sent a small army of matronly women armed with cleaning supplies and everything he would need to get the house set up for Caitlin's arrival. The ladies had a good time as he absorbed their suggestions on how to be a good housemate, all of which he listened to with a comically serious intent.

"Hey, I have something to show you. What would it take to get you to come down here for a visit this weekend?" Owen called Caitlin at Miss Linda's suggestion while the ladies attacked the house with furniture polish and more types of cleaner than Owen had ever thought possible. He waited with bated breath, praying she would say yes.

"The kids are at David's anyway, so I can come down," she said.

"Good."

"What should I wear?" she asked.

"Nothing," Owen replied, not caring what she wore.

"Um."

"No, that isn't what I meant. I meant you don't have to wear anything special. Although, technically if you didn't want to wear clothing I wouldn't be upset, but it's not a sex surprise. I mean, there could be sex, but there doesn't have to be…" Owen sighed in frustration as nothing would come out right.

Finley was not helpful. *What the hell are you doing? Stop talking like a lunatic, you're gonna scare her off! Although, I like the wearing nothing idea.*

You are not helping! Owen thought back in a panic as he struggled to stop himself from nervously babbling.

"Alright. Hey, are you okay? You've been a little off since you came up here," she asked.

See, you're freaking her out. Stop sounding like a complete moron or she's going to run away. She's already a little skittish. Finley coached.

"Yeah. I've been busy putting something together for you, that's all."

"Okay. So we're good?"

"We're great, as long as you think we're good? It's something big, and sort of involved. You'll see when you get here."

"Okay. We're still on for Friday, right? Should I bake something to bring for the station?" She asked, her voice sounding a little anxious.

"Yes we're good, and you only need to bake something if you want to. I love anything you make," he said sincerely.

When he ended the call he gave a loud whoop, turning around, finding Miss Linda standing there watching with amusement sparkling in her eyes.

"She said yes!" Owen said, sweeping the woman into a hug. "Now I just need to finish getting this place ready. I need… stuff."

"Come on, we've made a list of things you'll want before she gets here, and I'm going along to help you pick the right things out," Miss Linda said with a bemused smile.

"Oh good, I'll get my keys."

"I'm driving, you can keep me company," she said affably.

I'm so excited. She's going to love it! Finley wagged excitedly. Owen would have to go for a run later to run off his excess excitement. He was going to bring Caitlin home, and she was going to love it.

"Owen, honey," Miss Linda put her hand on his arm, grabbing his attention.

"Ma'am?"

"Did Jason talk to you?"

They had talked, but mostly Owen talked about Caitlin and the house.

"You know what's happening, right?" She asked gently.

"Caitlin is going to come?" Owen guessed.

"She is, but do you know what's happening to you, why you feel different?"

"You know?"

"I do," she assured, drawing him to the side. "Owen, you imprinted on her."

Owen's mind blanked, then made up for lost time by going full force ahead, his thoughts racing.

"If you feel around in your mind, you can probably feel the connection to her?" Miss Linda guessed.

"I imprinted," Owen said, his eyes going wide.

"Yes," the Alpha's mate confirmed.

"I imprinted. Oh shit," he said, sinking down to sit on the top step of the porch. "Shit, shit, shit."

"It's not all that bad. Caitlin is a lovely girl."

"She wants to be friends!" Owen exclaimed with growing alarm.

"You two can be friends. Friendship is an excellent foundation for being mates."

"No, you don't understand. She *just* wants to be friends. She's got... issues."

"I'm old, not stupid pup." Miss Linda said with a roll of her eyes. "I knew what you meant. It might take her more time than you like, just be gentle with her, and she'll come around."

"Like the Chief is with you?"

"Oh, he wasn't that way when we were courting," she laughed, settling down next to him companionably. "The first time he called on me I was at my boyfriend's house, it was the first time he'd brought me there, to meet his family. He was there to deliver a package, he saw me, walked right inside, and declared that I was his."

"Just like that?" He asked, incredulous.

"Just like that," she confirmed, shaking her head at the memory.

"What did you say?"

"Old Miss Mary chased him out of the house with a broom and we had dinner, but that fool was sitting outside the whole time, right up until we left."

A male voice came from the bottom of the steps, startling Owen.

"It was cold too, and raining." The Chief smiled up the steps at his mate, "And she wouldn't even tell me her name. It took me two years to get her to agree to be mine."

"Two years?"

"He wasn't as good-looking then," Miss Linda teased, standing beside her husband, "You'll be fine. Just know that it may take her some time to adjust to the idea. You two are welcome to come see us if she has questions or needs a lady friend to talk to."

It had been a long fucking week. Once the house was done he'd been left with little to do, so when his radio had gone off with a fire call nearby, he'd responded. The building had been more unstable than they'd thought, and Owen had barely been clipped by a falling eye beam.

"Chief, I'm fine!" He'd objected when the chief had ordered him to go to the hospital to get checked out.

"Kessler, don't." The chief had snapped, "Rules are rules. Get in the back of the damn rig and go get that shoulder checked out. I don't want to hear shit about it."

"Yes sir," Owen had said in a tone that was anything but resentful.

As he'd sat in the hospital bed he'd texted Caitlin as she'd told him about the baking she was doing for various groups or members of the community.

She'd been so excited about the business that he hadn't interrupted to tell her what he was doing. The hospital had verified that he'd dislocated his right shoulder, but he was healing well, and shifters always healed quickly so he would be fine. When he got discharged late that night she'd already been in bed, so he went to bed dreaming of when he would meet her and Brayden at the Fire and EMS base for Brayden's tour.

"Hey, there's my pal!" Owen bent down to receive an exuberant hug.

Caitlin noticed him wince as he stood. "Hey, you okay?"

"Oh yeah, I'm fine," Owen assured.

"I told him not to try to take on any more eye beams," Tyler laughed.

"Eye beams?" she looked alarmed, but Owen just shrugged.

"He was fine, just trying to be a hero," Tyler explained.

"Do you drive the trucks too?" Brayden asked Tyler, seeing Tyler's Fire & EMS t-shirt, his eyes widening in awe.

"I do. Wanna see them? If your aunt says it's okay, that is," Tyler looked at Caitlin for permission.

"It's okay," Caitlin said. When Tyler had taken Brayden away, she turned back to him and crossed her arms over her chest as Owen and Finley's light mood dissipated.

"Hey, I was fine. A beam fell-"

"Where were you that a beam fell on you?"

"A structure fire-" he reached out to her, but she stepped back.

"A *building* tried to fall on you and you didn't tell me?" She screeched, eyes bulging.

"It wasn't a big deal."

"When was this?"

"Yesterday morning,"

"If I told you a building tried to fall on me and I didn't call you, would you be mad?"

Of course, we'd be mad! Finley snarled.

"You're not a firefighter, so yeah I'd be mad but it's my job. Hazards are part of the package." Owen said.

"I'm not mad at you," she said, stopping when John McIntyre walked by and nodded politely to Caitlin, grimacing in sympathy.

Caitlin dropped her voice and waited for John to make his way to the kitchen. He didn't bother to remind her that shifters had exceptional hearing and John could probably hear them just as well from the kitchen, he appreciated her attempt at discretion.

"I'm upset because you didn't tell me. No call, no text, nothing." She pointed out. "We text all the time and you just... didn't tell me?"

"Because I was fine. You would have worried over nothing, and besides, I wanted to hear about your baking stuff. You were so excited," Owen explained.

"Okay, so you did think about telling me but you didn't want me to worry. So, you knew it was something worth worrying over, but chose not to tell me. That's just super." she crossed her arms tight in front of her chest.

"Caitlin," he started to speak, but she cut him off, her pain and anger cutting him more than angry words could have.

"It's fine. I'm going to check on Brayden," tears swam in her eyes as she hurried away from him.

I don't understand why she's upset. We weren't hurt? Finley whined, wanting to chase after her and make her listen.

"Want to bring her some water when you go after her?" John asked from the kitchen.

"May as well," Owen sighed. John came around the corner holding out two bottles of water and a juice box.

"Perfect. Thanks."

When he went out into the bay, Caitlin was up front in the engine, and Brayden was in the driver's seat.

"Hop in the back and we'll pull her out," Ryder was saying

"I can be in it when you drive it?" Brayden practically screamed.

"Yeah!"

Caitlin didn't talk to Owen for the rest of the visit, which was cut short when they got a call for an MVA.

"What's an MVA?" Brayden asked.

"A motor vehicle accident," Owen explained.

Owen and Tyler pulled out, flashing the lights on the rescue truck for Brayden, Owen didn't have a chance to text her until much later in the evening when the paperwork was done, even though he swore he could feel her connection to him wavering at times.

That sensation was what forced him to ignore Tyler's advice of giving her space, picking up his phone to text her.

> OWEN
>
> Hey. So, are you mad?

CAITLIN

Yes.

> OWEN
>
> I'm sorry I didn't call. I didn't want to worry you over something that wasn't a big deal.

CAITLIN

It's fine.

I DON'T THINK it's fine. Finley said, prickling uncomfortably.

She said it was fine.

She also said it was fine that her front door didn't lock. His wolf reminded him.

Fuck.

> OWEN
>
> It doesn't seem fine.

CAITLIN

I just figured I was important enough to warrant a phone call, that's all.

What in the dried-mud-caked-into-fur is she talking about? Finley demanded.

Owen picked up the phone, wanting some clarity. He was over this text message bullshit.

"What do you mean, you *thought* you were important enough to warrant a phone call?" He demanded before she'd even had a chance to say hello.

"If I was in the hospital, would you want to know?" Caitlin demanded.

"I wasn't *in* the hospital as much as I was at the hospital, there's a big difference," Owen argued.

"You had an *INJURY!*" She whispered furiously.

"Which is almost completely healed now. It wasn't a big deal. I basically got paid to sit at the hospital, with a bonus x-ray."

Silence greeted his joke and he had a sinking feeling.

She's still mad. Finley said uneasily.

No shit, genius. Owen retorted.

"Caitlin?" he prompted.

"Owen?" She retorted, matching his tone with an undercurrent of ice that made his stomach clench further.

Oh shit. She's 'stepped in the stinging nettles' kind of mad. Finley shied away.

"I am sorry," he said.

"Look, I don't want to be in the kind of relationship where communication is not a priority. I'm going to go. I'm glad you're okay, I just- I'm not interested in finding out important things through the gossip chain or because one of your buddies made a joke I wasn't supposed to hear."

"That wasn't what happened!"

"Except it was. Goodbye, Owen. It's been fun, but I don't want that. I've had relationships with secrets before and I don't want it ever again."

Did she just - break up with us? Finley asked.

She tried. You up for a drive? Owen asked, grabbing his keys.

We're sure as hell not sitting at home with our paws up our asses if she thinks she's not ours. What if she does that thing girls do where they cut their hair and go kiss other people so they don't feel so sad? Finley asked.

Rebounding? Owen suggested.

Yeah, that. We can't let her do that.

That hadn't even occurred to Owen. He was still reeling from her stark shift. She hadn't even given him a chance to really explain. Or, rather, she had and she hadn't listened properly.

Frustrated because this wasn't the conversation he wanted to be having with her, he hopped in the truck and drove to her shitty little apartment, stewing the entire forty-five-minute drive there.

CHAPTER EIGHTEEN

OWEN

Owen's truck roared into the parking lot. He called Caitlin's phone, she sent him to voicemail. He called again, same response.

OWEN

I'm outside, and I don't want to wake up the kids. Please come talk to me.

CAITLIN

No

OWEN

Then I'll wait here until you change your mind.

You can be mad at me all you want, but I'm not going anywhere until I understand what the hell just happened.

We had a misunderstanding and you just bailed. That's not okay.

You are important to me.

He waited for a whole five minutes in his truck, then he was too restless to sit still so he got out and paced in the parking lot. He paced for forty-five minutes before he heard the apartment door unlock and she was standing in the doorway, arms crossed over her chest, wrapped in an oversized sweater with baggy arms and a wadded-up tissue balled in her hand.

He bounded up the steps and stood before her, his heart pounding.

"Look, my life isn't that exciting. I go to work, I come home, and I talk to you. I volunteer at the fire department when I'm not working there and play on the sheriff's department's softball team. A couple times a month I go out and catch a game with the guys, sometimes get a beer at the Bar on Main," he said, the words tumbling out in a rush. "When I'm at home, I'm usually reading. Finley and I run a lot up in the mountains with the guys, and when I don't want to be at home alone I go over to John's or Tyler's and we play a game. That's as *secret* as things get for me."

He took a step back before he reached for her, knowing it would scare her if he did that right now.

"You know what I keep a secret? That I'm fucking crazy about you and I've been busting my ass to make my house as nice for you as I possibly can, so when you came down to visit this weekend you'd want to stay. But I'm terrified you'll get scared if I ask, so instead, I start more projects and keep my mouth shut so you don't think I'm moving too fast and being too intense. The truth? I want you to come home with me and never leave."

You're terrible at this secret thing. Finley observed.

"You...what?" She asked, her eyebrows all but disappearing into her bangs as they rose.

Good job not being too intense. Finley jibed.

"I've been coming up with all these bullshit projects like one of those walking path things you said that you like so much-" he said.

"Wait, you have a house? I thought you lived in an apartment."

"Well, it's my mother's house. She left it to me. I haven't ever lived in it because I hated it. I thought it would be a nice place for you, and I knew you'd want to be able to have the kids there to visit, and it has enough bedrooms for that, so I've been-"

"Hold up, you want me to move in with you?" She definitely

looked alarmed now, eyes wide, hands twisted in the sleeves of her shirt as she shifted nervously from foot to foot.

"Of course," he said, just on the cusp of telling her about the imprinting when she interrupted.

"But," she looked alarmed, "We've been dating for like no time. And I didn't even think we were officially dating. I mean, we never even discussed it, other than I'm really not ready for a relationship, and now this."

Owen, she's got the crazy eyes. Maybe we should stop. I think she's scared. Finley suggested, noticing how visible the whites of eyes were and the way she kept her arms wrapped around her body as she took a half-step closer to the door.

"Which is why I hadn't asked yet, but since you're accusing me of keeping secrets, I wanted to make sure I wasn't going to upset you for having an *actual* secret. I'm crazy about you and it's all I can think about basically all the time - making you happy. I don't know why you're so upset. If you want me to, I'll text you every day and tell you about all the stupid bullshit I have to do when I'm working, down to the paperwork I have to write out if you just need to know what I'm doing to be happy. Just - please don't give up on me."

"I don't need to know everything you do. I'm not that kind of crazy."

Owen was on the verge of arguing that she seemed to be that kind of girl when Finley stopped him. *Do not argue with her! It's a trap!*

"Then can you tell me what I did wrong and how to fix this? Because I'm very confused about what just happened between you and I," he begged.

"My ex pretended to imprint on me," she answered flatly.

"He- what?" Owen's face went from pleading to shocked in the half-second it took for him to process what she'd said.

Can you fake imprinting? I mean, clearly you could, but more to the point - why would you do it?

Steaming piles of scat. Finley cursed, his alarm growing with Owen's.

How could they tell her they were imprinted now? But also, she clearly had a deep issue with secrets - how could they *not* tell her?

"Yup. He acted like he was crazy about me and couldn't stop thinking about me, but he was really just- well I don't know. Determined to have me, I guess? It wasn't until we were already mated that I realized it was just a ploy to get me to commit to being his bonded mate."

"Oh, Caitlin."

"So, no, I don't like when people keep things from me. It sort of freaks me out, and I'm sorry I shut down. I realize it was an overreaction. It just... brought up shit for me and I should have communicated that better."

"Cupcake, I would never-" he started, taking an involuntary step forward even though he knew he shouldn't.

"You don't need to do that," she cut in. "Everybody lies, it's just how things go."

"No, it isn't," he insisted, incensed at the idea that she believed he would lie to her.

She gave him a polite, unconvinced smile that sent white-hot rage coursing through his body.

"Caitlin, I'm not lying to you," he said, his voice laced with a quiet intensity.

We have to tell her. We can't keep our imprinting on her a secret, Finley said reluctantly, shying away from the thought of her rejection, or worse, her disbelief.

Oh, right, Owen sniped back, *because I'm sure she'll just eat that up. Shit. I wanted her to realize how special imprinting was... how special* she is *to us.*

"Okay." She smiled that maddening, polite smile that made him want to hurt whoever made her so jaded. He ran his fingers through his hair. An idea struck him and his head snapped up, snapping and pointing at her when inspiration struck.

"I'll prove to you that I haven't lied to you," he said with determination.

She crossed her arms, making a face that he had to work not to close the distance between them to kiss away.

"And how do you plan to do that?"

"I'll take you to my Alpha, have him compel me to tell the truth to any question you ask."

"You'd do that?" Her expression was skeptical, but the relief that shone in her eyes erased all doubt.

"Why would I not?" Owen demanded, Finley's temper making his worse.

"Fine," she agreed.

"Where are you going?"

"To get my purse," she said shortly.

"What about the kids?"

"David came to get them a little bit before you got here."

"You'll come with me?" He asked.

"Yes. I want to believe you," she replied. "I want to know that you're a safe person for me."

They drove in silence for several minutes before she turned to face him.

"I'm sorry. This is crazy. Take me home, I don't need you to prove yourself to me-" Caitlin said, shaking her head when they'd pulled off the street.

"I don't mind," *And I just need you to see I won't hurt you.* Owen added silently, gripping the wheel tighter at the thought.

I don't want her to be afraid of us lying to her or hurting her. His wolf said, drooping at the thought. *We would never do that.*

"No, this isn't about you. This is about my damage, and it's completely unfair for me to ask you to prove yourself when I-"

"Good thing you didn't ask me to. It was my idea, remember?" Owen said, taking her hand and holding it in his as he continued to drive.

"Right, but that doesn't make it any less crazy," she said, her voice cracking.

When he glanced over at her face her lower lip was trembling, picking at her nails. Owen reached over and grabbed her hand, bringing it over so he held it in his lap.

"I don't care if you're crazy," Owen said.

Owen, you dumbass, you can't just call her crazy! Finley objected.

"What?"

"I don't. You're just - you. I accept you and your crazy," he said simply, giving her hand a reassuring squeeze.

"Shouldn't you be saying something like, 'No, you're not crazy,' to me?" She asked with a little laugh.

See? You're gonna hurt her feelings, Finley growled at Owen.

"I thought you said you didn't want me to lie?" He grinned, giving her hand a squeeze. "Seriously, everybody has their things. If I can help you feel better, I'm going to do it. This is something I can do."

The kitchen lights were on when they pulled up at the Alpha's house. Owen took Caitlin's hand and walked around to the side door. Before Owen could knock, a deep masculine voice called for them to come in.

"Owen," Chief Beckett sat at his kitchen island wearing jeans and a sweatshirt that hung loosely over his large frame.

"Sorry to come so late."

"It's fine. This must be the lovely Caitlin," the chief smiled kindly, extending his hand. "I'm Jason Beckett. The Pinehurst pack's Alpha. I imagine you have questions for me."

"She does, but not that kind," Owen cut in. "I need your help. She had... a bad experience in the past. She needs to know that I'm not lying to her or keeping secrets from her. I need you to compel me to answer everything she asks, fully and honestly."

"That's not how this normally works," Jason replied, crossing his arms and looking between them. "But, given the circumstances, I think I can do that, if that's what you want."

"I have nothing to hide," Owen responded.

"Alright then. Let's go to my office," the chief said comfortably, stepping back to allow them inside. They followed the chief through the house wordlessly.

"Alright. Owen, you're sure you want to do this?" the alpha asked when they were all situated in his alpha's office.

"Absolutely."

"Alright," Jason said, closing his eyes, rolling his neck in a circle, and then rolling his shoulders.

When the old alpha looked up, Caitlin took a step backward toward the door. Nothing had physically changed about the man in the room, but he seemed to fill more of the room now. The office that had felt spacious moments before now felt cramped and claustrophobic. When he turned his gaze on her, she took another half-step back.

"Ask him what you want to know."

"Have you ever lied to me?" She asked.

"Yes," Owen said, feeling more surprised than she was at the admission.

"About what?"

"I told you I like it when you wear your hair down, but I hate it." Her eyes widened as the truth tumbled from his lips, compelled by the alpha's magic. "It makes me crazy because all I can think about is burying my face in it and breathing in your scent. Or wrapping my fingers in it and-" he went on in great detail for a few minutes about the specific and very graphic things her ponytails made him want to do when the chief held up a hand.

"I think she gets the point," the chief broke in with a wry grin, pinching the bridge of his nose and expelling a long-suffering sigh.

"Have you lied to me about anything else?" she asked.

"I haven't lied, but I haven't shared all of my feelings for you because I didn't want to scare you away," Owen admitted.

"What feelings do you have for me?"

"I love you more than anything else, and I would give anything to make sure you were happy."

Caitlin's eyes widened and she glanced at the chief for confirmation and he nodded.

"Why?" She asked, looking genuinely confused.

What does she mean, why? Finley asked.

That puzzled Owen too. She was so wonderful, so caring and

innocent, she was worth cherishing. Why did someone telling her that they want to make her happy confuse her?

"Because you're mine. But I want that to be something you celebrate, not something you're scared of. I want you to *feel* safe, not just *be* safe. I can keep you safe and make sure you're always loved and cared for, but I want you to feel it too."

"If I didn't want to come live with you, would you force me?" She asked.

"I would want to, but I wouldn't do it," Owen admitted, not enjoying it when she looked scared at his admission. "Not because I would want to force you, I wouldn't want that, but because I wouldn't want you to be far away from me. And where you live is not safe. It makes me worry."

"Have you ever hit a woman?"

"Yes," he responded.

Caitlin stared at him, her mouth opening, then snapping shut, looking stricken.

"Explain," His Alpha commanded while Caitlin paled, scooting backward in her chair, looking at him like he was the monster hiding in her closet.

"We got a domestic violence call. The mother was crazy, out of her mind on drugs. She was hitting her four-year-old with a wire hanger. We got her restrained, but things got... messy. She went after the husband but ended up with her teeth sunk into the girl. I hit her."

"Oh," Caitlin sagged in relief.

"Have you ever raped someone?" She asked.

Owen's eyes widened in shock as he was filled with repulsion at the thought.

"No," he said, wrinkling his nose.

"Would you hit me? Rape me?"

"Never. I could never do anything like that to you," he said, shaking his head in horror, looking baffled and horrified, trying to rise out of his chair, but a gesture from Jason had him sitting back down.

"What's something you hope I won't ask?"

Oh, well, there goes your chance to volunteer that little bit of information, Finley pointed out.

The question hung in the air, filling the room until Owen felt choked by it, unable to speak. The chief cleared his throat and Owen swallowed hard, looked Caitlin in the eye and spoke to her, his stomach clenching as he waited for her to freak out.

"If I've imprinted on you," Owen says, his eyes sliding shut. He didn't want to see her reaction if she rejected him.

"Is that the truth?" Her voice came out surprisingly steady and Owen suspected that she wasn't asking him, but the magic compelled him to answer anyway.

"Yes," he whispered.

He opened his eyes as Caitlin rose to leave the room and Owen felt the Alpha's magic on him drop away. Owen went to follow her, but the older man stuck a hand out on Owen's chest.

"Give her a minute," Jason advised.

"I need to talk to her-"

"Sit down, son," Jason said gently.

"I don't understand how she could think -why would she think I would hurt her?" He suspected that her ex had been bad, and her confusion and appreciation of Owen for respecting her boundaries had seemed a little excessive, but she wasn't really afraid he would do *that* to her?

"Because someone else already has," Jason answered quietly.

Owen began to shake, rising out of the chair to find her but Jason took him by the shoulder and pushed him back to a leather chair.

"She said some things about her ex. I didn't realize the fucker raped her. I'm gonna kill him-"

"Son I know how you're feeling, but he's not here and you are. Let her process her feelings and she'll come back to you when she's ready." The chief advised.

"Someone hurt her," Owen said, running his hand down his face. "I mean, I suspected. But..."

Standing back out of the chair, he shook his head, pacing circles, raking his fingers through his hair.

"What kind of low life puts his hands on a woman who doesn't want it?" He demanded, his voice raising to match his temper. "What kind of monster -" he broke off when Caitlin came back, hovering in the doorway.

"Caitlin, I had no idea- fuck." He dropped into the chair, his frame shaking with rage as he dropped his face into them.

Walking across the room, she laid her hand on his shoulder but he didn't move. When he spoke his voice came out broken.

"I was so rough with you. The things you let me say to you...I had no idea, I never would have...why didn't you say something? Why would you let me do that to you, talk like that to you?" He looked up, his eyes red with unshed tears.

"I'll be in the kitchen," the chief said, closing the office door behind him on his way out.

"You didn't do anything to me I haven't enjoyed," she said, coming to stand between his legs, but Owen was shaking his head.

"Fuck - you said you liked it when I - gods."

He mentally replayed the times when he'd called her all the filthy names that turned her on, recoiling at the memories of his he'd hit her, tied her down, told her he would use her even if she didn't want it.

He wasn't sure if he was more upset about her for not telling him how traumatizing it had been for her, or at himself for missing it so completely.

He'd known she was scared sometimes, but he must have been blind not to see how he'd been making her relive what had happened to her. She smiled and sat down on his lap

"Caitlin," he began.

"I like my sex rough and degrading. I was raped. Those two things don't have anything to do with each other. Just because I had bad experiences doesn't mean I can't enjoy sex now," she explained calmly.

How was she so fucking calm? Finley was silent, horrified, and feeling small as they both relived all the times they'd hurt their mate.

"*Experiences*? As in, plural?" Owen finally asked.

"My ex was not a nice man. I don't want to talk about it right now, but yes he raped me more than once."

"But I…" he blew out his breath, shaking his head.

"You give me phenomenal orgasms that make me feel so good I worry I won't be able to survive, and you make me feel very loved while you do it."

"I would never do anything to hurt you," Owen whispered as his tears spilled over, "Not like that. Never."

"I believe you," she said.

He hoped to all the gods that she did. He wrapped his arms around her, burying his face into her neck.

"The idea of it makes me sick," Owen confessed, his breath warm on her skin.

They sat quietly as his breathing calmed. He kept his arms wrapped around her, holding her so her side pressed into his abdomen, her shoulder on his chest. Slowly, he calmed down. She believed him, and she hadn't run away.

She believed us! Finley yipped happily.

Owen gradually relaxed as she sat on his lap, snug in his arms.

"Come on, you. I want to see this house," she said, standing a few long minutes later.

"You…want to see the house?" Owen echoed, not sure he heard her right. Surely she would need time and space to process this before they went to the house.

"Well naturally. If you want me to come live there I need to know what it looks like," she laughed.

"Don't tease me," Owen groaned, standing and pulling her against him for one final hug.

"I'm not teasing," she assured.

He led her by the hand to the kitchen, where Jason sat at the bar, shaking his head as he sipped a cold beer and watched Miss Linda. A reusable grocery bag sat on the counter, Miss Linda was putting left-over containers in it.

"Linda, that's plenty," Jason was laughing.

"If they're going to be doing what I think they are, they'll need to refuel, and they won't want to be coming back into town for it," Linda said, pulling a few more containers out of the fridge and adding them to the bag.

"You two sorted?" Jason asked.

"Yes, thank you," Caitlin said, blushing a little. "I'm sorry."

"You don't owe anyone an apology," Jason said firmly. "You just let us know if you need anything. My cell's programmed in Owen's phone if you need me, or Miss Linda. There's not much one or both of us can't handle."

"Thank you, chief," Owen said, thanking Miss Linda for the food before heading out the side door onto the wrap-around porch.

CHAPTER NINETEEN

OWEN

Owen and Caitlin walked through the house, Caitlin's eyes were wide. She seemed to notice everything, stopping to admire every detail from the crystal door handles to the hardwood floors and rugs that covered them.

"You said this was your mother's house?"

"Yes,"

"She must have-"

"Been ridiculously wealthy," Owen supplied as Caitlin slid her hand along the fabric of the sheer curtains that hung in the windows of the front hall.

"I was going to say she had good taste, but yeah, that too." She looked uncertain, biting her lip as she bit back a question.

"You can ask me anything, Caitlin," Owen said softly.

Now that his imprinting was out in the open and she hadn't run away, he was eager to share his life with her.

"No, I- it wasn't anything."

"Please ask,"

"Are you..." She trailed off, still embarrassed.

Oh, she's damn cute. Finley said, enjoying the blush. *We should take her to bed.*

Finley, shut up. We're enjoying the moment. Owen chided.

"Am I wealthy?" Owen finished for her

"Yeah." She looked embarrassed, "Not that it matters, because it doesn't. I was just wondering."

"I have a trust fund. I didn't use any of the money until I moved in here and started using this place."

"Why didn't you use it, and the house?" She asked, wandering down the front hall with leisurely steps as she took in every detail, admiring the cream wallpaper with gold swirl designs.

Owen had always hated that wallpaper, but when Caitlin's delighted eyes traced the pattern with fascination, Owen gained a new appreciation for it.

"She left us when she got tired of living in a small town where she couldn't do what she loved,"

"What did she love?"

"Sex. She wanted to be a high-end escort, and there's not much call for that in Pinehurst, as you might imagine. She wanted to be in the big city, so she moved away and I only heard from her some years on my birthday, sometimes on a holiday."

"Oh, and you stayed here with your dad?"

"Yup. She didn't ask to take me, never had any interest. She finished the house and left, gifted it to me with the trust fund when I was eighteen. I resented her, so I didn't do anything beyond maintaining it until recently."

"You're here now because of me?" She guessed.

Owen stopped and looked at her with a self-conscious smile.

"I thought it would be a nice place for us to live if you wanted to."

"What if I didn't want to live here?" she asked, meandering into the large formal dining room.

"I'd sell it and buy or build you whatever you wanted. Do you not love it?" Owen asked.

Tell her we'll get a new one. She can pick it out! Finley urged.

"I adore it," She lovingly caressed the dishes hutch, peering at the dishes inside. "These are beautiful,"

She peered into the glass cabinet. He opened one and took it out, handing it to her almost carelessly. She took it reverently, tracing the gold rim delicately with the tip of her middle finger. The gesture was entirely platonic, but Owen couldn't stop himself from imagining her sliding that same finger over the head of his cock, on her knees before she took him in her mouth.

"Owen, I can't accept all of this. I don't even have a job, I can't pay for half of this or even a quarter of whatever it costs to maintain this place."

Why does she think she needs to pay us? She isn't a roommate, she's our mate! Providing for a mate is what you do for them. She's broken, Owen. Finley observed.

She's not broken. Well, she is, but lots of humans do that. They split things. Owen replied mentally.

Well, tell her we're not doing that. We're going to take care of her. Finley ordered. *Oh, wait! Tell her she can pay us in baked things and sex!*

"Who said anything about you paying for anything?" Owen asked her aloud.

"Well, isn't that what mates do, they split things?"

"What do you want to do?" Owen asked, following her while she wandered from the dining room to the den, eyes filled with wonder while she took in the dark paneling and the floor-to-ceiling built-in bookshelves.

"I've always wanted to bake, but not own a bakery. Like, for local places," she spoke softly, almost like she was talking to herself, remembering something in the past that wasn't in the room she stared at before her. Watching some memory play out that he couldn't see, her expression soft with something like regret.

"I bet Jared would buy your stuff. You can bake him some and leave them for him."

"I don't have a place to bake."

"You mean… like our kitchen?" He suggested.

Oooooh, show her the kitchen! Finley urged.

"Your kitchen," she said cautiously.

"Cupcake, the only things I've used in that kitchen are the microwave and the fridge. The only reason I know the stove works is because I tested it for you before you got here. It's safe to say the kitchen is all yours."

"You've never used the oven?" She said, eyes wide, looking horrified.

"Nope, neither of them."

"*Neither* of them?" she echoed.

"They're double ovens."

He watched her eyes widen in pleasure. The sight of her excitement made his chest swell. He never would have imagined he would get any satisfaction or pleasure from a damn oven, but he reached out for her hand, ready to show her to the kitchen.

"Come on," he beckoned softly.

"Oh, Owen." She stood spellbound, backing out of the kitchen until her back was pressed against his front. She covered her mouth, pointed feebly, then covered it again several times.

"You like it?" he asked.

Lights from the fixture reflected off the countertops, every surface spotlessly clean thanks to Miss Linda and the other women from the pack. From the tears in her eyes, he gathered she did.

"You have valances," she said, and he nodded, not understanding when she cried more.

"If you don't like them, we'll replace them with something you like," he assured.

"No, I like them," she replied, sniffing several times, then offering him a tender smile. "I want to see the rest."

THEY FINISHED up the house tour in the master suite. Despite the excitement of the day, she was so tired all she could do was manage a feeble smile, so he encouraged her to take care of whatever she needed in the bathroom, then they could go to sleep.

He stripped and turned off the lights. She came to bed naked too, sliding between the sheets with a sigh of relief.

"This bed is so comfortable," she moaned.

"Make more noises like that and I'll be making you uncomfortable when I make you deep-throat my cock," he growled.

I hope she makes more noises, Finley thought wistfully.

She chuckled but made no move to initiate sex, cuddling against his side, her arms pulled tight in front of her. Pulling one of her arms over his abdomen, she was asleep in no time, snoring softly. Owen lay awake while she slept, listening to the sounds of her breathing.

She is definitely broken, and the crazy kind of broken, but I like her, Finley said.

Everyone has their things, Owen thought back, his mind on the edge of sleep.

She smells nice, too. It makes me want to pull her close and just keep her safe. Finley thought. *Which is weird.*

Well, it's not like we've had a real mate before. Owen thought.

Yeah, but this isn't like that. It's... different. I don't know. She smells good. We're keeping her. Finley said. Owen agreed.

OWEN WOKE BEFORE SHE DID, amused that they both hadn't moved all night and she'd covered his shoulder with drool.

It's definitely broken. It's leaking, Finley thought wryly.

Caitlin sat up smiling and wiping her face off with a look of mingled embarrassment and disgust. He watched her without comment, not wanting to break the moment. What if she felt differently this morning? What if she wasn't ready for this? She looked pensive, and he didn't want to hear if she'd changed her mind, so he said nothing.

She yawned and stretched, then looked at him, studying his face.

"I'll stay," she broke the silence.

Owen thought his heart would burst. Finley practically pranced in his head, tail flicking with pleasure.

"For the weekend?" He asked hopefully.

"I'll move in," she clarified. "Charlotte comes home next week and

I've sort of been looking at places, but I needed to get a real job before I could look at anything."

"I have a suspicion that you're only saying that because of the kitchen," he said, grinning.

"It is not!"

"I was kidding."

"I mean....it is a really nice kitchen though," she added, tilting her head as she thought about it.

"Just wait till you see all the fancy baking...stuff."

"Like what?"

"I don't know exactly. There's some kind of fancy mixer that lowers up and down, the sales lady assured me it was the best. It's a commercial-grade mixer, but not too big. The mill is super quiet," he added. He didn't know shit about mills, but he hoped that made her happy.

"You got me a mill?" She looked amused now.

We should have let her pick out her things. Now she thinks we're idiots, Finley thought.

"Don't you need one?"

"I've never had one."

"Well, you have one now." She nodded dutifully as he talked about other things, but he could tell she wasn't really listening.

"You want to go use it now, don't you?" Owen asked.

She nodded and bit her lip with embarrassed pleasure.

"Go, play," he said.

Hey! We didn't sex her last night, we should do that now before she gets all worked up about the baking stuff. Finley suggested as she hopped off the bed and bounced to the bathroom on her tiptoes. Owen was definitely in agreement, but when she came out of the bathroom her hair was pulled back into a neat French braid.

"You sure you don't mind?"

Aw hell. She's so fucking cute. Finley said almost regretfully, resigning himself to waiting. *Hey, do you think she'll make us breakfast?*

"Nah, you go ahead. I need a shower, I'll see you down there," Owen said with a smile.

She turned to go, came back to the edge of the bed and crawled across the duvet, straddling him.

"Thank you," she kissed him softly, her hands resting on his chest as she pressed her lips to his.

"You should go or I'm going to make you thank me in other ways," his voice came out husky and rough.

"How about a big breakfast, then other things?" She offered.

"Mm-hmm, now get going, woman," he said, giving her a hard slap on the bottom.

Caitlin jumped and giggled, nearly falling off the bed in the process, but rewarded him with an enormous smile of hers once she'd righted herself before turning to go downstairs.

WHEN HE CAME DOWN to the first floor there was coffee brewing, and something was baking in the oven. She was still wearing his shirt she'd borrowed, but she'd tied an apron over it and she had music playing. He'd never liked country music, but the way she swayed her hips to it as she looked in the fridge for some ingredients was going a long way toward converting him. He took a seat at the breakfast bar silently and watched her sing quietly, gathering eggs, cheese, and milk out of the fridge.

When she turned around, she jumped, and then smiled at him.

"How do you like your eggs?" She asked.

"However," he replied with a shrug. As long as she was the one making them, she could serve them to him raw in a dog bowl and Finley would lap it up without any complaints.

Yeah, I would, Finley agreed. *Ugh, imprinting is weird. Now people are going to call us Moony Eyes, not just Ryder.*

She huffed and set the eggs down, placing her hands on her hips.

"Seriously, babe."

She pursed her lips.

"I'm not making you anything until you tell me how you like your eggs," she said, raising an eyebrow.

Ooh, look at how assertive and bossy she is. I like that! Finley praised.

"Over easy," he said, "Or scrambled, if that's too much work."

"Over easy it is. Coffee?"

"I can get my own coffee in a minute, I was just enjoying watching you work." His eyes lingered over her legs and the other delicious parts of her body that peeked out when she tiptoed to get a mug from the cabinet.

Owen's phone, which she must have plugged in, dinged. She poured his coffee and slid it across the bar, then handed over his phone.

"Mm, this a man can get used to."

TYLER

Hey man, you dead over there?

OWEN

Nah, just hanging out with Caitlin.

TYLER

Is it true you imprinted?

OWEN

Yeah.

TYLER

That's wild.

You holding up okay? Need anything?

OWEN

Oh yeah, we're great.

Thank the moon Caitlin's on board. It's not like when Ryder imprinted on Emma. It's been... easy.

OWEN'S EYES slid up to admire Caitlin for a moment until his phone buzzed in his hand, bringing him back to the conversation.

TYLER

Good, man. I'm happy for you. I'm glad it's easy, you deserve that.

> Don't take too long on your honeymoon or whatever you call it, I don't want to find a new partner.

OWEN

> Nah, I'll be back soon. You know me, I gotta keep myself busy.

TYLER

> Uh huh. Like Caitlin isn't keeping you busy.

> Don't forget to hydrate. *wink emoji*

> Talk later!

OWEN

> Heh, will do.

He put his phone away and watched Caitlin go from the pan of bacon to the eggs, somehow managing to have it all finished at damn near the same time.

"Thank you, cupcake," he said, inhaling the mouth-watering scent of the food wafting up from his plate when she slid it over the bar to him.

"I figured while I'm here, I might as well be useful, earn my keep and all that. I can start looking around for a job as soon as I'm settled in, I don't want to be a freeloader."

She really doesn't know how to let people take care of her, does she? Finley observed.

Apparently not, Owen thought as he took a bite of food. *But damn can she cook.*

"Caitlin, you don't have to earn your keep. You being here is plenty."

"I like to be useful, besides, I love cooking and making things for people," she said, walking around the counter with her food, setting her food in the spot next to his at the bar.

Owen grabbed her hand before she could sit down, waiting to speak until she met his eyes.

"Well, then if that's the reason, make all the food you want, but not if it's out of a sense of obligation. Also, you don't have to work. I have money for both of us. All I want is to take care of you," he brushed her hair to the side and kissed her cheek softly.

"I don't want you to resent me for having to work hard to provide for me. My ex- he did," she deflated in his arms.

You know, now that she knows we imprinted, we could ask her about him. Make sure he's dead, Finley thought with a nasty snarl.

I don't want to ruin the moment, Owen thought as she curled up against him. *Besides, I'm handling one thing at a time. First, she needs to let us take care of her. Then we'll handle the ex.*

"Cupcake, I love my work. The paycheck is nice, but if I never worked another day in my life we could live comfortably," Owen informed her.

The only time he'd touched his trust fund was to buy his truck, other than that it had sat there, growing. The thought of spending it on himself had no appeal, but he would empty that account in a half-second if it brought her a moment of pleasure.

"That's *your* money," she corrected, moving out of his arms looking sad.

It took an extraordinary amount of self control to not yank her back against him and kiss her until she forgot anything else in the world existed, especially any memories or ideas that made her look sad.

"You really don't get it, do you? Come here. Let me tell you how this is going to go." He stood and spun her stool around, taking her face in his hands, "You, ma'am, belong to me and my wolf. All we want is for you to be happy and healthy. Later on today, we're going to the bank and I'm putting your name on the bank accounts so you can always have whatever you need, or want."

"But," she objected.

"Then," he continued, raising an eyebrow. "We're going to the bookstore and wherever else you want to get; anything you want to make this place feel like home. You are mine to provide for, period. If you're working it should be because it's something that excites you and it's something you want to do."

"What if I don't want to do dishes?" she joked.

"Then I'll hire someone to do it," he said in all seriousness.

"I was kidding!"

"I am not kidding. I don't have unlimited money, but I've invested well and I've been saving a lot the last few years, waiting for the right thing to spend it on. I didn't know it, but that thing was a girl who was waiting to make me whole."

Very poetic. We should sex her! Finley suggested.

Luckily, even without the ability to hear him, Caitlin was in total agreement with Finley. Spreading her legs, she grabbed his t-shirt and pulled him into a gentle kiss. Her tongue slipped past his lips, sliding over his. She tasted like orange juice and happiness, Owen was sure he would never get enough.

CHAPTER TWENTY

CAITLIN

*C*aitlin woke to a savage growl from behind her, startling her from a dead sleep to instant alertness.

"Touch her again," Owen's words cut off in another growl that made the hair on the back of her neck stand up. She rolled over, putting her hand on his chest, and sliding it up to his neck.

"Owen?" she whispered, "Owen, it's just me here. No one is hurting me."

"My girl," he rumbled, pulling her as he shifted so her body was trapped beneath his weight. It would have been romantic if she didn't need to pee so badly.

"Finley?" she asked timidly, rubbing his neck with awkward small wrist movements, as her arm was now trapped beneath his.

When Axel had been in a bad dream, he'd been a nightmare to wake up. When he did wake, he was mean. With a deep breath, she reminded herself that she wasn't in Axel's bed. She was with Owen, she was safe.

"Owen?" She said a little louder.

"I'm up!" Owen exclaimed as his body shot up out of the bed, throwing the covers off and swinging his legs over the side. He stopped and looked around, confused.

"Oh, morning," he said sheepishly, blinking hard once.

"I'm sorry, you were on top of me and I really needed to move," she scooted off the edge of the bed.

"You're not leaving?" he asked, sounding alarmed.

"No, I just need to pee. And- that's a closet." She said when she opened the door, expecting a bathroom and finding a large empty walk-in room that was half the size of Charlotte's apartment.

"Other door," he reminded her with a bemused grin.

When she emerged, he was rubbing his hands down his face.

"Sorry about the rough wake-up, shift habits."

He was looking at her body with a hungry look that made her body heat. She shifted her weight from one foot to the other as she let the anxiety she'd had about his mood fade away. Clearly, he wasn't mad, and the only thing she had to be afraid of now was how many orgasms she was going to have to endure before breakfast.

Looking at the naked, and now very aroused shifter in front of her, Caitlin reflected that life with Owen was a huge improvement, in so many ways.

"I'm sorry I had to wake you at all," she said, letting her eyes linger on his erection as she offered what she hoped was a seductive smile.

"Mm. It was very rude. I may have to punish you," he said, narrowing his eyes as he gave her a dark grin that made her heart skip a beat.

"Is that so?" she edged toward the door as he stood and came around the bed, rolling his wrists and shoulders.

"Definitely. I brought you home and was so nice to you, you couldn't even wake me up nicely," he said in a light tone, but his body moved with the lazy grace of a predator who is supremely confident that his prey can't outrun him.

"Well, to be fair, you did growl at me in your sleep, then trap me under you."

She edged toward the door. She wasn't afraid *exactly*, but the look he gave made her want to run... but maybe not so fast that he couldn't catch her.

"I thought you liked being under me," he countered with a smirk.

She reached the doorway and hesitated.

"Cupcake, if you run I'll chase you and beat you like I own you," he threatened.

"You wouldn't want to hurt me, would you?" She said as a smile broke out on her face. He paused and neatly leaned down, catching his jeans from the floor from the night before. Sliding the belt out of the loops with one quick pull, he doubled it over and looked at her with a grin.

"I think I want to do exactly that."

Caitlin shot out the bedroom door as Owen lunged behind her. With a joyful screech she flew around the banister, making her way toward the east side of the house where a large bay window overlooked the driveway and the front yard.

"Come here, Cupcake," he said, cracking his belt.

"Got you!" She screamed, trying to twist away from him, but he pressed her to the wall, the windows letting in the light from the rising sun.

"Caught you," he said, giving her a kiss.

She bit his lip instead of kissing back nicely, he groaned and fisted her hair, jerking it back sharply.

"I was trying to be nice to you this morning," he growled, using his teeth to leave grazing nibbles down her exposed throat, licking the place where her pulse hammered beneath her skin.

"Sounds like imprinting has made you soft," she teased, her voice tight with laughter and a hint of nervousness. He wasn't going to *really* hurt her, right? Her whole body tensed.

"You think so?" He asked in her ear, his hand skimming up her body.

Turning her around, he ordered her to put her hands on the wall, flipping her nightshirt up so she was bare to him. He touched his belt to the apex of her thighs, rubbing it in her arousal then flicked it up so it struck her with a snap. Caitlin flinched away with a sensual cry, trying to reassure herself this wasn't a real punishment even as her arousal built in a confusing muddle of mixed emotions.

I am safe. Owen is safe. I am safe.

"Gods," she arched her back, pressing herself against it.

"Are you sure you don't want soft this morning? I could carry you back upstairs and worship your body with my mouth..." he murmured, using his belt to rub her more.

"I want you to beat me and fuck me."

"Nothing but my own little sex toy?" he asked in her ear.

"Yes,"

"Good. Because that's what you are. In fact, toys don't get clothes. Take off your shirt." She stood and took off her shirt, dropping it onto the floor in a heap.

"Spread your legs for me. I'm going to whip you until you're broken, then I'm going to claim this ass," he promised, "Because good girls let their mate have whatever they want, isn't that right, Cupcake?"

"Yes, sir."

"Tell me again what your safe words are, slut. You're gonna need them."

CHAPTER TWENTY-ONE

AXEL

*A*xel watched as the deputy took his mate right in front of the window. The happy couple were both so wrapped up in each other that they didn't notice him perched in the tree in the front yard. His mate's ass and thighs were a beautiful shade of bright red that contrasted with the rest of her pale skin beautifully.

Her hands gripped the railing around the top of the stairs as the deputy took her hard. Axel didn't look at the man's face, half closing his eyes as he pictured the last time he'd enjoyed his Kitty Cat's body, her tight little hole gripping his cock as he'd fucked her. Afterward he licked the tears from her face and then made her beg for forgiveness on her knees. The memory of how her skin had warmed as he'd slapped her and reminded her that bad girls had to earn forgiveness had his cock standing at attention, but he didn't indulge.

No, Axel wouldn't be coming again until he had his mate underneath him, writhing and fighting him off until he overpowered her, just like they both liked. Axel watched as she came, the deputy's fingers wrapped around the back of her neck as he brought her to orgasm. If it had been Axel, he would have grabbed her hair and jerked her head back. That always made her cry and gods how he loved it when she cried. Afterwards when he was satisfied and his carnal desires were met, the monster inside of him sated, she would curl against him and let him hold her, quiet and content in her submission.

When her lover had finished, he withdrew and turned her around to hold her close, saying words Axel couldn't hear. Axel almost pitied the man. He had no idea how secretly unhappy she was. She didn't want to be treated nicely, she wanted to be broken at the end of a scene, a tiny puddle of submissive nothingness. His Kitty Cat wrapped her arms around the man's naked body, snuggling into his chest while they held each other.

His poor little darling, he would have to make sure she had what she needed. When the couple had gone back into the interior of the house out of view of the window, Axel climbed out of the tree and made it to where his truck was parked in the woods a few miles away.

As he walked back alone with his thoughts, he considered what to do. He was going to have to rescue his mate from this pretender, which may take some doing. First, he had to separate the couple and make her realize that she wasn't any happier here than she was with her true mate. Formulating a plan, he drove back to Burlington with determination. He wasn't keen on leaving her alone with him, but the deputy would keep her safe enough for the time being, until Axel could return and reclaim his mate, but he would need time and supplies so it all went off without a hitch.

CHAPTER TWENTY-TWO

CAITLIN

*O*wen drove her back to Red River in time for David to bring the kids back to Charlotte's apartment. The drive back to her apartment was much more relaxed than the one to Pinehurst, with Owen holding her hand as Caitlin sang along with the country music he'd put on the radio. He didn't sing, insisting he couldn't carry a tune in a bucket, but hummed occasionally.

She got the kids settled in for bed and prepared their things for the morning so everyone could get out the door on time for school while she thought about the wild weekend.

Owen had imprinted on her. The idea still gave her little tremors of anxiety, but she ignored them. She wasn't a shifter, but even she'd felt the Alpha's magic working when Owen had been compelled to answer her questions honestly. As she switched and folded a load of laundry a knock at the front door startled her. Peering through the peephole, she squealed, unlocked the door, and threw it open. Her sister Charlotte, looking tired but pleased, stood on the threshold, a duffle bag at her feet and a backpack slung over her shoulder.

"Surprise!" she greeted, opening her arms.

"You're home!" Caitlin exclaimed, throwing her arms around her. Charlotte's frame, taller and slimmer than Caitlin's curves she'd inherited from their mother, Caitlin had never been happier to have her arms around her sister. Things were moving so fast with Owen, and while she was loving it, she also needed to be grounded in something that was normal so she didn't get too swept up in him and the newness of their, well... she guessed it was time to call it a relationship officially since he and his wolf were all in.

"Oh my god, you don't know how good it is to be home. Tell me how things are! The kids are in bed, I assume?"

"Yeah, they are."

"Well, what's going on with everything? Did they have an okay time at David's? How's the new guy who we 'aren't falling for' yet?" her sister asked, elbowing Caitlin with a teasing wink.

"About that..." Caitlin gave her an update on anything they hadn't already talked about regarding the kids' weekend with their father, then she poured out everything that had happened with Owen while Charlotte opened a bottle of wine. Charlotte listened with enthusiastic support as she drank, asking thoughtful questions and reveling in her sister's happiness.

"I mean, I think he sounds like the kind of guy you should have ended up with in the first place," Charlotte finally said when Caitlin finished telling her about Owen's imprinting and how they'd spent the weekend together.

"He *seems* great," Caitlin admitted. "I just don't know how to take it slow. I mean, I'm sort of not, I guess. But I know I have a lot of healing to do and I don't want to get so lost in this thing with him that I don't take care of me too."

"I mean, are you going to stop going to therapy and quit doing the stuff she's having you do that helps you?"

"Of course not," Caitlin said.

Therapy with Olivia was great for her and now that Charlotte was home, Caitlin planned to go see her therapist more, not less. Being with Owen was wonderful, but there were definitely times when she wished she wasn't always afraid and watching for signs that he was lying or manipulating her or feeling like Axel was just around the corner watching her, waiting to drag her back to her old life.

"Then I really think you're fine," Charlotte said. "And talk to Owen about what you're dealing with. I mean, he's imprinted, so it's not like you can scare him off or anything. In fact, I think this is probably the best thing that ever could have happened to you. A good man with an actual moral center loves you and can't stand the idea of hurting you, but does all that weird kinky crap you like."

Caitlin rolled her eyes and drank deeply from her glass of wine.

"No, really. Hear me out: he will do literally anything necessary to see you whole and healthy. He's the anti-Axel. And no matter how broken you are, he's never going to give up on you," her sister insisted, pouring herself more wine. "Heck. I think I need one of those myself."

"I hadn't thought about it that way," Caitlin admitted.

"Of course, you hadn't. You've been too busy getting dicked down." Charlotte laughed, "Of which I wholly approve, by the way. Whatever you two are doing, have him keep doing it,"

"Yeah?"

"So, not that I'm not happy to see you, but when are you moving out?" Charlotte asked.

"Well, I don't want to leave you in the lurch," Caitlin said, dropping her eyes.

"Oh, psh. We're gonna drink and catch up tonight, then tomorrow you're packing your crap to go live your best life. If David hadn't ruined me for the whole guys in uniform thing, I'd be jealous."

"I don't know. It's not too much too soon, is it?" Caitlin asked, worrying her lip with her teeth.

"He wants to buy you a library worth of books! If a nice man offers to buy you a library, you say 'Thank you, Daddy' nicely, get on your knees and suck his dick before you take his credit card," Charlotte advised with a twinkle in her eye, "I know you're into all that kinky crap. He'd probably love it."

They never had gotten around to going to the bank or the bookstore. Instead, they'd found all sorts of creative ways to christen the house.

"You're crazy."

"I'm right," Charlotte said, pointing at Caitlin with her wine glass,

"So, he can have you tomorrow. Now, I'm glad you're loved and safe and shit, but spill the deets on the sex. It's been too long and I'm going to live vicariously through you. First, how big is he?"

"Char!"

"Big, huh?" Charlotte guessed.

"I'm not talking about the size of his penis," Caitlin insisted.

"Fine, show me with your hands," her sister insisted, "so I can visualize properly. Are we talking about a pickle? Bratwurst? Hung like a horse?"

Caitlin laughed before holding her hands approximately nine inches apart, then held her fingers in a circle to indicate his girth. Charlotte threw her head back and cackled.

"You go, girl! I'm Charlotte, and I approve this dick for you!"

"If you run for office, is that going to be your slogan?" Caitlin teased.

"Hell yeah it is," Charlotte laughed.

They spent the rest of the evening enjoying the bottle of wine and reliving Caitlin's intimate activities with Owen in graphic detail, then catching up on the happenings of Charlotte's job before going to sleep together in Charlotte's bed. Sending Owen a goodnight text, Caitlin went to bed with her head delightfully buzzing from the wine, her heart happy that her sister was home safe with her kids as her excitement over being able to go back to Owen bubbled in her chest.

CHARLOTTE HELPED Caitlin pack her essentials, promising to meet up very soon to do lunch. Feeling sneaky in the most delightful way, Caitlin hopped into her car and drove to Owen's house, also now her house, she supposed. She didn't have a key, but he'd left the front door open and unlocked. He was in the kitchen making coffee, and eating an apple. The speakers in the kitchen played classical music, filling the room with a peaceful ambiance. She stood in the doorway until he looked up, his face breaking into a grin.

"Hey, where'd you come from?" he asked, setting the apple on the counter, not pausing when it rolled off, splattering little droplets of juice when it landed on the floor. He strode over to her and lifted her into his arms, kissing her thoroughly.

"Char came home early, so she sent me packing this morning with strict orders to christen every room of the house we didn't get to over the weekend," she grinned as he lifted her, wrapping her legs around him.

"Mm. I love that idea," he said, kissing her with a possessiveness that stole her breath, stopping only when her stomach rumbled.

"Have you eaten?" He asked, frowning at her.

"No, I wasn't hungry when I left the house."

"Hm, let's get you some food, then we'll work on your sister's suggestion." He kissed her nose lightly, then lowered her to the ground and walked back to the kitchen, bending to scoop up his fallen apple, and tossing it neatly into the trash can before opening the fridge.

Smiling mischievously, she quickly stripped out of her clothes.

"Take a seat, I'll rustle us up something," Owen said over his shoulder, "What are you in the mood for?"

"You," she said, walking around the breakfast bar.

"You have me, but what do you want to eat? I can make us-" He said, his eyes catching her naked body. "Um."

"Hm?"

"You're naked," he pointed out, the refrigerator door standing open, one hand still inside as if he'd forgotten it existed.

"I want sex," she said, pouting a little.

"You need food," he said, pupils dilating as his eyes rolled over her body.

"Olivia says that experiencing healthy, consensual sex reinforces the progress I've made in my recovery."

"She... said that, did she?" He asked, swallowing hard, then shaking his head. "Food first, then sex."

"You don't want me to service you before then, sir?" She asked, coming to stand in front of him, dropping to her knees.

"I, um, yes. Yes, definitely." He stammered.

· · ·

THREE MINUTES LATER, her hands were resting on his thighs, one of his hands fisting her hair as he used her mouth.

"You're nothing but a desperate cum slut, aren't you? You drove all the way home just so I could use you without even bothering to take care of your needs first," he thrust his cock deep into her throat, held it there for a few long seconds, then removed it as she gasped for air.

"Yes."

"Say it. Say what you are," he demanded.

"I'm a desperate cum slut for you," she said breathlessly.

"What are you going to do to earn my cum this morning?" he asked, stroking himself as he smirked at her on her knees before him.

"Anything!"

"Anything? You sure?"

"Yes!" She opened her mouth, tongue out, waiting for his cock.

"Mm. Suck my cock, my slutty little mate," he commanded, thrusting in so she gagged in an effort to take him all.

She sank into the submission he demanded, her hands itching to reach and satisfy the ache growing in her core.

"Stop."

She slowed but didn't stop, her eyes lifted to his with an impudent smile.

"Bitch, I said stop." He yanked her ponytail back, pulling his hand back to slap her face, pausing. "Do you want me to slap you? Hm? Is that what you need?"

"Yes sir."

"Fine." He slapped her on one cheek, then the other. "There. Fucking whore. I don't even know why I try to be nice to you. You don't deserve it." He hauled her to her feet. "Get in my bed, ass up, face on the mattress so I don't have to look at you."

Soon her screams of pain and pleasure echoed through the house, bouncing off the walls as he slammed into her from behind, slapping her ass as he plunged balls deep inside of her. When they'd recovered enough to move, she insisted on making him breakfast.

. . .

THEY SPENT the entire day finding fun and unique places to christen the house. After breakfast, Owen grabbed some rope from upstairs and stretched her out on the dining room table, and used a wand to edge her until she was in tears begging for release. Only then did he fuck her, her screams reverberating off the walls. They'd worked their way through most of the house when they paused for lunch.

"I need to run into town," Owen said reluctantly, standing behind her at the kitchen counter while she made sandwiches.

"Can I come?" Caitlin asked without pausing.

"I thought you had, many times," Owen teased, his teeth closing over the shell of her ear.

"Well, if you don't want me with you, I'll just stay home and play with myself," Caitlin teased as she cut her second sandwich.

"Oh no, cupcake. Your pleasure is all mine," he said, pressing against her back with a growing erection.

"Seriously, what are you going into town for?"

"Condoms," he replied. "Because I am definitely not done fucking you today."

"Oh, right," she said, blushing.

"You really are welcome to ride with me. I would enjoy your company," he brushed her hair aside and kissed her behind her ear.

"Actually, I think I'll stay here. I need to do my journaling and stuff for my next appointment with Olivia." She worked hard to keep her voice light.

"What's wrong?" Owen asked.

Caitlin took a deep breath. It was way too soon in a normal relationship to have this conversation, but Owen had put everything out there when Jason had compelled him to answer her questions honestly, the least she could do was return his trust.

Her hand shook, hoping he wouldn't think she was crazy, or at least, wouldn't be turned off by it.

"I sort of hate condoms, and I realize this is really crazy, so I'm going to discuss it and then we can pretend it never happened and just keep doing what we're doing if you don't feel the same way, okay?" She said, not looking over her shoulder.

"Okay," Owen answered cautiously, growing still behind her.

"I know it's way too fast. It's insanely fast to even think about this, but... I wouldn't be upset if we didn't use condoms."

Owen was so still behind her her heart started beating faster. Her mind whirred. *Was he mad?*

"You'd be fine with getting pregnant?" he asked quietly.

"Like I said, I do realize it's too soon," she hurried to explain, her cheeks burning.

She'd done it. She'd found the one way to scare off an imprinted shifter, by bringing up babies too quickly. Cursing herself, she put down the knife as her hands started to shake.

"Cupcake, I would absolutely love that."

"You don't think I'm crazy?" She asked, not looking at him, her cheeks heating.

He wrapped his arms around her gently, his hand around her middle, holding her close. His warmth and the pressure set her at ease somewhat.

"I have an unbreakable magic bond tying us together forever, and you're concerned about being the crazy one?" he asked with a chuckle.

"Well, yeah."

"The way I see it, we've got a lifetime together, and if you don't want to wait around, let's not," Owen was saying over the pounding in her ears.

She felt him push his sweatpants down with one hand, his erection springing out against her exposed flesh under his t-shirt that she'd thrown on. Lifting her up and placing her stomach-first onto the counter, he spread her cheeks and taking his cock in his hand, rubbed himself at her entrance.

"Caitlin Montgomery." He asked huskily, barely sliding the tip inside of her, holding himself back with shaky self-control, "Will you please have my baby?"

"Yes,"

He slid inside of her with a primal groan, his hand gripping her shoulder almost painfully as he entered her for the first time without anything between them.

CHAPTER TWENTY-THREE

OWEN

*H*aving Caitlin around just made everything nicer. They stocked the kitchen with everything she needed for baking. Owen asked around and quickly got her more orders than she could easily fill, which kept her busy and made her feel useful. It also kept her in his kitchen, which made the house feel like a home.

He happily washed the dishes and enjoyed listening to her talk about the pros and cons of different ingredients and methods while she baked and rearranged the cabinets to suit her. He didn't have a fucking clue what she was talking about half the time, but loved how passionate she could be about rising agents in quick breads and proofing sourdough. She liked to chat as she worked and he enjoyed that she shared about childhood or friends she had back in her hometown.

She'd been moved in officially for six days when he'd woken in the middle of the night and found she wasn't in their bed. He waited for several minutes but she never returned, so he'd gone looking for her.

His little mate had wrapped herself in a blanket he didn't know he owned and made herself a cup of tea that had long-since gone cold in her hands. She watched the tree line of the back yard, looking for something unblinkingly.

"Cupcake?" he asked her, his voice hoarse as he slid his hands around her waist over the blanket.

She screamed and recoiled from him, the mug slipping from her hands and shattering on the floor, sending cold tea all over.

"Hey, hey," he said, holding his hands up, taking several steps back.

"Oh, gods. It's you," she said.

"Yeah, don't move," he instructed, using his foot to scoot a particularly large piece of the ceramic mug out of the way so he could pick her up and carry her to the counter.

"Sorry," she said, looking embarrassed.

"I'm sorry I startled you," he said, waiting for her to explain herself.

"I woke up, and I couldn't sleep. So I went to make myself a cup of tea, but I thought I saw something."

"What was it?"

"I don't know. It sort of looked like a person was out there in the woods? Then I swear it was a wolf, but then I couldn't see anything and I got a little wrapped up in my head."

"I see,"

"I thought - maybe it was Axel," She explained, keeping her eyes on her hands.

Finley's growl ripped through their minds, savage and feral. It was the first time she'd said the dirtbag's name, and just hearing her say it made them both see red, but Caitlin was still sharing, so Owen begged Finley to be quiet so he could pay attention to Caitlin.

"I think I see him sometimes. A lot, actually. I'll see someone that looks like him out of the corner of my eye, or just other times. Olivia says it's PTSD, and also we lived together for such a long time that him being around is more normal to me than not."

"When?"

"Like, crazy times. The other day. I thought I saw him walking into the Bar on Main, which is just nuts."

"Are you sure?"

"Oh yeah. Axel was never one for subtlety." She said with a rueful laugh.

Why haven't we killed him yet? Finley asked irritably.

"You can talk about him." Owen said gently, "I know you went through things, but he was a part of your life, and I care about you, past, present and future."

"I know. I will, one day. I just don't want you to see me differently. Right now we're all sexy and fun, and I love that. You already know about some of the bad stuff, and that's plenty. Right now with you I can be a new me, one who isn't so broken. "

"You're not broken," Owen insisted, his heart constricting on the sadness on her face.

She is totally broken, Finley argued.

"The fact that you can say that to me with a straight face is why I don't want to talk about it. Look, I promise to talk about things. I just want to enjoy this right now, okay?"

"Alright, cupcake. But, no matter how broken you are, I'm not going anywhere."

"Thank you," she said, a fake smile plastered on her face.

She wanted to trust him, and she was giving him the opportunity to be trustworthy and that had to be enough for now. They had a lifetime together for her to realize he wasn't a bad man, and that instead of hurting her he would love and protect her.

"I'll clean this up, you go to bed," Owen said, but she didn't reach for his arms, drawing back when he moved to take her off the counter.

She hesitated, looking at the mess on the floor with eyes filled with anxiety.

"Caitlin. This is the thing we talked about. Fin and I take care of you. I'm not mad about the mess, or the cup. I promise," he assured.

She searched his eyes and he let her look her fill, not moving until she looked reassured, letting out a breath she'd been holding and scooting to the edge of the counter. She hugged him around the torso for a moment, clinging to him before she drew back and put her arms around his shoulders.

"Thank you for taking care of me and making me feel safe," she whispered.

"Always, cupcake. I swear I will always keep you safe," he assured her, lifting her and setting her down far away from the broken mug shards.

"I'll be up as soon as this is cleaned up, k?"

"Will you double check and make sure the doors are locked before you come up?" She asked, biting her lip.

"Yes ma'am," he said, tilting his head toward the stairs, watching her walk away.

You think she's naked under that blanket? Finley asked.

Finley, can you cool it? She's obviously not in the mood. Owen thought, irritated.

I didn't say I wanted to sex her. I just want to look. She's very nice to look at! Finley replied haughtily.

SHE WAS IN BED, snuggled up under the covers when he came upstairs. When he crawled between the sheets, she scooted over and almost held her breath, her heartbeat fluttering.

"Something wrong?"

"I'm working up to asking you something," she admitted.

"Mm." He said, turning so he faced her.

"I was thinking. You work weird hours," she began, sounding nervous.

"I do," Owen acknowledged.

"And I don't always feel safe here. I feel like Axel is going to come find me, or like he's watching me. I know that's crazy, Olivia and I have been talking about it, but she suggested something to help me feel safe when you're not home," she explained.

"Like a gun?"

"Maybe? I don't know. A gun is only so useful, and I'm not very confident with them."

"You're right," he agreed, taking her into his arms. "Well, whatever you need to feel safe, you can get it, you don't need to ask me. If you do decide you want a gun, I would like to go with you, or one of the other deputies if I'm busy. I want you to have something that would work for you."

"I'm not sure I want a gun," she said.

"And that's fine. But if you decide to go that route, let me or one of the guys take you. The chief would also take you, and he'll give you good advice."

"Okay, thank you. I didn't want you to be mad."

"Why would that make me mad?" he asked.

Because she's broken and she thinks everything will make us mad, Finley pointed out.

I'm giving her an opportunity to talk about it, Owen snapped.

Oh, right. Great idea!

"Because it's your job to protect me and all that. I should trust you to do that and maybe you'll think I don't trust you if I asked for something else to keep me safe."

"Cupcake, I'm not always here, and even when I am, if something makes you feel better then I'm happy to get it for you." He rubbed his nose against her jawline affectionately, "Especially when you're working on carrying my baby."

She laughed a little when he scooted closer, intending to hold and comfort her but she thrust her hips suggestively into his.

"Maybe we should try right now, is that what you're implying?" She asked with a little laugh, spreading her legs for him.

He climbed on top of her and pushed his sweatpants down so his erection sprang free.

"I'm not implying it," he said, his voice taking on a tight, dangerous edge that made her body quiver, "I'm demanding it, my little cum slut. I'm going to prove to you that the only thing you need to be afraid of in this house is how often I'm going to fuck you to put a baby inside of you."

Putting his hand around her throat, he squeezed as he entered her, keeping her breathing restricted.

"Are you going to be my good slut?" he purred.

She tried to speak but he squeezed her throat more, cutting off her air completely so no audible words escaped her lips.

"Sorry, I couldn't hear you. Are you going to be a good little mate and let me breed you?" He thrust into her hard and she made a strangled noise.

"Aw, I guess my slutty mate doesn't want to be bred tonight. I'll just have to fuck your ass instead." He released her throat and rolled off her, reaching for the nightstand where he grabbed a bottle of lube from the drawer.

"I'll be so good, please breed me, get me pregnant, I want it."

"I asked you and you didn't respond to me, it's too late for that," Owen said, "Now roll over. I'm going to fuck this tight ass of yours and fill it with my cum."

CHAPTER TWENTY-FOUR

CAITLIN

*I*n a flash, Caitlin wasn't in Owen's bed. She was bent over the couch in the little trailer in Burlington, her ass on fire from the beating Axel had doled out, her pussy wet not from arousal with her mate, but from Axel's cum seeping out of her.

Oh no, there's no safe wording out of a punishment, kitten. You can scream and cry all you like, but I'm going to fuck this pretty ass of yours. I'm going to ruin you, Kitty Cat. Axel's voice rang in her mind.

"Red," she whispered.

"What was that, slut?" Owen asked, leaning down, pausing for a moment, the tip of his shaft pressed against her.

"Red, red, red, red," she started whispering over and over.

"Oh, Caitlin," Owen said, moving away immediately and coming beside her on the bed. "Caitlin baby, what do you need?"

"Red."

"We're done, baby. I hear you," Owen assured her.

"Please don't punish me," she whispered.

"No, I won't punish you. You're always allowed to have a safe word, you *should have a* safe word and I'm proud of you. How can I help?"

"Sticky," she said aloud before pressing her head in the pillow as her whole body trembled.

"You want me to clean you up?" Owen confirmed.

The only response she could give him was a nod, too terrified to look at him. She felt material, a t-shirt possibly, against her thighs. He was going to resent her now, or he wouldn't want to have sex with her anymore because she was thinking about Axel in their bed.

"I'm going to wipe you off, but I'm not doing anything else," Owen said, placing a reassuring hand on her hip while he wiped her clean, then wiped off himself.

The dam of emotions broke as he cleaned her, wiping gently and tossing the fabric onto the floor. She began to shake in earnest, crying into the pillow while he sat by. She made her body small, pressing her thighs together as she pulled her arms underneath her.

When she calmed somewhat, she peeked out. His face was there, brows drawn down in concern, but no anger.

"Can I hold you? Would that help?" he asked, lying next to her. "I didn't want to touch you if that made it worse."

She nodded and he touched her awkwardly.

"Cupcake?" he asked when she didn't move.

"I'm stuck," she hiccuped.

"Can I move you?" he asked and she nodded, hiccuping.

"Shh," he said, pulling the blanket up over them both while she cried, crooning softly, "You're safe, I'm here."

She woke up the next morning to the sound of Owen's voice outside the bedroom.

"…not coming in," he was saying into the phone, "We're fine. Caitlin had a rough night, so Fin and I need to be with her. Thanks, Lawson."

Her mate walked back into the room, his face drawn.

"I hope I didn't wake you," he said, sitting on the bed.

"You didn't. You can go to work, I'm okay," she assured.

Owen's face creased into a scowl, and she recoiled, drawing the blankets up her chest and doing her best to sink into the mattress.

"You are a lot of things, fine isn't one of them." He said, his jaw ticking. "Do you want breakfast before we talk about what happened last night?"

"We don't have to talk about it."

"You might not want to talk about it, but I need to," he said. "Something happened and I need to know what it was so I don't make it happen again."

"Okay," she said, sighing, "I need to pee first."

In the bathroom, she gathered her thoughts and stared at her reflection in the mirror. She hadn't wanted to talk about things with Axel because she didn't want Owen to see her differently, didn't want him to look at her like she was broken, but that ship had sailed.

Emerging back out into the bedroom where Owen was pacing.

"I'm not going to talk about everything, but I'll tell you about the couple of days before I left Axel."

CHAPTER TWENTY-FIVE

OWEN

"I hate leaving you alone after last night and all the stuff we talked about this morning, but I have to go. There's an evaluation this morning for the medics and security positions for James and Emma's project and I have to be there. After that's done I can come home and grab you for lunch if you like?"

"Okay. I was thinking I might go to the bookstore while you're gone," she said, walking to the doorway between the kitchen and living room, eying the empty bookshelves. "The owner, his name is… Jared, right?"

"Yup, he can be a bit gruff, but he'll take good care of you. Here," he pulled out his wallet.

"No, I didn't mean that," she objected, but he wasn't listening.

He'd listened to her recount the period shortly before she'd left her ex that morning and was in no mood to let her think that he would be anything but provide for everything she needed, happily.

"Cupcake, I'm not asking you," he said, pulling out his bank card.

He felt bad now that they hadn't made it to the bank last weekend, but he was going to remedy that today when he went in to do a magical tolerance test for the security position he'd applied for with Emma and James.

"I don't want to take your money," she said, refusing to take his card.

"Fine," he pulled out his phone and called Jared.

"Hey, Caitlin might come up there today to get some books. Don't let her pay for them, I'm covering it. Yup, thanks."

She crossed her arms and made a face at him, but he just shrugged. She was going to have to learn that he would take care of her, period.

"Sweetheart, you're broke. I have money and I like spending it on you," Owen explained patiently.

"I don't want you to feel like-" she began.

"You're my mate, I want you to be happy. That's all there is to it."

Now he gave her a stern look that made her drop her eyes. Timidly, she put her arms around him; he pulled her against his chest and asked what she was really worried about.

"What if you hate what I buy?"

Why would we care about a bunch of books? Finley asked.

"You could buy every book with some shirtless Fabio guy Jared has in stock if it made you happy."

"Oh really?"

"Mm-hmm," he answered, rubbing her back gently.

He was on the verge of telling her how much he loved her and apologized again for last night, but she spoke first.

"What time do you need to leave?" she asked coyly.

"In about forty minutes, why?" She raised her eyebrows in response, looking at him through her lashes with a sly, coquettish smile. "Are you trying to seduce me, cupcake?"

"Well, if I'm going to be your sugar baby, you might as well benefit from it."

"I'm not buying things for you so you'll have sex with me," he said seriously.

When a flicker of doubt passed her face, he frowned and took her by the hand, leading her to the bookshelves. He placed his hands on her shoulders pushing her backward so her back rested against the empty shelf and then knelt down in front of her.

He spoke gently and kept his eyes on hers so could see he wasn't angry with her, because what he was about to do was not going to be particularly nice, or gentle. She needed to learn that his love didn't come with strings, and she didn't need to do anything to earn it. If words didn't work, he was going to show her in a way that he might understand better.

"I want to please you, to let you know how safe and loved you are. I also want to have sex with you. I also enjoy buying you things, so you have what you want in *our* space." As he spoke he slid his hands up the outsides of calves, sliding up her thighs till he found her underwear. Sliding them down, he had her step out of them.

"What would make you feel loved?" he asked.

"Be mean to me," she said breathlessly.

Owen grinned and nodded, his eyes flitting over her body in quick assessment.

"As my good girl wishes."

His head disappeared under her skirt. His firm hand lifted one of her thighs to his shoulder, closing his mouth around her clit without any warning.

"Owen!" She cried out as he sucked hard, gripping his hair through the thin material of her skirt. "Holy fuck, slow down!"

He sucked harder, his hand reaching up and gripping her wrist tight so she released his hair, holding it against her abdomen.

"Owen, fuck," she cried out.

He removed his mouth from her, snatching the material of her skirt from over his head. He gathered the fabric and shoved it into her empty fist.

"Shut up, slut," he commanded. "You're not here to talk."

"If you talk again, I'll make you choke on my dick until you see stars," he threatened.

He went back to her, sliding one finger inside of her. He licked, sucked and teased her until she was whimpering with need.

"Owen- please," she begged.

Immediately, he removed his mouth from her and stood, leaving her panting. Placing his arms on either side of the shelf at her back, he said in a low, threatening voice.

"What did I say about talking? Get on your fucking knees," he growled, undoing his belt.

"I want you to touch yourself while I fuck your mouth, but if you orgasm you don't get to swallow my cum. Understand, slut?"

She nodded, opening her mouth. As he pushed himself inside of her mouth, she spread her legs for him, her fingers finding her clit as she sucked him with an eagerness that almost made him forget what he was planning for her.

"You can do better than that," he coaxed, shoving himself further into her mouth.

She gagged as he hit the back of her unprepared throat. Gripping her hair, he held himself there, filling her throat for a few seconds, pulling out as she gasped for air. His other hand went around her throat, squeezing lightly. As her body struggled for air, she swirled her juices around her clit.

"Slap your clit, hard," he commanded.

She whimpered, slapping herself. The sting of pain made her moan around his cock.

"Again," he withdrew and thrust into her mouth.

She hit her clit again, moaning louder, the vibrations sending a glorious feeling through his shaft.

"Fuck, like that. Moan on my cock like you want to, my good girl. Make that pussy I own feel good while I use your whore mouth. If you cum, I'll punish you."

Caitlin made unseemly noises, desperate with need and Owen fought hard for control over his own body.

"Don't you fucking come, I get to take care of that pussy," he growled.

She slowed her pace, but she was trembling and desperate. Her eyes met his. Looking deep into her eyes, he slid almost entirely out of her mouth.

"Choke yourself on my cock," he ordered.

She took as much of him as she could, taking him as deep as she could until her stomach heaved. His breathing became ragged, his self-control waning as he fought the urge to release into her throat.

"Fuck, just like that," he grabbed her hair and shoved himself into her mouth, pushing to the back of her throat cutting off her air.

She rubbed her clit in small hurried motions, rubbing at just the right angle to make her orgasm. As her vision blacked at the edges she lost her control, making obscene noises as she felt her arousal gushing out of her in a puddle on the floor. He pulled out, releasing her hair.

"No!" She objected, reaching her hand out to stop him but he batted her hand away mildly.

"I told you not to come, Caitlin, that I get to take care of you," he said, stroking himself.

"No, please," she begged.

"Close your mouth," he ground out, resting one hand on the bookshelf as he leaned forward, jerking himself hard and fast.

"Please Owen, I want to," he took his hand off the bookshelf and slapped her cheek, his orgasm shooting through him with a low growl.

Thick ropes of his cum landed on her face, eyes and mouth closed, looking considerably less happy than she usually did after an orgasm.

"You know, I would have loved to fuck your throat. It would have felt a lot better than fucking my hand," he commented, keeping his voice low and cold.

"I'm sorry," she said, not opening her eyes to avoid getting his cum in them.

"Only obedient girls who let me take care of them get to make my cock feel good, cupcake," he said when he was finished, gripping her face so her jaw opened. "Now clean me off."

She sucked him eagerly. When he was satisfied, he used her hair to pull her off him with an audible pop.

"I guess I'll have to see if you can please me like a good girl later," he said, stripping his t-shirt off to wipe off her face.

When she'd cleaned her face off well enough to open her eyes, he'd tucked himself away, standing shirtless before her, a smirk on his lips. He offered her a hand up from the floor.

I don't know if she got it, but damn, that was hot! Finley cheered.

She frowned a little, but accepted his hand up.

"I wanted to take care of you," she said.

"You're not in charge of how I use your body." He kissed her gently on the lips. "Also, you're still trying to use sex to pay me back for taking care of you, which isn't how this works. As long as you think you're using your body to buy my caring for you, I'm not going to let you satisfy me in the ways you know I like."

Her face went from a slight frown to outrage.

"That's - awful!" She protested, crossing her arms.

"No. You're mine. You are enough, without sex, and until you learn that, you're going to be very frustrated," he pulled her into a hug. "I need to get another shirt, but I love you."

"You love me?" She blinked in surprise.

I don't know why that's a surprise. What does she think imprinting means, that we just have a lot of sex? Finley asked, amused at the idea.

Well, I mean... Owen thought, pointing out that that was almost all they'd done since he'd imprinted on her.

Fair point, Finley conceded.

"More than anything." Owen didn't release her. "I'm thrilled to have you as my mate, my future baby momma, and the love of my life."

He pulled away and sighed, glancing at his watch with regret.

"I wish I didn't have to go, but I won't be too long. Be a good girl, get some books if you want to, or if you want me to drive you I'll pick you up when I'm done. But I love you, Caitlin. You don't have to earn it, alright? It's just a fact."

CHAPTER TWENTY-SIX

CAITLIN

*A*lthough their time christening the house and shopping for books and knick-knacks to fill the bookshelves had been wonderful, Caitlin was glad when Owen had taken a shift at the EMS base to fill a hole in the schedule. Caitlin ran some errands, not expecting to see Owen until when she dropped off dinner for the whole shift, a delicious stew that was sitting at home in a crock pot. She'd even planned to make fresh-baked rolls with honey butter, requested especially by Tyler, Owen's usual work partner whom Caitlin immediately took a liking to.

Now all she could think about was the fact that she couldn't remember if she'd put salt in the dough that was sitting in the fridge overnight. Caitlin walked into the base unsteadily, her entire body shaking like a leaf. Clutching her purse, she put on her best fake smile. Everything was fine. The dough would be fine, and so would she. Probably. Maybe.

A broad-shouldered medic was sweeping the floor and laughing with a coworker.

"Yeah, my brother's in that program, he said she had to transfer out because they caught her with three guys in the supply closet, one of them was the program director. That's why he 'retired' out of the blue," the medic whose shirt read CUTLER in bold, white letters said, wiggling his eyebrows, breaking off when he noticed Caitlin.

"Ma'am," the EMT, whose shirt told her his last name was Bailey, stepped forward to greet her. "Can we help you?"

"I'm looking for Owen Kessler," Caitlin said, biting her lip as she tried not to cry.

"Caitlin," Brian said from the hallway leading back to the supervisor's office, his face lighting up in a genuine smile, "what brings you here? Please tell me you have cookies."

"I don't, I was just looking for Owen." She gave a tremulous smile.

Brian searched her eyes for a moment, his smile fading into a thoughtful expression.

"He's out taking some supplies to Base 4, can I help?"

She didn't know Brian, not well enough to talk to him about this. Despite how his eyes seemed to invite confidence, she didn't want to bring her personal drama to Owen's work, especially not during his first shift back.

"Oh, no. I'm fine. I can come back."

She turned to go, but the big shifter insisted.

"He's not gonna be too long, hang out. You want some water?"

"No, thanks," she said, wrinkling her nose at the idea.

"Soda?" he offered.

"Do you have any lemonade?"

"Let me check," Brian left her in the front hall, returning a moment later with a glass of lemonade. "It's the powdered stuff, but it tastes okay. Come sit in the office."

He placed a hand between her shoulder blades and escorted her down the hall.

"What's up?" Brian asked.

"Not much, you?" Caitlin said, sipping the lemonade as tears filled her eyes.

"Caitlin, I know we don't know each other, but it's my job to make sure that everyone on my shift is okay," Brian said gently, reaching behind him for a box of tissues which he plunked down on the desk.

"I'm not part of the shift, I don't work here." Caitlin pointed out.

"One of my guys imprinted on you. You're a part of the shift as much as any of us now, so…" he folded his arms and leaned back in his seat, the leather creaking beneath him.

"I… I'm pregnant." She said, hot tears spilling out over her cheeks.

"You didn't know," Brian surmised.

"Not until this morning. Owen and I were talking about it, which I realize seems crazy considering we just started seeing each other, but," she shrugged and took a sip of her drink, "It felt right, you know?"

"I do know," Brian said sincerely.

"Well, I figured I should get checked out so I went to the doctor, and surprise, I'm already pregnant."

Owen's voice came down the hallway.

"Yeah, let me check in with Lawson, then I'll give you a hand," he was saying.

Caitlin only had a moment to compose herself before Owen was in the doorway. Instantly his face changed from relaxed to alarmed.

"Hey - what's wrong?" Owen knelt before her on the floor, taking her hands in his as his eyes searched her face.

"I'm sorry, I know you're working," she leaned forward and folded down on herself so her head rested on his shoulder as she dissolved into incoherent hysterics.

"Cupcake, what's going on?"

She sobbed into his chest, clinging to his shirt when he tried to pull away to get a better look at her. He held her while she cried, only releasing her when she gathered herself, sitting up and taking a shaking breath.

"Please tell me what's wrong," he pleaded softly, as if her tears pained him, "Are you hurt?"

"Not exactly," she laughed, dabbing her eyes and nose with the tissue from her hand.

"I'm going to need a bit more than that. Where does it hurt?"

"It's not that kind of hurt," she said, her lower lip quivering dangerously.

"Hey, let's go outside," Owen said, glancing over his shoulder at Brian.

"No, I'll go, you two stay," Brian said, evacuating his chair. "It's time for my lunch anyway. Take as long as you need."

"Thanks," Owen said without looking as his captain left, shutting the door behind him.

"Please tell me what's wrong. Whatever it is, we can fix it."

"I- I'm pregnant. I went to the doctor to get a blood test... I'm too far along," Caitlin said, desperately trying to get control of herself so she didn't start crying again.

"Too far along for what?" He asked.

Not wanting to spell it out, but knowing she needed to, she took a fortifying breath.

"When I left Axel, he'd just..." She bit her lip, closing her eyes, not wanting to see Owen's face when he understood. "We had sex, the night before I left."

"And that was the night that he..." Owen trailed off.

"Raped me, yes." Owen sat still, not moving a muscle so she continued, "He hurt me really badly. I bled. I've had some bleeding since, so I figured my period was just weird. I've never been regular. I haven't felt sick or anything, just tired, but I figured that was because of all the sex. But after our talk the other night I wanted to get things checked out."

She opened her eyes when he didn't respond. Owen nodded his encouragement, his hand patting her leg in a mechanical, detached way as his eyes burned a hole into hers.

"It's not yours. I'm too far along, it has to be his," she said, tears spilling out again.

Owen's eyes slid closed as his body began to shake. His jaw tightened and he took her hand gingerly, bringing it and pressing his lips to the back of her fingers.

"I need a minute. I'm walking outside, but I'll be right back, okay?" He assured her, "I'm not upset with you. I am not mad at you. I just need a minute. Don't go anywhere, just... stay."

She nodded, her lower lip trembling. He left her alone in the office. After a few minutes, she began to cry again. She was absurdly relieved that her pregnancy was why she'd been so emotional, and why she'd been so willing to cling to Owen. Owen may not be the father, but shifter babies tended to make even human mothers act a little wolfish with their clinginess, or at least so the doctor had assured her.

"Caitlin, you okay?" Brian asked from the doorway.

"No," she said.

Owen said he wasn't mad, but how could he not be? She was carrying another man's baby. How could he be okay with that? She'd only brought up Axel's name to him one time and he'd looked downright murderous... how much worse was it going to be when she was carrying around Axel's baby for months, then raising it? What if it looked like Axel? Would Owen be able to live in the same house with it?

Brian hovered for a moment before coming in and she realized she was still sitting in his office and probably keeping him from doing his job.

"I'm probably in your way. Sorry, I can go."

"Sit down, honey," Brian said gently and she started to cry again.

"Gods, I'm so sorry."

"Is the baby okay?" He asked softly.

"I- it's fine I think," she replied.

When Brian waited, the whole story poured out of her. Axel and his last punishment, how she'd left, and how she'd come here, and then Owen and her meeting at the bake sale, not expecting any kind of relationship. Brian listened, his eyes sliding closed for a moment before opening them. His eyes, which she could have sworn were blue a moment before, shone chocolate brown, but when he blinked they were blue again - his wolf was trying hard to surface.

"Where's Owen?" he asked quietly.

"He left, he said he'd be back," Brian held up a finger.

"Aiden!" he barked.

After a few moments, the young man who'd been in the ambulance when Owen had picked up the batch of cookies from her for James appeared in the doorway - this must be Aiden, Owen's normal EMS partner. Owen had mentioned him before, but they hadn't been officially introduced.

"Yeah?" Aiden popped his head around the doorframe, eyes flicking to Caitlin briefly and his eyebrows drew down into a frown of concern.

"Find Owen, stick with him till he comes back here," Brian ordered.

"Everything okay?"

"Everything's handled here. Don't let him take a truck anywhere. Call for backup over the radio if you need it."

Aiden hesitated ever so slightly before he responded, looking like he wanted to ask, but instead he just slowly nodded to Brian, a look passing between them that Caitlin couldn't read.

"Will do," Aiden said with a polite nod in her direction, disappearing back into the hallway with a murmured, "Miss Caitlin."

Brian picked up his phone and dialed someone.

"Hey chief, we need you down here. It's Owen- yes, right now. There's a problem- yeah."

Had she gotten Owen into trouble? Caitlin worried her lip, fighting more tears. If he wasn't mad about the baby, which she clearly was, he was going to be mad that she brought drama to his workplace. Good mates didn't bring their dirty laundry and drama to where their mates worked.

"I'm sorry. If Owen isn't okay, we may need some extra support for him, and the best people for that are his partner and the chief," Brian explained, "Imprinting makes your feelings difficult to manage, especially when it comes to your mate. Protective instincts can be overwhelming, as I understand it."

"Yeah, that's probably a good idea," Caitlin said woodenly.

She could sure use some extra support herself, but Charlotte was working for several more hours and Caitlin didn't want to bother her with a problem that there was no fixing, and that wouldn't be solved by interrupting her sister's work day.

"What do you need right now? Is there someone I can call?" Brian asked.

"No."

"Do you know Emma, Ryder's mate?" he asked, scooting the box of tissues several inches closer as she blew her nose into her wadded-up tissue.

"Yeah, we met at the bake sale," she said.

"She might be able to help you feel better. Want me to see if she can come down?"

"I don't want to bother her," Caitlin said, shaking her head.

Brian rolled his eyes and pulled out his cell, sending a quick text.

"Look, Caitlin, this is what we do. We're all family here. We take care of one another, and that's that."

At his insistence, Caitlin drank her lemonade while they waited, still sniffling on occasion as she tried to calm down. Emma showed up a few minutes later, phone in hand. Ryder stood behind her, holding her purse and jacket. Emma pulled her curls back into a chaotic bun at the base of her neck and gave Caitlin a professional smile.

"Hey, I hear you can use a pick-me-up," Emma said in a crisp and professional tone that set Caitlin at ease.

"Yeah," Caitlin said in a tremulous watery voice.

"I don't think another man hovering around is going to help her feel any better," Emma said, raising her eyebrows.

"Right. I'll go check on Owen," Ryder said, vacating the room.

"So, a little about me. I'm a dual mage, I control sound and emotions. I don't know how much you know about charge magic, but here's how it works. This track I'm about to play is a relaxation charge. Here - put these in," Emma instructed, handing her headphones to Caitlin, but not turning the music on. "It won't hurt the baby. In fact, it will probably help both of you feel calmer, okay?"

Music floated through the headphones, Caitlin suppressed a reluctant sigh, glancing at Emma. "I'm not sure this is doing anything."

"Give it a second," Emma said. "I haven't started the charge. I can't make how you feel go away, but I can help you not feel everything quite so strongly."

"Okay," Caitlin closed her eyes, suddenly realizing she felt completely at peace. She listened to the soft music, sinking into an almost trance where all she could feel was calm. When a hand touched her leg, she jumped.

"Sorry, Cupcake," Owen said when she started, taking out an earbud.

"Hi," she looked down and frowned.

Had he changed his shirt? What had happened to his knuckles? Before she could ask, he was checking in on her.

"Feeling a little better?" he asked, concern etching deep lines in his forehead.

"Yeah," she admitted, sitting up when she realized she'd slumped in the chair.

"Good. Leave that in," Owen said when she went to remove the other headphones. "Emma said to keep it in. She took your phone to load some charged music on it."

"I don't want to be any trouble," she objected, trying to get out of her chair.

"We're a pack. We take care of someone when they need it. Stop fighting it, please," he said tightly, his jaw ticking as he chewed the inside of his cheek.

"Okay."

She had the fleeting thought that at least if he hated her, they were in public so he wouldn't hit her, but she pushed the thought away. Owen would never do that to her.

I am safe. Owen is safe. I am safe.

"So, you're how far along?" He asked.

"Four months," she said, resisting the urge to cover up her belly. She'd known that she was gaining a little weight, but she thought that was because of all the baking she'd been doing.

"Oh wow."

"Yeah," she said uneasily, not sure what to say, and not wanting to press him in case he gave her an answer she didn't want to hear.

"So, we're having a baby in five months, give or take," he said, pursing his lips, nodding. "Miss Linda said to let her know our due date and she'd make sure we had everything we needed."

"I need to say something, and I need you to not be mad," she said.

Owen's eyes narrowed dangerously.

"If you're going to say something like-" he began.

"You don't have to do this," Caitlin cut him off.

"Like that," he finished, scowling fiercely.

Kneeling in front of her, he took her hands in his, holding them captive even when she tried to pull them back.

"Stop pulling away from me," he snapped, then got a hold of his temper. "I love and adore you. Unless you plan on leaving me because you don't want to be with me, then please don't push my buttons by suggesting that again. Ever."

"I just-"

"Caitlin," he growled, gripping her hands in warning, "Don't."

"I need to say it."

"Fine." He set his mouth in a tight line.

"I don't want you to feel obligated to raise a baby who isn't yours just because you made a mistake and imprinted on a girl who was knocked up," Owen's upper lip was curling into a snarl, but she continued anyway. "I know you're probably mad because now you're trapped in this, and I just wanted you to know, you have a get-out-of-jail-free card if you want it."

"Are you finished?"

"Yes," she replied.

"You're sure?"

"I said yes!"

"Good." He stood, leaning over her, placing his hands on the arms of the chair so he towered over her. She tipped her head back, shrinking into the chair at his black look.

"I don't really get mad, mostly I see it as a waste of energy. But if you ever call yourself a mistake, or call our relationship a jail again, I will lose my mind. I am barely holding myself together as it is. And since I doubt you would appreciate being locked in my bedroom until you push out *my* baby because the only thing you're allowed to do is let me love you until you realize that I'm thrilled to be here... please refrain from that in the future."

He held his body still, staring at her with an intensity she could feel burning into her soul.

"Yes sir," Caitlin replied, offering him a nervous, placating smile.

"Good girl. I need something from you," he said.

"What?"

"I need his name," Owen said.

"What?"

"Your ex. I need his real first and last name. There's no one named Axel in Burlington," he said shortly.

She wasn't sure if it alarmed her more that he'd looked, or that his eyes had turned from their normal blue to dark brown. Was this him, or Finley talking? She wasn't sure it mattered.

"Why?" She asked. Owen raised an eyebrow. "No. He's a - bad man. Scary."

"Sweetheart. I might be the hero who's a good man every other day, but today I'm prepared to drag the very gods to hell with me if that's what I need to do to make sure you and my baby are safe. There is nothing I would not do to protect you, and I don't want anything out there existing that might have a claim on either one of you."

"I'm not telling you. I couldn't stand it if something happened to you because of me," Caitlin said, her throat tightening.

"Cupcake," he pleaded, kneeling in front of her again.

"You're not going to out-stubborn me on this one," she said, shivering. The idea of Owen being in the same space as Axel made her gorge rise like she was going to be sick.

"I can find out regardless," he informed her, resting his elbows on his thighs as he surveyed her as if he was trying to gauge how far he could push her on this.

"But you won't, because you want to be around to raise our baby together," She said, taking his hand and placing it on her lower abdomen.

"Fine, but if he ever shows up…" Owen said darkly.

"You can sell your soul to the gods of darkness and kill him if he ever shows up and I won't say a damn thing."

"Alright, I can live with that. Now, let's go home, baby momma."

CHAPTER TWENTY-SEVEN

OWEN

Two weeks had passed since they'd found out about the baby. At first, it was quite a shock. He'd been so worked up that he'd spent a full night on the full moon running on the mountain with the unmated males, picking fights with other rough-and-tumble wolves just to blow off steam. After that, he and Caitlin had been showered with love and affection from so many people from the pack that it had been difficult to see their baby as anything other than a blessing and a cause for joy and excitement.

Today he'd been kicked out of the house so the women of the pack could host an unofficial shower for Caitlin. When he'd asked if it was a little early for a shower, Miss Linda had informed him that it was his job not to come back until it was time to clean up and that they were waiting for him to report at the EMS base.

"Hey man, what's up?"

"This woman, man," Calen grumbled, bloodshot eyes cutting to Owen meaningfully.

"What's going on with Cheyenne now?"

"Same shit, different day."

"Well, if it's any consolation, you look fucking terrible and you smell like a distillery."

"I wonder what it's like to be a human without a wolf in your head talking all the damn time," Calen mused.

I bet it's awful. We're great! Finley chimed.

"Boring." Owen offered Calen coffee, his friend nodded gratefully.

"Simple," Calen corrected, "I just don't know what I'm supposed to do. I can't just - not have her. I don't know. I mean, maybe I could. But something about her just won't let me see her with someone else until she's given me a chance," Calen said, adding sugar to his coffee.

"She did give you a chance. You fucked it up. That full moon was your audition and you blew it, man," Matt said smugly as he pulled a drink out of the fridge.

"You shut the fuck up, beta," Calen growled.

"Oh please, Merrick, as if you have any room to talk to me about how I talk about a woman. You can't get a girl unless you're scooping someone else's date."

"That's funny coming from the guy whose full moon 'date' was my sloppy seconds," Calen shrugged.

"Man, you left her hanging. It wasn't my fault she would rather run out of your house without her socks than deal with you for one more round. I did make sure to leave the window open in case you wanted to jerk one off while you listened. She's like a fucking porn star when she *really* comes, I wanted to make sure you knew what it sounded like since you hadn't heard it before," Matt said with a smirk and a wink.

Calen launched himself across the room, the two went tumbling as fists flew. Patrick Lawson was standing in the doorway, sighing heavily.

"It's too early for this shit," he muttered. "Chief!"

A few moments later, the chief was peering over Lawson's shoulder.

"Stupid pups," he grumbled, "It's too early for this shit- move over."

Stepping around Lawson, Jason inhaled deeply and bellowed.

"Oi! Have you lost your fucking minds?" The chief bellowed.

"No sir!" Matt said as he hauled back and got in one more punch.

"Alright, you, in my office." He pointed to Matt. "Owen, look at Merrick's eye."

Owen chuckled as he went to grab an ice pack. "I'll get Ryder's student to do the evaluation. He could use the practice."

"Thanks,"

"Owen! Did you see what happened?" Lawson stopped him on his way out to find the student.

"Uh, no sir. Didn't see a thing. I went temporarily blind in both eyes. Must be the imprinting," Owen said, wanting precisely nothing to do with the drama. His phone dinged and he pulled it out of his pocket.

> CAITLIN
>
> Is it okay to come in? There sounded like there was something going on.
>
> OWEN
>
> Let me come to you.

Owen went out front, greeting Caitlin with a kiss on the cheek.

"Hey, cupcake. Thought you'd be a while longer."

"The ladies said I looked tired and needed a nap, so left me to it and I escaped to come see you. What was going on inside?"

"Meh, a fisticuffs with some of the guys, nothing big," he said, reaching for her, but instead of leaning into him, she stepped back a half-step. "What's wrong?"

"You weren't... fighting, were you?" she asked, her voice tight with anxiety.

"The other day when you found out about the baby, I just- I didn't want to ask, but," she rubbed her lips together.

"The other day Ryder and I traded punches to blow off steam. We weren't fighting, in the sense you're thinking," he promised.

"And today?" She looked at the ice pack he still had in his hand.

"No, babe. I was just watching. This is for Merrick, who took a nice one to the face," she sighed in relief, wrapping her arms around him.

When she didn't let go after several seconds he kissed the top of her head and made a quiet noise of inquiry.

"Some guys fight a lot over their mates," she explained, raising her head and searching his eyes for reassurance that he wasn't that type of man.

I'd fight somebody for her if she won't let us take care of her ex. Let's take that Aiden kid, he's annoying, Finley said.

Finley, we like Aiden, Owen reminded him.

You know I live in your head, right? Finley asked. *We don't like him, we tolerate him.*

We are not fighting Aiden. Owen insisted.

"I'm not one of them," Owen assured Caitlin.

"My ex used to do that. Any time somebody was talking to me or looked at me too long. I hated it," She shuddered.

Tell me again why we haven't hunted him down and killed him, Finley said.

Because she asked us not to, Owen said. He could feel Finley considering that, then rejecting it.

She's hormonal, she doesn't know what she wants, Finley reasoned.

I am not telling her that, Owen said. *Firstly, because being hormonal doesn't make her incompetent, secondly, because no male in his right mind would ever suggest anything like that to a female.*

"I'm not that type. I'm kind of the opposite. As long as everything's on the up and up, I like when my girl gets looked at in a way that makes her feel good." He put his lips close to her ear. "I like to see another man's eyes on your ass in a skirt like the one you've got on, knowing he's picturing doing the same thing I'm going to be doing to you when I get home."

"Oh?" she said, blushing a little.

"Mm-hmm. Knowing you're looking like a fruit ripe for the picking, I'm thinking you're probably wearing that butterfly thong you like when you're feeling frisky and all it would take is one little movement of my hand and I could be inside of you, using my fingers to see how wet you are for me."

"Owen," she blushed.

"Mm-hmm. I could bring you in through the bay door, put you in the back of my truck and sit you on the gurney, spread your legs, and eat you out until you-"

"Owen, oh my god," she said, covering his mouth.

He kissed her fingers with a chuckle.

"Just saying, I don't mind. I've got no need to fight for some bullshit claim. You're mine, it's that simple. You could have two other men balls deep inside of you and I wouldn't care if it was what you wanted."

Oh, that's hot. I like that idea, watching her with somebody else, Finley agreed.

"Oh, right," Caitlin laughed, rolling her eyes.

"Seriously," he said, looking at her with a frown, trying not to let it irritate him that she didn't believe him.

"Seriously? You wouldn't be mad if I wanted to fuck, like, a coworker?"

Ooh, she wants to do it! Finley's ears perked up. If they had been in wolf form, their whole body would have been wagging in delight.

"Who?" He asked, a wicked grin spread over his features. "Who do you want to fuck, cupcake?"

"It was just a general question," she objected, casting her eyes downward, trying to hide the truth in them.

"When you lie, you look at your cleavage. Did you know that?"

"I do not!" She insisted.

She's adorable. Also, don't tell her how to tell when she's lying, Finley said.

It's not like she's good enough at it to matter, Owen pointed out.

Well, that's true I guess, Finley agreed.

"You do. It's adorable. Also, I want to know," he said with a grin.

"I'm not telling you!" she insisted.

"So, there *is* someone you want to sleep with?" He teased.

"Owen Kessler! You're ridiculous."

"Tell me I'm wrong," he challenged with a smirk.

She glanced down at her chest, then said, "You're wrong."

Realizing what she'd done she promptly turned crimson and tried to turn away with an exasperated huff.

"Oh not so fast there, ma'am," he said, grabbing her waist and turning her to face him.

She gave him the side eye and glared, half irritated, half amused.

"Tell me," he bargained, "And I'll make it happen for you. Unless it's Patrick Lawson, he doesn't swing that way. But I bet Brian would be on board, especially if you cook. He has a thing for pregnant women."

"If you're having people over for dinner I want an invite," Tyler strolled up, leaning against the wall casually.

"No, we were just talking about-"

"*Nothing!*" Caitlin said with emphasis, her blush deepening by several shades.

"I can go," Tyler said, looking from Owen to Caitlin with amusement, "If you are having a moment."

"No, it's fine. Do you think everybody would like to do another dinner?" Caitlin asked, going for coolness.

Owen looked from Caitlin to his partner, his grin widening slightly as she pointedly did not meet his eye.

"If you're cooking, you'd have to beat people off with a stick," Tyler said enthusiastically, taking a long draw on his vape pen, and blowing the vapor away from Caitlin.

"What about this weekend? We could do it Saturday after the next black shift," Owen suggested slyly.

"I'm always down for food. I'll bring beer," Tyler volunteered.

"Hey, I actually need some help with something. Wanna come over early and help me put in a fence if the weather holds?" Owen asked.

"Sure." Tyler shrugged, "I'll be there."

Tones dropped over the radio, and Tyler and Owen both listened for a moment. Tyler gave a nod to the couple before walking back into the ambulance bay to head out on a call.

"There, will that satisfy you, ma'am?" Owen teased.

Instead of looking pleased, her face was pinched with worry.

"Oh baby, you don't have to do anything you don't want to do. I was teasing, okay? We can just have dinner if you want to host and feed people."

"I don't want you to be mad about it," she confessed, her breaths increasing as she started to panic.

"I really need you to hear me on this: I have no problem sharing you. You're mine and I'm yours. Besides, you'll like Tyler in the bedroom. He's very sadistic, more than me even. He would leave you so sore you'd feel it for days," Owen winked.

"Yeah? And you're *sure* that you don't mind?"

"Why is this so stressful for you?" He asked, pulling her close.

"I can't imagine a mate being just… fine with it."

"Sex brings you pleasure," Owen shrugged, "If you want it and I can give it to you, it doesn't mean you love me any less. I don't need to be your only lover any more than I need to be your only friend."

She closed the distance between them, snuggling into his chest. Hands fisted his shirt behind his back as her arms squeezed his torso.

Is she…happy? Finley asked.

I'm not sure, Owen thought back, hoping to hell she was.

"Hey, you okay down there?"

Caitlin nodded, then sniffed.

Oh shit. You made her cry! Finley panicked, *Why is she crying? Is this a hormone thing, do you think? Or is this because she's janky?*

I don't fucking know, Fin. Owen grumbled as he held her against him.

"Cupcake?" Owen prompted.

"I don't know why you're so nice to me. It scares me."

Owen, unsure how to respond, just rubbed her back.

She's scared because you're nice? She's definitely broken. Maybe she should go talk to the talky lady some more, Finley suggested.

She's not used to being treated well, she doesn't know how to handle it, Owen thought back, rubbing her back while she cried. *Also, yes, I think it's a hormone thing.*

Calen walked outside, interrupting their moment. Owen tossed him the ice pack, which Calen caught neatly.

"Owen, Lawson needs you in the office," Calen said, giving a questioning thumbs up, nodding toward Caitlin in silent inquiry.

"Be there in a sec," Owen confirmed, cupping his hand around an imaginary water bottle and tipping it.

Calen nodded and disappeared back into the base.

"I'm sorry," Caitlin said, pulling away, "I'm keeping you from working."

"Nah, I'm on base bitch duty today, it's no problem."

"Miss Caitlin," Jason said, strolling out of the base holding a bottle of water.

"Hi, chief," she said, a little embarrassed.

"I'm glad you're here, I was going to order some snacks for the next training day and your name came up. Are you still taking orders?"

"Oh, I am, yeah," she said, straightening and brightening at the prospect of another order to fill.

"Well, how about we walk down to Lillington's and discuss it over a little lunch? I'm famished, and we can't have the baby mommas getting peckish."

"Good idea," Owen agreed, giving her a side hug before planting a chaste kiss on her temple, "Enjoy."

"Thank you," she said with a rueful smile.

"Now, how are you feeling, momma?" Jason asked as they walked away.

I really, really love her, Finley said wistfully. *Do you think she'll ever feel safe with us?*

I think one day she might. When she realizes that she can trust us to love and protect her, not hurt her. Owen thought back as he made his way to the office.

CHAPTER TWENTY-EIGHT

OWEN

"We are facing a problem," The chief said without preamble, "In the last three hundred years this town has been standing, we haven't had a single documented case of imprinting. Our first imprinting happened in October of last year. It's now October and in the last several months, that number has grown significantly. All of the imprinters have been male, all of whom have a close connection to the Fire, EMS, or deputy's departments in this county."

"The males who have imprinted are as follows: Ryder Marlow, Owen Kessler, Patrick Lawson, John McIntyre, Arion Easton, and a number of others on our volunteer roster."

CAITLIN

Hey, I got something, can I drop by?

OWEN

We're in a meeting, but we should be done in half an hour, maybe one hour tops.

CAITLIN

That's fine, We're coming home from Red River anyway!

OWEN

We?

CAITLIN

That's the surprise. Love you, see you soon!

OWEN

I can't wait.

Drive safe, Cupcake.

CAITLIN

Will do, sir!

The meeting dragged on, going over new protocols for accountability for everyone, particularly imprinted individuals. Owen bounced his leg while he waited for everything to conclude, wondering what Caitlin's surprise was.

"So, to recap, anyone who has imprinted is on base duty until cleared by me personally," the chief was saying, "Also if you see anyone acting strange, report it to a supervisor. I don't need to tell you how dangerous it can be to have an unfocused medic on a truck."

The chief looked around, making eye contact with every team member before he continued. The group was uncharacteristically quiet, only the shuffling of bodies and the occasional cough made any sound. No one made jokes under their breath to their neighbors or popped off with a witty rejoinder.

"I know that pranks and fun are a part of the culture here," the chief began. "But let me make one thing crystal clear: if *anyone*, shifter or otherwise, wants to fuck around with one of our imprinted males by making them jealous, you will no longer have a job in this county and I will make it my personal mission to make your life hell. You will treat the mates of our imprinted brothers with the utmost respect and professionalism. All first responders in this county will set the tone for the rest of the pack, and the rest of the community, on how we treat the ladies who are finding themselves in a... challenging situation."

197

"Is anyone unclear on the new rules and protocols?" Lawson asked from beside the chief.

Choruses of no's filtered through the room.

"Alright. I'll be here all day if anyone has any questions or issues, and obviously you can go to medic one for any issues on shift. Thank you for your time, I know some of you are here on your day off and I appreciate you making the time and effort. You're dismissed."

Owen walked over to the table where Caitlin's batch of scones, donuts and muffins were all but decimated. Some medics filtered out into the bay while Owen snagged the last muffin.

CAITLIN

We're out in the bay!

OWEN

Coming

One of the other medics snickered as they let Owen through the bay door before him, but Owen ignored him. Coming around the truck in bay two, Owen stopped.

"He's a protection dog?" The chief was asking, fighting to keep his composure as he bit back amusement.

She got a - what? Finley asked. *A dog? To keep her safe? Seriously?!*

"Yeah! The guy said his whole line was bred for this kind of thing, but he gave me a deal on him. His name's Toten, it means 'to kill' in German," his mate was gushing, eyes bright with excitement.

A fearful Rottweiler was cowering in front of the chief, pulling the leash in his mate's hands taut, its eyes wide with terror.

She thinks that thing will keep her safe? Finley scoffed, *I know we're not supposed to say this because she's our mate, but she's fucking crazy.*

Owen watched as the chief got down on his haunches and held his knuckles out to a Rottie who was cowering on the floor beside Caitlin, ears slicked back. The chief avoided eye contact and held the pose, looking at Caitlin.

"How good of a deal did you get, honey?" Jason asked nonchalantly.

We're sending it back, Finley said.

Agreed, Owen said.

We should phase and show her how I can keep her safe. That thing is two seconds from running away and the chief isn't even all Alpha-y at him.

"A really good one," she assured, smiling with pride.

"Surprise!" Caitlin exclaimed when she saw Owen hovering.

Either the noise or the sudden movement of his leash made the dog start, leaping into the chief, knocking him backward. Promptly, he let out a stream of urine, yelping when the chief flailed.

"Oh no!" Caitlin exclaimed.

"Motherf-" the chief said, Owen extended a hand down to help him up.

Jason, completely unamused, gave Owen a silent look from him to the dog and back.

"Are you *so* surprised?" Caitlin asked, grinning from ear to ear.

"Shocked," Owen agreed, tearing his eyes away from the chief's.

"I'm going to take him outside, I'm really sorry-" Caitlin said, but the chief held up a hand and waved it off.

The moment she was out of earshot, the chief looked at Owen.

"What does she think she needs protection from that *that* thing's going to help with?"

"She thought she saw something at the house right after she moved in, and she'd worried because I work at night sometimes. Plus, she gets scared, a PTSD thing. I've got to go talk to her, there's no fucking way she's keeping that thing."

"Good luck with that," the chief said. "One time Linda got a bird, I hated it."

"What happened?"

"I tried to talk her out of it," the chief admitted, running his hand down his face, shaking his head at the memory. "The horrible thing lives in the bedroom and has an enclosure that's about the size of our first apartment. That's what happened."

Owen rounded the corner and found Caitlin kneeling in the grass, the dog wrapped up in her arms.

"It's okay. I know things are scary sometimes. Lots of things are scary for me right now too, we can learn to not be scared together, okay?"

The dog laid its head on her shoulder while his mate held it.

"Wait till you meet Finley, you'll love him. And Owen's nice too. He takes good care of me, and he'll take care of you too."

Um, Fin? Owen thought, resigned.

We're stuck with it, aren't we? Finley asked sulkily.

Looks like it, Owen thought back.

Fine, but it's not sleeping in the bed, Finley thought.

I'll at least try to get her to see reason, but she looks pretty attached, Owen thought.

Caitlin rose and patted the dog affectionately, then turned to Owen, a nervous smile on her face.

"It's okay? He's okay?"

"You know, we could probably find you one who's a little more suited to protection work," Owen said, not stepping closer to Caitlin when her dog pulled on the leash in fear when it saw him.

"You don't like him?" She asked, her face crumpling.

She fell in love faster with that thing than she did with us, Finley accused, his mental voice taking on a distinct edge of jealousy.

"I think another dog might be a better fit," Owen tried to say gently, but when her eyes widened and she gripped the dog's collar tighter, Finley's voice interrupted.

Oh, stop. She can keep the little flea-ridden mongrel. Maybe we can, I don't know, train it, or something, Finley suggested.

Are you sure? Owen confirmed.

Well, if you want to be the one who tells her she can't have it, then by all means, go ahead. You're the idiot that told her she could have 'anything she wanted' to make her feel safe.

I had no idea she would want a dog, let alone this one. I was thinking more along the lines of a security system, Owen said as Caitlin stood there.

"I was thinking it would be a nice friend for Finley!" She said, looking unsure.

"Yeah," Owen agreed.

"Maybe he could go on the pack runs with you when he's a little less afraid?" she asked, hopeful.

No. Finley said flatly. *We are absolutely, positively not letting that thing -*

"That's usually just for wolves," Owen said diplomatically. "Plus, you'll want him with you when I'm out on a run right?"

"Oh yeah, good point," she agreed. "I'm gonna load him up, one sec."

The dog loaded up into her car, she rolled the window down and came back to kiss Owen.

"You're sure you don't mind?" she asked.

You should just kiss her. Finley suggested, and Owen agreed, so he lowered his lips to Caitlin's soft ones and gently pressed them together, his tongue slipping between hers.

She pulled away from his kiss, looking back at the car.

"Alright, Toten and I are heading home. The breeder says he loves to snuggle, so we're gonna take a nap in the bed," she said, wiggling her eyebrows in excitement at the prospect.

Tell her that thing can't sleep in the bed, Owen! Finley practically screamed.

Look at how happy she is. Owen thought as he walked her to her car. *I mean, I will if you really want me to.*

No pets in the bed! Finley insisted.

"Hey cupcake," Owen said as Caitlin buckled herself in.

"Mm-hmm?" she said, giving Toten an affectionate rub.

"Finley says that," he hesitated, not wanting her to be sad.

Oh forget it. Finley relented when a little worry line appeared between her eyes.

"He says he's excited to have the dog here to play with," Owen finished.

I hate you so much right now. Finley thought savagely.

Owen smiled as she backed out of the parking lot and went back in the bay.

"So, how's your new buddy? You gonna let him keep you safe too, Kessler?" Someone taunted.

Fin, I don't think you hate this anymore than I'm going to, Owen sighed.

THE ONLY THING that made the ribbing from his coworkers endurable was the selfie that Caitlin sent from their bedroom, curled up with her dog looking so pleased with herself she could barely stand it.

CAITLIN

I might be too excited to nap. *eyes emoji*

OWEN

Take a nap, or you'll be asleep at the dining room table again.

CAITLIN

That happened ONE TIME!

OWEN

Yeah, that one time you were tired and didn't take a nap.

The dog will still be there when you get up.

CAITLIN

Thank you for letting me get him.

I can't wait to see him and Fin playing in the yard together! They're going to have so much fun.

OWEN

Nap!

CAITLIN

Fine!

I'm putting my phone down and napping.

She hadn't texted in several hours, so he assumed she was getting the rest she needed. Now he needed to talk to Tyler, who he found working on inventory in their rig.

"Hey, Tyler," Owen said, rubbing the back of his neck. He and Tyler had shared women in the past, but this felt different and Owen felt uncharacteristically awkward.

"Hey man. Something on your mind?" Tyler asked.

"Yeah, wanted to talk to you - you still good to come over after next shift?"

"Yeah, I was. Why, you need something?"

"Sort of. A favor, of sorts?"

"Okay," Owen climbed up in the rig, taking a seat in the captain's chair. "So, you know how Caitlin's into degradation and all that?"

There were very few, if any, secrets when you spend a quarter of your life running calls with someone. Tyler knew more about Caitlin and Owen than anyone did.

"Yup," Tyler said, checking the expiration dates of the supplies of their rig.

"Well. She has this thing, and I trust you, she wants..." Owen sighed in frustration.

"Spit it out," Tyler said.

"She wants to be - shared. And since you're experienced with her kind of kinks, and we've done it before," Owen trailed off.

"Yeah, sure. You just tell me when you wanna do it," Tyler said, marking something down on the checklist.

"Yeah? Thanks."

Tyler looked up, grinning at Owen.

"I mean, look, it's not a hardship." Tyler pointed out. "There aren't a lot of women around here who like it as intense as I do, at least not that I've found. It will be fun to play with someone who plays on the same level. You two want to do like a threesome thing?"

"Um," Owen didn't know what she wanted, and while he didn't dislike the idea, he mostly just wanted her to be happy.

"If this is your first time sharing her, plan to stick around," Tyler suggested, "You can at least watch, and be there to make sure she's all good. She may want you too for aftercare."

"Alright, thanks, man."

"Alright. Cool. She's gonna feed me dinner, right?" He asked hopefully.

"As if I could stop her. I'm gonna look like the one having a baby if I'm not careful."

Tyler stared at the airway bag open in front of him thoughtfully.

"I have an idea," he said, looking up at Owen with a grin.

CHAPTER TWENTY-NINE

CAITLIN

Caitlin was making tea when a text from Owen made her phone ping.

OWEN

Hey cupcake.

Don't forget Tyler is coming over to put those posts in for us for the fence. I told him you'd be around to show him where things are.

CAITLIN

Yup, I've got it.

OWEN

Thanks, love you.

"Hey," she called from the porch as he walked up.

"Morning," Tyler greeted.

"Owen said you were working on the posts? I can show you where things are, let me get my boots. You want some coffee before you get started?" She blushed when she noticed that his gaze was lingering over her erect nipples and the way her blue t-shirt dress hugged her curves.

"Sure, thanks."

He strode ahead to open the door for her, "Ladies first."

He enjoyed some coffee and a scone before she showed him where things were and he got to work. She'd cleaned the kitchen, made a batch of baked goods for the knitting club when she stopped for a tea break, checking her phone to see a message from Owen.

> **OWEN**
> Tyler there?

> **CAITLIN**
> Yup! Gave him some coffee and he's out there.

> **OWEN**
> Alright, good. You doing good?

> **CAITLIN**
> Yeah.

> **OWEN**
> You sure?

> **CAITLIN**
> I'm really, really horny.

> **OWEN**
> Me too. Last night was fun. :)

THEY'D BEEN in bed in the middle of a hard fucking. Owen had suggested that he would just let Tyler have her for the night as payment for helping out around the place. She'd come so hard he thought she would pass out. Desire rushed through her at the memory while she watched Tyler through the side window.

> **CAITLIN**
> Yeah it was.

> **OWEN**
> You thinking about it right now?

CAITLIN

Maybe.

OWEN

Good. I bet he'd fuck the shit out of you in that dress you were in when I left.

CAITLIN

Can I put on panties now?

BEFORE HE'D LEFT for training he'd ordered her to wear no panties all day, pocketing the ones she'd put on that morning before kissing her goodbye.

OWEN

Nope. But there is something you can do.

CAITLIN

Okay?

OWEN

Go to the front room.

She walked around to the front room, spying Tyler out the window, working in the hot sun.

CAITLIN

I'm there.

OWEN

Unbutton your dress.

CAITLIN LOOKED AT HER PHONE, pressing her lips together as she considered, then put her phone down and unbuttoned the soft fabric so she was bared to the waist. She sent him a picture to prove she'd done it and waited for his response.

OWEN

I want you to sit at the window seat and play with yourself.

Think about what you'd do for Tyler to thank him for doing all this work for us.

Don't stop until you cum. Get a toy if you like, but don't stop, not even if he sees you.

She went upstairs and grabbed her favorite dildo with a suction cup base, fixing it to the window seat. At first, she just teased her nipples with her left hand while her right hand circled her clit expertly until she was so aroused her core ached with a need to be filled. This one was a present from Owen, one modeled after his dick, but with a knot added. She shivered as she felt it stretch her, forcing herself to relax to let her work more of the length inside. Once she was satisfied with the depth, she began to bounce, her breasts jiggling as she rode the cock, imagining it was Owen inside of her.

As she looked out the window though, it was Tyler's muscles that glimmered with sweat, she was picturing his hands around her throat as the tingle began to build in the base of her spine. She whimpered as her body made obscene noises as she bounced on the dildo again and again, her slick fluids coating it and making a mess on the smooth wood of the window seat beneath her.

She went harder, moving her hand from her clit to steady herself on the window frame, watching Tyler's muscles strain. As she let out a loud moan she was grateful he was too far from the house to hear her. As if he heard that thought he paused to drink the water she'd brought out for him, glancing at the house. She swore he looked right at her, his jaw lowering slightly as he squinted, then adjusting himself, he continued to watch the window where she was. Surely he couldn't see - the sun was too bright and the interior of the house was too dark to see in, wasn't it? But the idea of him watching was enough.

Her orgasm tore through her as a sharp cry escaped her lips, as she squirted all over her toy, coating her thighs and leaving a mess on the hem of her dress. She almost stopped at one, but began to ride again, this time hiking up her dress and setting up the camera so she could take a video to send to Owen.

It didn't take much to get her going again. Even though he'd said it was fine for her to want to sleep with Tyler, she would have been too embarrassed to let Owen see she was getting off while watching another man.

As she worked herself on the dildo, her thighs aching as she went faster and faster, she kept both hands on her nipples this time, spreading her juices over her nipples and teasing them to points, telling Owen she wished it was him here.

When she felt herself reaching the crest she moved one hand and slapped her clit hard three times in succession. This time, she wasn't certain Tyler was too far away to hear her carrying sharp scream of pleasure, but she screwed her eyes shut, milking every drop of pleasure from her body before stopping.

She sent him the video and took a picture of the mess she'd made before going to get the cleaning supplies for the window seat and taking her toy upstairs to be cleaned as well.

OWEN

Damn, cupcake. I can't wait to get home and eat that pussy tonight.

CAITLIN

I think he saw me.

OWEN

Really?

CAITLIN

Yeah.

OWEN

I bet he enjoyed that. Did you?

CAITLIN

Yes.

OWEN

Good girl. I've got to run, but I'll be home soon. Love you.

CAITLIN

Love you too!

OWEN CAME HOME and kissed her gently.

"Hi there, baby momma," he said with a wink.

"You want some lunch?" she asked, "I was just about to make something."

"Yes please, let me go shower off the shift first. I had to go into a patient's house," he shook his head in disgust, "it was bad, I need a shower, and these clothes are going straight to the laundry."

"I thought you were just doing training?"

"I lost a bet," Owen said, rolling his eyes.

"Okay, I'm gonna go tell Tyler lunch will be served shortly."

"Oh, are you?" Owen asked, raising his eyebrows, "You gonna offer yourself up for a pre-lunch snack?"

"Owen!" Caitlin blushed.

"What? I told you, I don't care. Tyler's a good guy, hell, I'd fuck him if I was into guys," Owen shrugged. "Besides, you're the one who enjoyed putting on a show, hoping he'd see."

He grinned at her and she pursed her lips in response, trying to hide her smile.

"Mm-hmm," Owen's eyes traveled from her hair down to her bare feet, "I bet if I put my hand in your panties right now you'd still be soaked."

"I'm going outside," Caitlin informed him, rolling her eyes.

"If Tyler gets to have you for lunch, I want to watch!" he called as he made his way upstairs while she headed for the back door and out to the side yard.

Tyler had taken off his shirt, his body glistened with sweat as the sun beat down on the unseasonably warm October afternoon. The mason jar of water Caitlin had brought outside nearly slipped from her hands. Cradling the jar, dripping condensation into her palm, she walked forward. He grinned and took a jar from her, drained half, then dumped the remainder over his head with a sigh.

Oh, sweet gods have mercy on me. Caitlin thought as water droplets cascaded down his chest.

"Hey I'm about done here," Tyler said as Caitlin struggled to maintain her composure, "just another two posts."

"Okay. I'm about to make lunch if you want to take a break and cool off?"

"Let me finish up here, then I'll take you up on that."

"Sure," she hung around, he looked at her expectantly.

"I can take that back in," she said, indicating the empty jar.

"Oh, yeah, right." He handed her the jar.

She swore she could feel his eyes on her, but didn't look back to check as she walked into the house to finish the lunch prep. She jumped, slicing her finger cutting vegetables for a salad when the back door opened.

"Shit!" she cursed, holding the finger.

"You okay?"

"Yeah, I just cut myself, it's no big deal."

"Let me see," he said.

Caitlin grabbed a clean towel from the drawer and held it to her finger for a moment while Tyler kicked off his boots and came to stand next to her at the sink. Washing his hands and forearms, he took her hand in his and opened the towel.

"Yeah, that smarts. Hang on, I'll get you doctored up."

"I'm fine, it's just a cut-" she said as it oozed dramatically.

"I'm not arguing that you're fine," Tyler said with a wink. "But you need something on that finger."

"What's up?" Owen asked, coming through with his uniform held away from his body on his way to the laundry room.

"She sliced her finger, nothing too bad. She said she was fine, I said I wasn't arguing that fact but that she needed to put something on it."

"Yeah, let him take care of you baby, I'll be back in a second, I'm gonna start this laundry."

"Don't forget to check your pockets!" She called over her shoulder.

When they turned back to face Tyler he was looking at her with an almost wistful expression.

"What?" she asked.

He blinked and went back to cleaning then putting a small bandage on her hand.

"You two are good together. I'm glad Fin picked you."

CHAPTER THIRTY

OWEN

*C*aitlin was so aroused that he'd smelled it the moment he'd walked through the front door. Owen couldn't decide if being a shifter made it better, or worse when your mate was pregnant and couldn't get enough sex. Maybe if you couldn't smell it, human males weren't tortured by it all the time.

This is definitely better, Finley said as he watched the hungry way Tyler kept stealing glances at their mate, making it clear Tyler had definitely noticed too.

After they devoured the roast chicken with broccoli, carrots, and mashed potatoes she made and fell upon the cake she'd baked earlier in the day like starving men, Owen and Tyler had insisted she sit while they cleaned up. After the meal she'd made, both men were looking to take care of her before they spent hopefully the rest of the night using her for more recreational purposes.

Caitlin voiced her frustration, but before Owen could respond to her, Tyler jumped in.

"Miss Caitlin," Tyler said, dropping his chin and lowering his tone slightly so that while his gaze was even and his tone was respectful, he was definitely not asking her permission to clean her kitchen, "You fed us; let us clean up."

"I want to be helpful," she said, looking around the mess in the kitchen, her brows drawing together in an anxious frown.

"I'm sure we can find ways for you to be helpful," Tyler said, his voice heavy with meaning. "Owen, your woman needs a job."

"Set her up on the counter," Owen suggested as he collected the lunch dishes, his pants noticeably tighter at the tone Tyler took with Caitlin and how he knew she would react to it.

Careful not to inhale too deeply and fill his nose with her scent before he could get his job done, Owen walked through the kitchen and placed the stack of dishes in the sink where the hot running water was creating a small mountain of bubbles.

"That's not a job!" Caitlin objected as Tyler put his hands around her waist and lifted her on the counter easily.

"You're - oh hell what does Scott call it?" Tyler asked Owen.

Owen thought for a moment, then snapped his fingers as he remembered, holding a soapy finger in the air in triumph.

"Counter decoration," Owen supplied.

"That's it, you're counter decoration," Tyler said with a wink at Caitlin.

When the rest of the dishes were gathered, Owen let Tyler take over washing while Owen dried and put everything away.

"You can just put them in the dishwasher," Caitlin objected, "You don't have to go to all that trouble, really."

Tyler and Owen exchanged a look, Owen put down the dish towel he was holding and walked over to where she sat on the counter and put one hand on either side of her bare legs that rested on the cold marble.

"Will you let us take care of you?" Owen asked with a hint of playful exasperation, then grinning mischievously he leaned in to whisper in her ear. "If you play your cards right, the two of us will make sure you're so well-fucked that by tomorrow you'll be too worn out to empty the dishwasher."

He knew that Tyler could hear every word, seeing them both squirming at the suggestion made him grin with sadistic satisfaction. A little flush crept up her cheeks and he kissed her there, his lips pressing against the hot skin with a knowing grin before turning back to make polite conversation with Tyler.

"Thanks for working on those posts. I didn't want to leave Lawson in a lurch, you know how flaky these new guys are," Owen said, chatting with Tyler as they finished cleaning up. When they were finished, Owen suggested they watch a movie.

"Sounds good. Do you care if I use your shower first?" Tyler asked. "I don't want to sit on your couch all sweaty and crusty."

"Sure, top of the stairs, door on the right side."

"I'll get you a towel." Caitlin volunteered, trying hard not to get too worked up at the image of Tyler naked in her shower.

When she came back, Owen was erect and ready for her. He drew her into his lap even as she objected, her cheeks scarlet.

"Owen! He said he was going to be really quick."

"So will I."

"What if he comes back down?"

"I don't care. He'd probably ask to join." While she processed that, he pulled up her dress and pulled her down so he slid inside of her.

"You would like that, wouldn't you? If he came in here and fucked you?" He whispered in her ear as she rode him. "You were probably wet all day thinking about when he watched you touch yourself in the window."

"You told me to!" She objected.

"And you liked it. You got him all worked up all day, wearing this 'fuck me' dress and no panties, making yourself cum watching him like a slut, inviting him over to stay. You're a fucking cock tease, Caitlin" he whispered in her ear.

"No. I didn't mean to-"

"You did. Admit it, you want him to fuck you tonight."

"No!"

"No?" He stopped her, gripping her hips painfully, "Are you lying to me? Do you know what happens to girls who lie?"

"Yes, I want him to fuck me," she mumbled, embarrassed.

"Good. After you fuck me, you're going to take care of him. It's the least you could do after teasing him all day."

"Oh god."

"You better hurry up, he's probably about done in the shower. Unless you want him to see you with your skirt up."

She came, burying her head in his shoulder as she desperately tried to muffle her sounds of pleasure.

"Don't stop." He ordered, "Fuck, don't stop."

There was a noise in the kitchen, and she paused. In response, he slapped her ass hard, then once more with equal force, making her yelp.

"You're going to make me come, whether he's here or not." She bounced hard, her breasts brushing against his chest. "I want to suck on your nipples, baby. Get them out for me."

She quickly undid the front of her dress, sliding her breasts up so they were perched on top of her bra.

"Damn, that's hot." He sucked on one nipple, gripping her hips to work her even harder. "Fuck, like that."

He grunted, filling her with his seed.

"God, cupcake, that was good," he groaned, holding her there for a moment.

"Now, be a good girl and come sit in the middle. Open your legs so he can smell you."

Tyler came in, smelling amazing. He offered Owen a beer and asked if he could get Caitlin anything.

"I think I'll get myself some water. Anyone want popcorn?" Caitlin offered.

"I'll come give you a hand," Tyler replied.

When they were alone in the kitchen, she was reaching up to get her wine when she caught him staring at her.

"You look nice in that dress," Tyler commented casually.

"Oh, thanks," she said, blushing.

"It was nice earlier, in the window." He pitched his voice low. "Did you want me to watch?"

"Yes."

"Why?"

"Um…"

"Do you want to fuck me?"

"Yes," she admitted. She couldn't get her head around Owen being okay with this, but not only did he not mind, he seemed excited about it, like he was the one who wanted it. The idea of another man using her while Owen knew what was happening made her core heat.

"Owen said you like it when he's nasty to you in bed. You like that?"

"Yeah, I do."

"Well, I like treating little whores like they deserve." He touched her thigh, lifting her dress ever so slightly. "Especially when they tease me all day and invite me to stay on the full moon, walking around smelling like you'd fuck anything that ordered you to bend over. Should we ask your man what he thinks?"

"H-he knows."

"Yeah?"

She nodded in reply.

"Hey, Owen?"

"Yeah?"

"Mind if I fuck your girl? She's been a little fucking cock tease all damn day."

"Have at it. She likes it rough," Owen's voice carried from the other room.

"Do you like it rough, Caitlin?" Tyler asked with a smirk.

"Yeah,"

"How rough?" He asked, his eyes sharp, watching every micro-expression, every minute movement of her body.

"Really rough," she whispered, a thrill of excitement and fear shooting through her.

"Tell me what else you like." He stepped between her legs, pressing his growing erection against her abdomen as he stared into her eyes and waited for her answer.

"I like being spanked."

"I bet you do. What else?"

"Slapping, sometimes."

"How do you feel about being choked?"

"I really like that," she said, blushing.

"Good. You know, I can smell you from here." He put his hand between her legs, pressing the palm of his hand across her clit, rubbing where her and Owen's juices now covered her labia and thighs.

"Couldn't wait to get plowed, huh?"

"Owen made me," She said, tilting her pelvis up to give him better access.

"He *made* you, huh? I bet he barely even asked you and you just let him fuck you," she gasped as he put several fingers inside of her easily, staring into her eyes."If I'm going to let you have my cock, you may address me as sir or master."

"Yes, sir."

"Can you remember that?" His fingers were sliding in and out of her noisily.

"Yes sir."

"If you forget, I'll punish you, hard, until I'm sure you won't forget. I don't like disobedient fuck toys."

"Yes sir."

"Good. Bend over the sink and spread your legs," she complied, then he ordered, "lift your dress, I want to inspect you closer. In fact, take it off." She took off the dress, then bent back over, shivering from excitement.

"You were mean to tease me." A drawer opened behind her, then slid shut but she didn't look behind her, keeping her eyes forward. "Apologize."

"I'm sorry I teased you, sir."

"I'm going to enjoy you tonight. I like it when a woman's mascara is running down her face from having her ass beat when I fuck her." He played with her pussy, sliding his hand over her clit, then wiping his hand in the evidence of her recent encounter with Owen. "Your body is going to be so full of my cum that by the end of the night, you won't be able to stand up without dripping."

He smacked her bottom once, then again. After warming up her cheeks so they glowed with a healthy pink, she heard Owen's voice from a few feet away.

"She's got a great ass, doesn't she?"

"Oh yeah, she's a real pleasure to look at," Tyler agreed.

"It's great to grab too," Owen commented.

"Oh yeah?" He took the full force of his hand and slapped her, grabbing a full hand and squeezing it as she yelped. "You're right. I hope it's okay if I bang her around a bit. I had to jerk off three times after watching her."

"She deserves it, don't you, cupcake?"

"Yes, sir," she gasped.

"You'll call him sir or master tonight too, whore. Do you understand?"

"Yes sir."

Gripping a wooden spoon from the drawer, he gave her a gentle swat, then set into giving her a proper spanking. Soon she was up on her toes, yelping and wiggling as he gave her swat after hard swat

"You got off watching me while you played with yourself, teasing me. Maybe later I'll tease you."

"Yes sir."

"For now, I'm going to show you what happens to whores who tease," Tyler said, his voice hard.

Briefly the swats stopped.

"Owen, are you sure she's pregnant?"

"Yeah, pretty sure," Owen said with a chuckle.

"Well, just in case, we should both fuck her tonight. Doctors get things wrong all the time," Tyler said.

"They do," Owen agreed with a laugh.

"You hear that, whore? Your mate doesn't even care if I breed you."

"Yes, sir."

"Stand up." When she was standing and facing him, he threw her over his shoulder and carried her to the formal dining room, sitting her down on the table, her bare bottom stinging against the cool wood. He shoved her back roughly and grabbed her breasts roughly, he stroked himself for a minute, considering her.

"You'll do for a quick fuck," he said with a dismissive shrug.

Sliding in between her legs, she whimpered as he bent her legs up, his jeans rasping against her hot tender skin. He wasn't as long as Owen, but he was wide. He watched her face carefully as he pressed inside of her, stretching her to the point of pain. He got all the way inside of her, pausing as he struggled not to release.

He slapped her breast hard, then the other as he moved with small motions inside of her, barely pulsating. She cried out, moaning in pain and pleasure, her hands reaching for her clit, but he slapped them away.

"You got yours already, slut. Owen, grab her hands."

Owen appeared beside the table, grabbing her hands, watching hungrily.

She moaned when Tyler resumed slapping her breasts again, he growled harshly, "Shut that bitch up."

They slid her over to the side of the table, Owen forcing his cock in her mouth.

"That's better. Nothing better than a bitch choking on your dick," Tyler commented, watching as Owen's cock invaded her mouth, making her gag.

"That's right."

Tyler came inside of her, digging his thumbs into her hips as she felt the warmth of his seed inside of her core.

"I want her on her knees for me," Owen said, so they pulled her off the table onto her knees. Tyler knelt behind her, positioning an arm around her neck, his elbow just below her chin so when he squeezed, her vision darkened.

"Good thing you like being choked, fuck toy. If you don't do a good job, I might not let up," Tyler threatened. Her pulse quickened as he gave a little squeeze that left her light headed.

She was pretty sure he was just playing, but what if he wasn't? The little tinge of fear made her that much more aroused and she whimpered.

"What do you say, slut?" Tyler asked in her ear, reaching around to give one of her nipples a sharp pinch.

"Yes sir!" She cried out, twisting to test his grip.

Tyler tightened his grip on her throat, watching her closely while Owen fucked her mouth with little restraint, loosening slightly each time she nearly passed out. Finally when her jaw began to ache Owen came, shoving himself deep in her throat as she gagged.

When both men had finished she stayed on the floor, glancing up at Owen and Tyler, looking between them.

"She looks well-used," Tyler commented, picking her up from the floor and carrying her to the couch.

"Yeah she does," Owen grabbed a cloth while Tyler cradled her in his lap.

"Good enough for now, anyway," Tyler winked at Owen then bent to clean off her face gently, then handed the wash cloth back to Owen as Caitlin burrowed into Tyler's shoulder.

"You did so good," Tyler murmured, stroking her. "You were perfect, baby girl."

When she started to cry, Owen looked alarmed.

"You're safe. Owen is here, I'm here. We're going to be here for as long as you need us, okay?" A nod let him know she was hearing him.

Wrapping her in a blanket, Tyler sat with her curled on his lap, her head resting on his chest.

"Movie?" She asked softly some time later.

"Sure thing, baby girl," Tyler agreed, "You need anything?"

"May I have a drink?" She asked with wide eyes.

"What do you want?" Owen asked.

Caitlin's eyes widened in alarm at being asked to choose for herself when her brain was still submissive and not inclined to make her own choices. She glanced up at Tyler, trying to convey that she needed help.

"You want pineapple juice or water?" Tyler asked, his face softening into a tender smile as he caressed her cheek.

"Juice please," she said, snuggling back into his chest, burrowing into the blanket, whining a little as her sore bottom pressed into his lap.

"You'll feel that for a bit," Tyler said with a chuckle, "You took that all so well honey. I can't wait to play with you again when you're feeling up to it."

She enjoyed more juice, her feet resting in Owen's lap. Eventually she moved to the middle of the couch, her head resting in Tyler's lap and her legs curled on top of Owen, peacefully dozing and existing in the afterglow.

Owen and Tyler bumped knuckles over her form with a nod of satisfaction.

CHAPTER THIRTY-ONE

CAITLIN

*B*y the end of the movie, she'd cuddled with both men and started to feel aroused again. It was a good thing the doctor warned her that carrying a shifter's baby might make her more sensitive to the full moon the further along she was in her pregnancy. Normally she would have been in bed ready to sleep after a scene like the one they'd just shared. As she lay there with the movie going, Tyler playing gently with her hair and Owen rubbing her feet tenderly, she felt a heat pool in her core. She looked uncertainly at Owen, then Tyler, biting her lip.

"What's wrong, baby girl?" Tyler asked, smoothing her hair.

"Cupcake, we're both here to make sure you have fun. Neither one of us are going to have our feelings hurt if you just want one of us," Owen said.

"Not at all. The other one can watch, or not. It's whatever you're comfortable with," Tyler agreed.

"Will you watch us?" She asked Owen, gesturing between her and Tyler.

"I would love to, if that's what you want," he said, standing to lean over and kiss her softly.

As their lips connected he grabbed the back of her hair roughly and pulled her away, all softness and affection gone from his eyes.

"I expect you to make his cock feel good, little slut," he said in the low commanding growl.

"Yes sir," she said breathlessly.

He kissed her again, then used his grip on her hair to direct her lips to Tyler's, she scrambled to rise up and meet his lips.

Tyler kissed his mate passionately, drawing her onto his lap so she straddled him, grinding against him. For one brief moment, she cut her eyes over to Owen, eyes uncertain, but Tyler forced her chin up so she looked at the ceiling, sucking on her neck.

"You mind marks?" Tyler turned and asked Owen who gave a thumb's up.

Caitlin shook her head that she didn't mind, but Tyler grinned against her neck.

"I wasn't asking you, slut. You don't get to make decisions here. If I want to mark you when I fuck you, I'm going to do it." With that, he pressed his lips to Caitlin's neck and sucked as he toyed with her nipples, pinching them.

Caitlin nearly came undone on his lap. She thought it would take time for her to be ready to actually have sex after the last time, but her body ached to be filled.

Caitlin enjoyed Owen's hard eyes on her as he watched Tyler tease her, edging her again and again until she cried, begging for release.

When Tyler allowed her to present herself on all fours on the rug for his use, Owen stroked himself as he watched her fall apart on his partner's cock while Tyler took her from behind. She felt Tyler's grip in her hair, yanking her back. Owen's cock was in her face, his hands rough on her cheeks, prying her jaw open. He shoved his cock roughly past her lips. The blood was pounding so loudly in her ears she couldn't hear anything else, her body lost to the world of sensations. Every thrust of Tyler's girthy cock filling her shoved Owen deeper into her mouth, providing only a moment of relief before the process was repeated. She was so torn between the building orgasm and trying to struggle for breath that she felt dizzy as the world started to spin, the tingling of her impending orgasm building everywhere, not just her spine.

When she did orgasm, her hearing came back with a snap as she heard Tyler roar his release. Owen moved around behind her and slid between her wet folds, Tyler's multiple loads dripping out of her onto the carpet. Every thrust her mate made pushed some of the fluid out so her thighs were covered, even more so when Owen gripped her hips and buried himself inside of her with several deep sharp thrusts. She felt his cock jerking inside of her as he filled her, more cum sliding out of her used body and down her legs as he withdrew.

"Stay on all fours and clean us up like a good whore, and maybe we'll let you come again," Tyler said.

"We've got some nice implements up in the bedroom," Owen suggested. "Those thighs look awfully colorless."

"Oh she could definitely use some color," Tyler said, moaning in approval as Caitlin sucked him clean. "Good girl, now show me that cum-filled pussy."

She made her way around and wiggled her ass in the air for him.

"Spread them for me, I want to take a good look."

She used her hands to spread herself for him, her cheeks flaming in embarrassment as he swiped some of the cum that leaked out and shoved it back up inside of her.

"Don't waste it, now. Go upstairs, on all fours. Be waiting on the bed. If we see any cum has leaked out onto the floor, we'll punish you." Tyler promised.

"Yes sir," she whispered, humiliated as she crawled away while they watched, her body already ready for more.

If this was what the full moon felt like when she was pregnant, she and Owen were going to have to look into adding more rooms onto the house.

CHAPTER THIRTY-TWO

AXEL

*S*he was in the window, touching herself like a common slut. He itched to touch his straining erection in his pants, but he mastered himself and watched. The man working on the fence line noticed, but he didn't go back into the house. That was interesting.

He stayed in the woods until the evening when the sun set. Once the deputy was home, Axel crept closer. They didn't even shut their windows, so Axel had a perfectly clear view of the deputy pulling Axel's mate on his lap, using her before sending her to the kitchen to service the other male.

Rage boiled up within Axel. She was being passed around like a community whore. Maybe he hadn't been perfect to her, but he'd never let his friends use her, even when they begged. She was a pretty piece of ass, but he knew that a woman who needed more than one man to be satisfied wasn't a happy woman. She deserved better. She deserved to have a real man back in her life and in her bed.

He watched until the three of them went upstairs and the sounds of loud sex floated through the open bedroom window. Axel made his way quietly through the woods and climbed back in his truck. He thought about driving home, but the need for violence had grown as he'd watched the two men enjoying his woman. He needed to hurt something, badly. Instead of heading back to his hotel, he drove to the mountain trailhead and found a game trail the pack used. Around midnight he found a deer, taking it down easily. Ripping the carcass to shreds did little to abate his anger, but the goats he picked off a herd before the inhabitants came outside had sated him - for now.

He wasn't going to be able to wait much longer. Every day that passed that she spent it in the arms of another man was making him crazy.

CHAPTER THIRTY-THREE

AXEL

TWO DAYS LATER

*I*t was a complete fluke that he'd seen the brochure sitting in the passenger seat of her car. *Pregnancy in Mixed Species: A Guide for Human Mothers.*

Pregnancy? The word stopped him short. Was Caitlin pregnant, or did she want to be? She'd always been curvy, she'd been wearing lots of dresses since she'd moved to Pinehurst, but Axel had thought she'd just put on a little weight. Gods know with all the baking she was doing that she had the opportunity enough to eat more than she needed. When he got her home, if she wasn't pregnant, he was going to encourage her to go on a diet.

If she was pregnant... he pictured her in a fitted pregnancy shirt, one meant to emphasize her growing belly, and grew hard at the thought. He watched her, cursing the apron she was wearing as she was sipping a drink on her back porch, enjoying the swing when her phone rang. She answered it, then stood and walked back into the house.

Axel watched her disappear into the house, drinking in the sight of her. He'd always wanted to see her pregnant with his child. He'd never imagined that he'd get to see it once she'd left. He heard her fire up the deputy's big truck and pull down the long driveway.

He walked across the lawn and went to the back door unchallenged. The back door was unlocked, which was foolish of her. He'd have to train her to keep their doors locked when he got her home. What if it had been someone who wanted to hurt her? Tsking, he slipped out of his boots and left them on the back deck.

Her kitchen was clean and tidy and smelled of coffee and baking. God, he'd missed her baking, he'd have to tell her. The living room had one of those fake paintings that hid the tv. He'd remembered her talking about them, bitching to him when he'd watch a game with a few beers about how the television threw off the aesthetic of the house. Her bookshelves in the living room held a lot of the kinds of things he'd expect her to read: cookbooks filled with all kinds of recipes, from the modern to the classics. He spotted her favorite: Mastering the Art of French Cooking, volumes one and two. She'd raved about them, but he'd been stubborn, insisting she make him his tired favorites. Maybe when she came home he would let her introduce him to some new things.

Then his eyes came to another shelf that made him growl low in his throat. Criminal Psychology, Arresting Communication, and a title called Blood Lessons that had been opened and read so many times the spine was cracking. Below that shelf were a handful of psychology books and the next shelf held copy after copy of legal thrillers, well-worn. Picking up a copy of one, he saw that the pages had been dogeared in many places. Walking back out to the kitchen, he opened the cabinets and found a stack of disposable cups, and then several mugs. A local sheriff's department mug, a police academy mug, and several feminine cups that could only belong to his Kitty Cat.

A thought stopped him cold as he noticed a pair of work boots on a rubber mat by the back door. Was this deputy the one who'd fathered her child? Maybe that was why she'd run. Things hadn't been so bad between them. Sure, they'd had the same problems every couple had, but they were both spirited and stubborn. Of course they'd fought, everyone did.

He'd had times when he suspected someone else, but never any proof. Was this child the proof of her cheating? Or just something she'd kept from him when she'd left?

He heard a strange scrambling and chuckled. Her 'protection dog' was locked in its crate, whining to be let out. Axel grabbed a few treats from the canister. She'd had the deputy mount a floating shelf for all of her dog things, all of which were perfectly matched and coordinated. Axel threw the dog a few treats and kept going through the house.

After investigating the things he couldn't see easily through the exterior windows, he proceeded upstairs to the room that was the primary goal for this visit. A two-sided glass desk sat with an apple laptop neatly plugged in, a neat black journal laid out beside it with a pen carefully placed on top. He opened the journal, and then checked the first entry. Damn. It was after she found out she was pregnant.

Axel flipped through the pages, at first looking for his name, finding that he was featured in many of the earlier entries but less and less of the more recent ones. When he came to a printout of a sonogram he stopped and read.

I can't believe I'm pregnant. Pregnant. It doesn't even feel real. I insisted about a dozen times to the doctor that I couldn't be pregnant because I feel fine. I feel great, actually.

Thank goodness for Miss Linda. I would have been freaking out with all the things I'll need, so she's handling all of it. Apparently, the pack does this for all the moms, whether they're first-time moms or not. Even though the shower isn't going to be for a couple of months, random women keep stopping by and bringing me things. I put them in a box in the office closet until I have a place set up for him or her.

He scanned a few of the prior pages, stopping when he saw his name again.

There are times when I miss Axel, at least the good parts. Olivia says this is normal, and that I need to process that. I do miss him. There are a lot of things I don't miss. The drinking, the fighting all the time, how he made me feel small…but it's all mixed up because if he hadn't raped me, I wouldn't have Jamie.

What luck, the baby was his. He wanted to read more, to find out if it was a boy or girl, but he heard a car in the drive. Making his way quickly out of the house, he left through the back door, making for the woods with his baby's name on repeat in his mind.

Don't worry, Jamie. Daddy's coming back for you. Axel thought as he walked toward his truck some distance away.

CHAPTER THIRTY-FOUR

AXEL

THREE WEEKS LATER

*H*e walked across the lawn and went to the never-locked back door. Going inside, he'd walked through the house, giving the dog a handful of treats before making his way to the spot where he'd ended the last time he'd come in the house. He'd spotted the journal just before Caitlin had come home from the store, but he hadn't had time to read it on his last visit. Now she would be going to her therapist's office and getting the dog from the vet, leaving him plenty of time to peruse her latest entries and work on his other project.

He read her latest journal entry, pleased to know their baby was doing well at the last checkup, then put it away so he could accomplish the real thing he'd come here to do. Axel worked quickly, making sure to clean up after himself as he went so she wouldn't suspect anything.

He went through the rooms until he found the bedroom. There were so many pillows on the bed, Axel shook his head. Clearly this guy let her run the house, Axel was going to have a lot of retraining to do when she got back. Letting her bake and make her fancy stuck up food was one thing, but letting her cover the bed in pillows like it was some kind of harem? No, definitely not.

Muttering darkly about the ways he was going to punish her for making him work this hard to keep her safe from her own stupid choices, he worked fast and was done in no time. Checking his watch, he had a few minutes before she was home so he did something impulsive.

Opening the closet on the left, it was full of men's clothes, so he closed it, barely resisting the impulse to begin tearing them to shreds on sheer principle. The closet on the right was much fuller with bright dresses and adorable sweaters, as well as a small basket of dirty laundry. That he shifted through, looking for his prize. He found a pair of lace panties, put them to his face and inhaled deeply before he stepped into her clothing, trying to absorb as much of her scent as he could.

God, he missed her like a missing limb. He needed to find a way to get rid of this asshole she was with now and make her see how much happier she would be back home with her true mate. This visit would help him a lot.

He stuffed the panties in his pocket then on an impulse he went to her nightstand and opened the drawer which was filled with sex toys. He sniffed. She would be lucky to be rid of this guy who obviously had no idea how to keep a woman happy with what the gods gave him.

He heard her in the driveway and made his way carefully out of the house, careful to make a beeline for the woods so the dog wouldn't see him and come to play with him like Axel had made a habit of doing when his Kitty Cat was out of the house.

CHAPTER THIRTY-FIVE

CAITLIN

*C*aitlin sat in the driveway for a moment after she turned off the truck. Today's therapy session had been rough, leaving Caitlin feeling raw and exposed. Owen would be home any minute and she needed to calm herself down and explain to Owen that she needed some space. He would understand, he always understood, but it still gave her anxiety to take space for herself.

In the span of their relationship, she hadn't seen him angry once. Normally, she would think that was a good thing but it left her imagination to fill in the gaps in her knowledge about the man she now lived with, and one who she would be raising a baby with. The only frame of reference she had for it was her father who got sullen and withdrawn, burying his feelings in a bottle of scotch when her parents had problems, and Axel.

Obviously, Owen wasn't anything like Axel, but the little voice of doubt always lingered in her mind, whispering that each time she told Owen no or took space for herself, this was the time he would lose it, when he would drop his mask and she would see all the things she hadn't been able to see before, all the things that made him less than the seemingly perfect man he was.

Really, the only thing she suspected was wrong with him was that she suspected he was sneaking her dog the treats that upset his tummy, even after she asked him to stop repeatedly. It was odd, and she didn't understand why, but he'd insisted he'd had nothing to do with it so she'd taken Toten to the vet in town and bought more of the treats that didn't upset his stomach, intending to replace the ones in the jar above his crate so he wasn't taking midnight trips outside.

After she calmed down, she eased herself down from the truck, which Owen had insisted she drive to town so the dog crate could go in the back, she waddled around the truck to open the back door, then opened the door to Toten's crate.

"Aw buddy, are you glad to be home?" She asked as he wiggled.

She stepped to the side, then said "Out!"

Toten launched himself out of the box, flying out and landing on the ground, twisting and jumping around her, barking his pleasure and excitement as he pranced around her in a joyous circle.

"Yes. I'm glad you're home. Did Amanda treat you well?" He ran around the front yard barking joyfully while she got her groceries out of the passenger seat, cursing when a plastic bag of groceries split down the side, sending a cascade of canned goods flying in hard-to-reach places for a woman who felt like she had the coordination of a drunken monkey with an enormous mixing bowl strapped to her stomach.

A cold wind bit through the air. She sighed when she heard Owen coming up the drive as she strained to reach a can, grinning in satisfaction when she grabbed it, then groaning when she spotted another can just beyond, trying to maintain her temper.

Owen was going to fuss at her again for not wearing a jacket, she just knew it. The idea made her clench her jaw in irritation, but it wasn't her fault she was hot all the time, she blamed Jamie. She was a little over a month away from her due date and this baby had turned her into a human space heater.

Saying yet another prayer of thanks that she wasn't in this stage of pregnancy in the heat of summer, she strained to reach a can of green beans and slipped on the step, crashing down hard onto her extended belly. With a cry of pain, she dropped the other bag of groceries. She slid to a sitting position in the gravel as Toten came barking over to her, Owen appearing seconds later.

"Hey, are you okay?" A sharp pain rippled through her stomach as Owen crouched in front of her. "What were you doing?"

"A can rolled under the seat," she said, closing her eyes and fighting back irritation as she reminded herself that she wasn't actually irritated with him.

"Aw, I would have gotten it for you," he offered, offering his hand to her to help her up.

She gave him a dark look, her effort to be nice and understanding failing.

"I wasn't base jumping. I just wanted to grab the can," she snapped.

"Come on, I'll get it, Let's get you into the house," he reached for her hand, but she snatched it back.

"No!" She yelled, snatching her hands back, eyes wide with fear.

"Aw, did karma punish you for being a bad girl?" Axel chuckled, standing over her. Sharp pain blossomed from where she'd fallen, but his voice remained pleasant, "Come on, let's get you into the house."

Reaching down, he'd taken her hands and yanked her none-too-gently to her feet.

Forcing her eyes shut, Caitlin repeated her mantra.

"I am here, I am safe. I'm with Owen, I'm safe here." She repeated it under her breath until she felt her breathing calm. Toten wiggled around her feet, nosing at her.

Owen's whole body was still, his hands raised palms-up, regarding her with dark brown eyes filled with anxiety.

"My cupcake…you're safe. I'm not going to hurt you."

Two paws appeared in her lap, a warm nose on her belly.

"Oh. Toten," she leaned against her dog, putting her arms around him as the pain in her belly subsided. He stood there, waiting for her to release him, panting.

"Off," she commanded, then gave Owen an embarrassed, watery smile, "Sorry I freaked out."

"Unnecessary apology. Can I help you up?" At her nod, he helped her. "Does it still hurt?"

"Yeah, but I don't think I'm actually injured, just hurt."

"Okay." Scooping her up with a grunt, he carried her to the front porch.

"Put me down! You're going to put your back out."

"You hush, mate. This is why I go to the gym. You're nowhere near as heavy as my PR." He grinned at her.

"Give me a month." She grumbled, without any real malice. When he set her down on the front porch she leaned into him, turning her belly to the side and sighing.

"Now woman, get in the house, get on your comfy pajamas and sit down somewhere comfy while I make dinner."

"You've been working all day," she objected, but he silenced her with a finger in her lips. She closed her eyes, tensing.

Moving his hand to her cheek, he said quietly, "Yes I did, and now I'm making you dinner, and then we're having movie night."

"Isn't tonight cards night?"

"Not if you're hurt," he kissed her forehead, rubbing his nose against hers, "not to mention triggered. Now, pajamas and pick a movie."

HE'D BROUGHT her dinner on a tray, then sat down with his own food.

"What are we watching?" He asked, picking up the remote.

"Nothing. You're going to card night. I have a date."

"A date?"

"Mm-hmm. Toten!" She called and Toten bounded into the room, sitting next to the couch, standing up, then sitting down again, giving a little bark. She patted the couch and he launched himself up, bounding next to her, laying next to her legs, his head resting on her baby bump.

"If you're sure that you're okay…" Owen said, looking unsure.

"Some alone time would be nice," she admitted, fighting the anxiety rising in her chest.

"Okay then. What can I get you before I head out?"

"Sunflower seeds?"

Shaking his head at her latest strong pregnancy craving, he went to the kitchen. She settled in, settling a thin throw blanket over her and her dog.

"Hey maybe you could bring me a bottle of something-"

He appeared at the living room doorway, holding a bag of sunflower seeds and a bottle of coconut water.

"Oh, you're the best. Thank you."

"Mm-hmm. This baby is going to come out smelling like coconuts."

"There are worse things. It could be salt and vinegar chips."

"Hey, I like salt and vinegar chips!"

"I know, and they smell terrible," She said, wrinkling her nose when she remembered the bag of chips he'd opened in the truck that had triggered her only bout of morning sickness.

"Mm. Anything else?"

"No, thank you for everything. Have fun!" He gave her a gentle kiss on the forehead, grabbed his keys, and left out the front door, locking it behind him.

She heard the car start, then switch back off, the front door unlocking and Owen appeared at the door with a gust of wind that brought in the scents of the pines outside.

"No washing the dinner dishes! I'll get them in the morning."

"Okay! No washing dishes!" This time, he really left, giving her two brief honks before pulling away. She snuggled down, enjoying her dog and her snack, enjoying My Best Friend's Wedding.

After the credits began to roll she'd woken Toten up and let him outside, sitting on the top step of the porch, enjoying the chill of the night air. "You up for another movie, boy?"

He stood, stretched, and got into the recliner, turning around several times before curling into a circle and going to sleep.

"Some date you are."

OWEN

Hey. Want me to stay here tonight?

She wanted to say no, wanted to want him close, but the thought of a man's touch on her made her skin crawl. She was in the process of reminding herself that it was okay for her to take space for herself when another text came through.

> OWEN
>
> It is okay for you to say yes you want/need space.

> CAITLIN
>
> Will you be mad or upset?

She cursed herself for needing the validation, waiting on pins and needles for his response.

He opened the message but didn't respond and her heart sank. Then her phone rang with a video call, startling her.

"Hi," she answered shyly.

"Cupcake, I don't mind staying here, and I wanted to call so you could see my face and hear it in my voice that I'm being genuine."

"Let him stay!" Tyler called out, an arm appearing around Owen's shoulders, Tyler's scruffy face bumping into the frame, kissing Owen's cheek.

"Fuck off," Owen growled, shoving Tyler off with a laugh before rolling his eyes into the camera.

Clearly, he wasn't upset, and she really could use the night to herself.

"Okay. Yes, please? We can have bacon scones in the morning when you get home."

"Sounds perfect. Bacon scones are my favorite."

"Hey! Caitlin is making scones for us in the morning." Brian yelled, several of the guys whooped in delight.

"You guys can fuck off," Owen responded with a laugh, then spoke quietly, "We're okay baby. You enjoy your evening. Call me if you need me, love you."

"Goodnight, have fun, love you too."

She walked to her bedroom to change for bed, opening the closet. A sickening scent that punched through her with visceral force assaulted her senses. She looked around the room, but everything looked normal. Irrationally, she looked out the bedroom window as if she expected Axel to be peering in, but she saw nothing but the darkness.

She shook her head. Of course there was nothing. What had Olivia taught her when she was panicking?

Heat rolled through her, her breathing was too fast. Ice. She needed ice, but she couldn't make her feet move.

"Toten," she whispered, then louder. "Here, Toten! Come here, baby!"

Toten woke up with a bark from his place on the couch. He nosed her hand, nudging Caitlin with his big, solid body. She backed up, then slid down the wall.

"Good boy," she pulled the dog close, he laid across her lap, licking her hand. "You're a good boy."

Once she'd come back to herself she released him. He heeled with her after she rose, walking to the bed to find her phone. Owen answered on the third ring.

"Hey baby," he answered with a laugh.

"I need you, right now," Her voice came out sounding scratchy and foreign. "Come home please?"

"On my way," he ended the call.

After opening the window so the crisp November breeze wafted in, Caitlin sat herself on the floor on Owen's side of the bed, her hands shaking so badly her phone fell from her hands, making a soft thump on the beige carpet.

There was no way Axel had been here, but she had definitely smelled him. Nothing products Owen owned smelled anything like the smell of Axel's cheap bargain store deodorant mixed with cigarettes. She was triggered, it was just her imagination. No one had been in the house.

"I am here, I am safe. I'm with Owen, I'm safe here."

CHAPTER THIRTY-SIX

OWEN

wen walked through the front door, calling out her name. Toten barked in answer - Caitlin must be upstairs. When he entered the bedroom, Toten ran out to find Owen, then darted around the bed and back to Owen. Caitlin was sitting on the floor, eyes widened in panic, her skin deathly pale against the backdrop of the red duvet behind her head.

"What's happened? Is it the baby?" He asked, crouching down in front of her.

"I smelled him. It was in the closet. *I smelled him*. He must have been in the house, he found me-"

"Slow down, cupcake. No one has been in the house."

"I smelled him!" She screamed, her voice so loud and shrill that Toten whined and stepped back.

"Where, specifically?" Owen asked carefully.

"I went to get my shirt, my laundry basket was open and it smelled like him. It all smelled like him." Owen rose and walked to the closet, sniffing.

He turned back around, approaching her slowly, like he would a panicked patient.

Is she... okay? I mean, clearly she isn't okay, but what's wrong with her? How do we help? Finley asked.

"I don't smell it," he said. She started to talk, but Owen continued, "I believe you, I'm not saying *you* didn't smell it. I am just saying I can't smell it now. What do you want me to do? Check the house?"

She nodded. He pulled his nightstand drawer open, opened the fingerprint safe inside, and took out his pistol.

"Stay here." He seriously doubted that anyone had been in the house, but he went through, checking every closet, leaving every light on as he went.

We're not supposed to lie to our mate, Finley accused.

I believe that she thinks she smelled something, and that's what matters to her right now, Owen replied as he made his way to the kitchen.

He grabbed small ice packs to lay on her wrists out of the freezer then made his way back up to the bedroom. She was still sitting there on the floor, frozen in place, Toten was lying across her lap, his body pushed up against her belly. Caitlin gripped his leather collar so tightly her knuckles were white.

"No one is here. I checked everywhere." Owen informed her.

"You believe me, don't you?" his little mate said in a small voice, her chin trembling as her eyes begged him to believe her.

We believe you're crazy, Finley offered.

Shut up, Fin. You're not helping, Owen snapped and Finley retreated, saying nothing else while Owen handled their mate.

"Yes, I believe you smelled something. I'm going to tuck you in with Toten, and I'll sleep in the other room-"

"No! Stay with me," she said, the whites of her eyes showing.

Tucking her in with her ice pack in her hand, he put Toten in front of her on the bed and spooned her from behind so she would be sandwiched between them.

Can I talk now? Finley ventured a little while after she fell asleep.

Not if you have any more snide remarks, Owen bit back.

I'm worried about our mate, Finley admitted, *this isn't normal, even for her. We should call the talking lady in the morning. Even the stupid dog didn't make her feel better this time.*

Yeah, I'll have her call Olivia tomorrow if she doesn't do it herself. I'm worried too, bud, Owen replied, tucking the blanket up around Caitlin as she snored softly. *I'm definitely worried too.*

THE NEXT MORNING Caitlin slept in. Owen had barely slept, waiting in case she needed to be woken from a nightmare as she sometimes did after a triggering therapy session. When Toten needed to go out in the morning, Owen had thrown on a jacket, let the dog outside, and made himself a pot of coffee.

Walking out to the back porch he sat on the top step and sipped his coffee while he basked in the cool morning air, thinking maybe he'd take Caitlin and Toten out of the house today to the park in town. Being home wouldn't help her, but then considered that maybe he should take her somewhere she would enjoy that didn't involve much walking. Although she didn't like to admit it, she got tired easily these days. He was contemplating where they could go when a bug landed on his foot. He flicked his leg to get it off but something caught his eye.

Leaning forward slightly, Owen's throat went day. A muddy boot print that wasn't his was on the bottom step. Someone had been at his house.

Carefully, he walked down the steps and measured the footprint against his own foot. Tyler was the only one who'd been here since the last rain when there had been enough mud to leave tracks, and he wore a size smaller than Owen. He looked around at the tree line surrounding the yard, the hairs on the back of his neck rising.

Wouldn't we have smelled someone if they were in the house? Finley asked uneasily.

I don't know. Owen thought back, his mind racing.

Calling the dog he went back inside to grab his phone, dialing his partner.

"Tyler, yeah, I know it's early. I need your help with something. Remember that security system we were talking about? Yeah. I need to put it in - today." Tyler agreed and said he'd be right over.

Someone had been here who didn't belong, and Owen was going to make damn sure it didn't happen again.

CHAPTER THIRTY-SEVEN

CAITLIN

"*W*here are you going?" Owen asked her when she came downstairs fully dressed, her hair done in a French braid.

"Therapy."

"Ah, good girl. Want me to drive you?" He asked.

Was it her imagination, or did Owen look tense? She couldn't blame him after last night. She'd been a mess over a whole lot of nothing. If it had been real, he would have smelled it too, which meant this was all in her head and she was losing it. This emergency appointment with Olivia had to help because she was not okay.

"No, I'm good," Well, maybe good was too strong of a word, but at the very least she could drive herself.

"Mm-hmm. Drive safe. Tyler's coming over this morning to install that new security system."

"Okay, I'm taking the car, love you."

Caitlin wiggled her fingers at Tyler who was coming down the driveway in his red pickup as she drove out. He nodded in greeting, looking tired, and Caitlin felt a surge of emotion made up of equal parts of gratitude and guilt. She hadn't expected Owen to take her seriously, she'd been crazy last night, but she would also feel better with the cameras up to watch the doors so she could feel safer.

The road she got on five minutes from the house was long and straight, a rarity in this part of the state. She put her foot down on the accelerator, one eye on the road as her anxiety that hadn't diminished much from the night before melted away. With each tick she passed on the speedometer as her speed increased, she felt a thrill.

Lowering the windows and turning up the music, she breathed a sigh of relief. Nothing could touch her here. She was safe. Her mother had always swore that belting it out with Shania Twain and a glass of wine would fix just about any problem. Pregnancy put a damper on the wine part, and she'd never had much of a taste for alcohol anyway. But speed... that she'd always had a penchant for. She rarely indulged, because these days she had healthier coping skills, but right now none of those things were working. She just needed to feel something good, so she cranked the radio up louder.

Next on her playlist was Reba McIntyre's *Independence Day*. She was singing at the top of her lungs when she passed a county car, which immediately pulled out onto the highway behind her, blue and red lights flashing in her rear view. She cursed, the good feeling evaporating.

"Caitlin, is everything okay?" Deputy Scott Barrington leaned on the car, looking at her with concern.

"Yeah, why's that?" She asked, trying to look nonchalant as her heart tried to beat out of her chest.

"I clocked you going 86 in a 45. Any particular reason why you're going so fast?" He asked.

"I was just jamming, must have been distracted," she laughed uneasily.

"I was at poker night last night at the Lawson's. I know you've been having some trouble." Scott said, not unkindly, "Look, I know-"

"I was actually on my way to therapy." she said, looking at her watch and giving him a look. "If I promise to watch my speed, can you let me go?"

"Give me just a minute, sit tight," he walked back to his car, shaking his head.

When he got back to his car, she shut her eyes. The blue and red lights in the rearview were not helping her anxiety, so she flipped up the rearview mirror, turning her music back up. She texted Olivia to explain she'd be a few minutes late, then practiced her deep breathing.

She heard the familiar rumble of a big truck then a bark she knew all too well. Opening her eyes, she flipped the rearview back down as her stomach dropped. Owen and Scott were standing outside of his cruiser having an intense conversation. She didn't need to be able to hear what Scott had to say to see Owen's body tense up, his posture shifting as he squared his shoulders. He shook Scott's hand and clapped him on the back before walking toward her car. Caitlin folded her hands in her lap, a nervous smile sliding into place as she waited.

She didn't know how it worked for other people, but a friend whose husband was in the army had told her once that she really had two husbands. There was the caring, gentle, loving man who changed their baby's diapers and sometimes enjoyed being the little spoon. Then, her friend had explained, there was her army husband. She said she'd only seen it once, but that had been enough.

Now, looking at her mate's posture, his hard expression, and the way he walked toward her car she realized she was about to meet Deputy Owen Kessler, and he didn't look nearly as nice and understanding as the Owen who would soak in the flowery scented bath with her in their enormous clawfoot bathtub or paint her dog's nails to match Caitlin's after she got a pedicure.

Irrationally, she rolled up the window, locking the doors. He walked up to her window and made two sharp raps with his knuckle then motioned for her to roll down the window. She stared at him, shaking her head. Rolling down the window was very low on the list of things she was willing to do with him looking at her like that. She trusted Owen, mostly. He'd never harmed her, but he'd also never looked at her like he'd *actually* wanted to punish her...until now.

"Caitlin, roll down the window," he commanded and her treacherous body moved instinctually at his tone, rolling the glass down half an inch. "All the way please."

Once she'd complied, Owen said in a professional crisp voice, "Please step out of the car."

Shaking, she fumbled with her seatbelt, unlocked the doors, and stepped out. Toten barked in the truck, she glanced toward him. Scott leaned on his car, studiously not watching the two of them.

"Follow my finger," he held out his index finger in front of her.

"Owen, I'm not drunk-"

"Follow my finger," he repeated sternly.

"I will not!"

"Fine. Take nine steps-"

"Oh my god!" She interrupted, exasperated, "I am not doing that. I haven't been drinking, you know that. Don't be an ass."

"Are you impaired in any way?" Owen asked in his professional tone that showed no emotion, his dark brown eyes narrowing.

"For gods' sake, no."

"Then why, in the name of the bright moon above, were you driving more than forty miles over the speed limit?" He whispered.

She realized with a start that he was as far from calm as she'd ever seen him, his whisper not a sign that everything was fine, but a measure to keep himself from shouting and losing his cool altogether. A little voice in her head said it was good that they were finally seeing how he reacted when he was truly angry, but the larger portion of her brain told that tiny voice to shut the hell up.

"Owen, give me a minute, step back please," she felt the panic rising in her again, her chest squeezing, her head spinning until she thought she might pass out.

"No. There is no minute here. What the hell is wrong with you? Forty over the limit is reckless endangerment, Caitlin. What were you thinking?"

He leaned in as he spoke and it was too much for her. What little self control she'd been holding herself together with despite her extreme anxiety snapped. The proximity of an angry man, the fear that Axel had found her the night before, and hormones that made everything seem bigger and scarier - all converged inside of her, and the need to act in any reasonable manner evaporated like vapor in the wind.

She pulled her hand back and slapped him across the cheek, the palm of her hand stinging as if she'd burned it. His face snapped to the side and he took a half-step back, turning to face her slowly, his eyes narrowing.

Before he could say anything in response Caitlin did something she'd never done before. As he opened his mouth to respond she clenched her fists, squeezed her eyes shut tight, opened her mouth and screamed. The sound ripped through her throat, the shrill undulating sound echoing off the hills around them until her body refused to make any more noise.

When she opened her eyes, Owen was staring at her, his eyebrows nearly hidden behind some of the jet-black hair that fell across his forehead. Her throat ached but, surprisingly, she felt much better. It was probably terrible for her throat, but who knew that a good scream could be so good for the soul?

"It made me feel calm, and therefore safe," she explained calmly, clearing her throat.

Toten was going crazy in the cab of the truck, barking and slobbering all over the window, his paws scratching the glass of the driver's side window but they both ignored it. Owen stared at Caitlin with a measured, searching look before shifting, tucking his thumbs into his belt.

Scott was out of his car, standing a dozen feet away, no longer pretending not to notice them.

"Say that again for me?" Owen finally asked, tilting his head like he was trying to confirm that he'd misheard her the first time.

"I felt too crazy last night, like lost deep in the forest of crazy. I thought if I got some sleep I would feel better, but I woke up feeling like everything I was afraid of had come true - like he'd found me and he was going to take me and Jamie away. I have all of these healthy coping skills to make me feel better and none of it was helping. So I called Olivia and then I just... I don't know. The faster I went, the more dangerous it was, the quieter my head got."

Owen looked at her, then shook his head and walked a few paces away. "You can go, Scott. Thanks. I'll make sure it doesn't happen again."

"Thanks a lot, Scott," she called angrily after him.

Owen's eyes cut to her, but he said nothing, his hands resting on his belt as Scott climbed into his car and passed them. Then his eyes cut back to Caitlin. He spoke in a commanding voice that was most definitely not one she'd ever heard before, even in the bedroom.

"You will drive, slowly and carefully, obeying all the laws of traffic, back to the house. Once you are there, we will sit down and have a calm, respectful, reasonable discussion." *Hello, Deputy Kessler.* He took his keys from his pocket, turning to go to his truck.

"I have therapy," she supplied.

He turned, looking her up and down slowly to see if she was really going to make a thing of it. When she stuck her hand on one hip and raised her chin, he sighed.

"Alright, there first then, then home," he replied in the same measured authoritative tone.

She nodded and made her way to her car. She could feel his eyes on her, but she didn't look. Buckling up, she pulled off the shoulder. He followed in the truck, but instead of getting off at the next exit to head back to the house, he followed her to her therapist's office, raising two fingers off the steering wheel and nodding in farewell at her as she walked inside.

THEIR SESSION CONCLUDED, Olivia got up and walked to the window, and looked outside. Caitlin couldn't hear his truck, but he wouldn't have left it running with the weather so nice. Toten was probably lolling with his head out the window.

"Is he still there?" Caitlin asked, anxiety rising in her chest.

"Yes. Did you expect him to leave?" Olivia asked calmly.

"Not really," Caitlin admitted.

"What are you feeling?" Olivia asked.

Guilt tightened her chest as she looked at the clock. She was well past the time limit of their session and although Olivia didn't seem phased or upset, Caitlin always tried to respect the boundaries others set, and taking more of her therapist's time was definitely not respectful. As much as Caitlin wanted to get up and leave, for the first time in their whirlwind of a relationship, it was the first time she'd made him angry. Even worse than him being angry, he'd been angry at *her*. What would he do?

Not that it wasn't justified. She'd been reckless, and to put the cherry on top of the sundae of dysfunction, she'd slapped him and screamed like a banshee when he'd tried to have a discussion with her.

She had no context for how he would behave, but as Olivia pointed out, maybe that was what Caitlin needed. Maybe she needed to see him angry, to see what his worst was in order to feel safe. Owen obviously cared for her, even before he'd imprinted there had been feelings there. She knew better than anyone that having feelings for someone didn't mean you wouldn't hurt them. Axel told her how much he loved her, how much he'd wanted her and wanted their relationship to be good as he'd done terrible things to her. Feelings didn't mean you were safe.

The only other ideas she had of how Owen might handle her were how they acted in the bedroom. Caitlin knew intellectually that Owen had never done anything to her that made her feel anything other than loved. The way he treated her in the bedroom wasn't what anyone would call nice, but he stayed within her boundaries, paid attention to how she reacted and felt, and when they weren't engaging in sexual activities he was so tender, kind and respectful it almost felt like she had two different men living in the house along with her. But which man would she be going home to? Was he just waiting for an opportunity to be hateful, like Axel did? Even as she felt guilty at how unfair it was that Owen had to defend himself against things he hadn't ever done, she couldn't let her guard down.

Not knowing how he would react kept her body frozen on the couch, unable to move or think of anything else.

"I don't know how to go home," Caitlin said.

"Why?"

"I don't know what he'll do. What do normal people do when they're mad?" Caitlin asked.

"Let's bring him in and talk about it," Olivia suggested.

Caitlin gave Olivia an unimpressed look, but the therapist's face remained neutral.

"I hate that idea."

"Good job expressing your feelings," Olivia said with a hint of amusement that didn't diminish the seriousness of her suggestion.

"Also, I hate you," Caitlin muttered, simultaneously grateful and frustrated that Olivia was pushing her.

"That's your choice," Olivia said.

Caitlin could feel the crazy eeking out, and she was not only judging herself for it, she resented it. When Caitlin reluctantly agreed to have Owen come inside to talk, Olivia fetched him, letting him sit on the couch beside Caitlin. He didn't move to give her the usual reassuring love pat on her leg, and Caitlin couldn't decide if that hurt her feelings or made her feel relieved because he was trying to give her space.

"Caitlin expressed to me that she's afraid to come home, because she doesn't know how you'll react to her," Olivia explained.

Owen looked surprised, but directed a carefully measured reply to Caitlin.

"I told you how I'll react. I want to sit down and have a calm, reasonable conversation," Owen said.

"You won't yell at me?" Caitlin asked.

"I am working very hard not to," Owen replied evenly.

"What's the worst thing you think he could do?" Olivia

"Beat me, rape me, probably both," Caitlin responded Owen stopped, the color draining from his face.

"I would never do that. I hate the idea of harming you," he said, his eyes searching hers as he begged her to believe him.

She noticed in an abstract way that his eyes were back to blue.

"Axel said that too," She said and Owen flinched as if she'd slapped him. "And afterwards he told me he was sorry, that he'd 'misunderstood' when I said no, and that it would never happen again. And again. And again. Every time I said no to anything, he bulldozed right through it, and then he promised me that he'd never hurt me on purpose, and that he loved me."

He stared at her in silent horror, throat too dry to swallow. Olivia got up and handed Owen a bottle of water then motioned for Caitlin to continue.

"People don't usually hit you the first time you make them mad. It's the first time you make them the right kind of mad. I want to believe that somewhere there is gold at the end of the rainbow, that somehow, this time it's different, but maybe it isn't. Maybe this time is the time you'll be too mad, and it all goes to hell. When is the time when my 'no' doesn't matter? This time? The next? When do I make you mad enough that you just don't care about me and my feelings, and I become a body to stick your dick in, no matter what the damage is, or a woman who really needs an actual beating to make me small so I don't defy your wishes?"

"You...still see me that way?" Tears pooled in his eyes and he cleared his throat, his hand shaking in his lap.

"Yes."

"Then why didn't you say? Why do you stay with me?"

"Because I know you're a good man. I know because a hundred times a day that you prove it in a thousand little moments that you're good to me." She began to cry too, "That doesn't mean my brain isn't screaming all the time that at some point you are going to violate this trust we've been building, and it's just a matter of when."

Owen raked his fingers through his hair, shaking his head.

"Gods," he whispered.

"Yeah."

"So, do you want to go home with me?" Owen asked, sounding broken but resigned.

"Yes."

She did want to go home, but she wanted home to still be a safe place.

She couldn't stand the thought of having another home morph into a prison, or having the place she'd started to feel happy and secure turn into another place where she couldn't stay and live, but was afraid of the consequences if she'd left.

She didn't know if Axel had ever looked for her or simply let her go, but Owen and Finley? Since they'd imprinted she could see the strain of everyday things like letting her out of their sight long enough to walk into the grocery store or drive to therapy without them. There was no way that they would tolerate it if she wanted to leave permanently, she knew that much.

"But you're still afraid," Owen prompted, shifting on the couch.

"Yes. I'm always afraid."

"Do you want me to go somewhere else?" He asked, steeling himself for her answer.

"I play a game everyday," She explained, wiping her tears away. "How much space can I ask for? How much damage can I reveal? How much trauma do I get to talk about this week before it's just too much? When does my crazy become too much of a burden? Sometimes, it's better to keep you close so you don't suspect how broken I am, and I can take it just long enough so you won't grow to resent me." She touched her belly, "To resent *us*."

"Don't ever do that. Not with me," Owen said emphatically, his careful control over his tone slipping slightly.

"You say that. But I see it when you want to talk about a normal work day and I'm stuck on the couch having a panic attack because you said something that was sexy two days ago, and now isn't fine."

"That is my choice. I choose to give you space when you want it because that's what love is. It's not all making bacon scones and making sure to take the notebook out of my pants pocket before you wash my work pants." They grinned at each other. "Will you please come home with me? I'll make you tea and get your favorite blanket. We can cuddle on the porch. Nothing else."

"Okay."

"Well" Olivia said, eyebrows raised at the two of them. "Glad we got that settled. Caitlin, are you okay to go home? You feel safe?"

"As much as I can," Caitlin answered with a confident nod, despite the nervous flutter in her stomach.

"Okay. Then I'll see you Tuesday at two."

They got home, and he waited for her to get out of her car, walking behind her with a hand hovering over the small of her back.

"I'm not a decrepit old lady," she joked with a half smile he did not return.

"You're mine to protect. And so is Jamie," he touched her belly, letting his palm rest there for just a moment.

"Even though I'm crazy?" she asked, not looking at him.

"I've never known you any other way. If you were all fixed, I wouldn't know you. So yes, I love you, crazy and all."

She turned to go into the house, but he stopped her with two fingers on her arm.

"Caitlin," he began seriously, his blue eyes boring into hers, "I know. On the days when you fake it, I notice. You don't have to fake it. Just because I don't say anything doesn't mean I don't see."

"Where would you like me to sleep?" Owen asked, one arm leaning against the doorway between the master bathroom and bedroom, arms crossed over his chest as Caitlin spit her mouthwash into the sink.

"In our bed, with me." She left the sink and walked over to him, pressing herself against his hard body, hands tracing the seam of his T-shirt's neckline, but he didn't respond.

Taking his hands in hers, he said quietly, "You don't have to say that, I'm fine sleeping on the couch."

"I want to sleep with my mate," she replied.

"But you're afraid I'll..." he shook his head, taking a step back but she grabbed his shirt and pulled him close.

He let her pull him, unresisting and she felt a little rush of grateful-ness for this man who was so gentle and considerate in all the ways that counted. It made her feel that much more guilt for her brain's constant doubt, knowing he'd never done anything to deserve it.

"I'm always afraid. This is what love is for me. Every day I have to give you opportunities to prove to me that you're not the monster my brain says you are. And every day I make a little progress. Some days are harder, and that's okay," she replied, resting her head on his chest as he settled back against the doorframe, putting his arms around her lightly.

"And right now?" he asked, barely breathing.

"Right now, I want you to remind me what it feels like when a man is inside of me, in a way that feels good."

"I can't be mean to you right now." Owen spoke softly into her hair, "I want to be intimate, but please don't ask me to hurt you or say things to you that aren't loving. Tonight, I just want to make love to you. I need you to know how much I love you, cherish you, and I can't-"

"I would love that," Caitlin said, then stepped back and tilted her head up at him. "You know Deputy Kessler, you make that door frame look pretty sexy."

"Deputy Kessler?" he laughed, pulling her close and stepping back so she found her in his place, her back against the doorframe as he rested his arm above her head, leaning down so their lips barely brushed.

"Mm-hmm," Caitlin said breathlessly as she kissed him.

Unlike most of the times they'd enjoyed one another's bodies, this time was slow and gentle. He kissed her against the door frame before kneeling in front of her. He planted a soft kiss on her abdomen, then reached up and hooked his fingers inside the waistband of her sleep shorts and panties.

"Oh, no, I haven't shaved or anything," Caitlin objected, but Owen's eyes met hers, blazing with need.

"I cannot express how much I don't care," Owen laughed, slowly pulling her clothes down until they pooled around her feet, then grabbing one thigh he placed it on his shoulder, used his fingers to spread her wide, and licked her.

Pleasure exploded from her core, making her cry out as she struggled to stay upright.

"Owen," she panted, grabbing his hair as he licked and sucked on her clit, "Owen, I need you inside of me,"

Wordlessly Owen readjusted his position, using his finger to find her entrance. He teased her for a moment, then shifted his body, his fingers disappearing and he slid his tongue inside of her. The unexpected sensation sent her into an animalistic frenzy of pleasure, grabbing his hair to hold him where it felt best, crying out against his mouth as she cried out.

He made no effort to slow or stop, letting her ride out one orgasm, quickly followed by another. She thought she was finished when he pulled back just enough to speak in a hoarse whisper.

"That's right, cupcake. Use my mouth, I want to taste you while you cum for me."

Then his tongue was inside of her again, his thumb working her clit. She saw stars as the world around them imploded. She heard herself screaming in ecstasy, felt the slick coating of her arousal gush from her, covering his face as he wrung every iota of pleasure from her until she was shaking, spent and unsteady. Carefully, he moved her leg from his shoulder and steadied her before standing. He bent to kiss her but she turned away, nose wrinkled.

"I love you, but that's nasty," she said, wrinkling her nose, "Not that it wasn't mind-blowing, I don't want to taste myself. Ew."

Owen laughed and nodded.

"I'll wash off. I need to take Toten out anyway, then we can go to sleep if you're done."

"Oh, I'm not done," she assured.

"Alright," he said, walking into the bathroom to wash his face.

"When I come back, I expect you to be waiting in my bed, beautiful," he commanded, his voice low with sensual promise, then mischievously rubbed his still-dripping wet but clean face on hers.

"Hey!" she exclaimed with a laugh, pushing him away.

Toten, roused by her exclamation, rose from his corner of the room and barked, watching the two of them. Owen rolled his eyes.

"I hear you," he said to the dog, then looked back to Caitlin, smiling a soft smile. "You know, I'm pretty damn lucky. I've got the whole package with you. You're sweet, kind, you do magic in the kitchen, and you're gorgeous. I don't know how I got so lucky, but I'm glad I have you."

Kissing the tip of her nose he used the hand towel to dry off his wet face and tossed it into the waiting hamper. She felt tears rush to her eyes and hurried to blink them away, but he saw, his softening further into an understanding smile.

"One day I won't be so broken, you know. Don't give up on me. I promise one day I won't be like this," Caitlin said.

"I'm not waiting for you to be healed, Cupcake. I'm waiting for you to realize it's safe to heal. I'm not going anywhere. Even if I wanted to, Finley wouldn't let me," he winked.

Toten nudged his hand.

"I know Finley is only staying for Toten," she teased.

Owen gave her a flat look then shook his head.

"You need anything from downstairs?"

"Nope, just my two boys," she replied.

"Alright, hop in bed and we'll be back in a few," he said, making to leave.

Before he got to the door of the bedroom, Caitlin took a deep breath and said what she'd been thinking since he'd gotten his knees in front of her.

"If you, uh, wanted to use your bossy deputy voice, I wouldn't mind," she said, blushing scarlet.

"You like that, do you?" Her mate said, eyebrows raising.

"When I'm not in actual trouble, yeah," she admitted.

He worked to keep himself from smiling, saying in a stern drawl, "Well then ma'am I'm going to have to take myself over there, get naked and wait on my bed, if you don't comply I'll have to get my cuffs and subdue you."

She dissolved into a peal of helpless giggles as he left the bedroom.

CHAPTER THIRTY-EIGHT

AXEL

The house was quiet. He'd taken out the security cameras easily enough. Axel was irritated when the deputy took her car to work instead of his truck, but it wouldn't matter, she would be gone with Axel soon and he would end up driving it eventually.

Using the hidden key that Owen had placed after they changed the locks and installed a security system with cameras watching the exterior of the house, Axel let himself in, chuckling as he did so. He never would have known where the key was without the camera in their bedroom he'd placed on his prior visit last week when he'd stolen her red panties.

He eased open the door and made his way to the living room where the sound of a loud movie was playing.

The deputy hadn't left Caitlin alone, even with that joke of a protection dog since Axel had carelessly left that damned boot print on the porch steps.

Tonight the other deputy, Tyler, was the one guarding the house, which suited his plan perfectly. He wanted a way to make sure the men who had touched his mate were brought to justice, with as little inconvenience to himself as possible, leaving him free to handle Caitlin. Luckily for Axel, Owen had been near one of Axel's interior cameras when he'd given his Kitty Cat the app, login, and password for the new security system, allowing him to enter silently by putting in Caitlin's code.

It was almost too easy. Axel crept forward then in one swift motion gripped the blonde hair, jerking the head upward, and drew the knife across the man's throat. Returning to the kitchen he washed his hands and his knife. He didn't want to scare her more than necessary, people said that kind of thing wasn't good for the baby. He took his time setting up the enchantments he'd purchased around the house, opening windows to give the spell plenty of air.

He turned on the attic fan to suck air into the house, hearing the gentle whir as it kicked on. Finally he grabbed the keys that hung on the hook by the door so she wouldn't be able to go anywhere, pocketing them before he headed upstairs.

He couldn't wait to see her running barefoot through the moonlight, wearing that tempting little nightie that clung to her enhanced curves, draping over the swell of her stomach and cradling her swollen breasts. He wouldn't let her get too far though, he didn't want her to fall and hurt herself.

He walked upstairs, going for the master bedroom. She'd left the curtains open. There were two days until the full moon, so plenty of light shone through the window to illuminate the room for what he needed to do. The lock on the bedroom door was finicky, but he managed to lock it. It wouldn't keep her there, but he would enjoy seeing her panic as she fumbled with it.

She was curled up in the middle of the enormous bed, covered with just a sheet. She barely moved when he sat down on the bed, took the pre-filled syringe out of his pocket, uncapped it carefully then carefully straddled her, his bodyweight pulling the sheet taut around her body to help keep her still. He allowed himself one minute, just sixty seconds to savor the feeling of her beneath him.

She made a little noise of approval as he ground against her, his empty hand moving the sheet down just enough to cup one breast, squeezing it. He couldn't wait to fuck her but he wouldn't do it here, not in the bed she'd shared with other men. He also wanted her fully awake and aware when he took her and reminded her exactly who she belonged to.

When his sixty seconds were up he held her arm, pinning her body between his thighs, and injected the drug into her arm. He anticipated her starting, holding her steady while he pushed the drugs into her vein as she struggled, her terrified scream piercing his ears making them ring. He moved off her reluctantly so she wouldn't injure herself or the baby as she struggled, but not before he noticed how good she felt struggling beneath him. There would be plenty of time for him to play with her later.

"I've missed you, Kitty Cat," he said as she thrashed around in the sheets, desperate to get out. The dog rose and greeted him with a happy wag of his tail, rushing to Axel in greeting. Caitlin was scrambling out of the bed, calling her dog, horrified when it hopped up on the bed and play growled at Axel. His little mate was hysterical as she watched him reach out, pull the dog against his body as if for a hug, then drew his knife around its throat the same way he had with Tyler downstairs.

Caitlin's beautiful screams served as his theme music as he pulled another few enchantment activator pods out of his pocket and tossed one in the middle of the bed. The silver disc bounced lightly against the sheets, then lay still. Satisfied, he crossed the room to open the window. She made it to the locked door , glancing back at Axel as if he was going to try to prevent her. She fumbled with the lock as her hands shook while Axel admired her body. Chest heaving, eyes wild, her muscles taught with fear... she'd never been more beautiful.

"Don't touch me!" She screamed. "Tyler! Tyler!"

"Tyler isn't coming, Kitty Cat." He crooned, walking toward her.

He checked his watch lazily. It was time, so he pulled the last part of the enchantment kit from his pocket, took the small remote, and pushed it. Flames erupted in the middle of the bed, and Caitlin screamed again. When he reached for her she drew back. He stepped forward and unlocked the door with a salacious grin and then stepped back with a mocking bow, beckoning her to go before him through the door.

"Axel, please, don't..." she said.

She gave a hopeful glance at the door, the knowledge of her predicament causing her face to fall. Then, as he knew it would, she hardened herself, steeling herself with determination.

"WHAT'S THE RULE, KITTY CAT?" Axel's arms boxed her in.

"If I run, you'll find me. If you find me-" A sharp pinch to her nipple, his fingernails digging painfully into her tender flesh made her yelp in pain. She looked dazed, but he didn't give her any pity. "When you find me, you'll punish me with an effort equal to the time and effort you had to put into catching me." She recited, wiping the snot from her face, wincing as her hand brushed across the busted lip she'd given herself when he'd pushed her into the doorframe on the way out of the house.

"That's right, Kitty Cat. Now, do you want to run some more, or do you want to come home like a good girl and stick with the punishment you've earned?"

HE COULD SEE the memories of the other times she'd tried to run and defy him behind her eyes. She'd only been successful once, but then the other times had been a game between them where she'd actually wanted to be subdued, otherwise, why would she run, knowing the consequences? Sure, she said she just needed a walk, or just needed to go to her parents for the night, but he knew: she needed to be captured and taken, made to submit.

"What will it be, Kitty Cat? Do you want to come home like a good girl and stick with the punishment you've earned?" he taunted her softly, "Or do you want to rack up some more?"

As he'd hoped, fear won out. She bolted out the door like a scared rabbit, the purple of her nightie catching the light. He grinned and went to open one last window to feed the fire that would be burning from all corners of the house, the attic fan sucking in air through the open windows.

He knew his little kitten would run to find Tyler, trusting that useless boy to keep her safe. She would find him dead and then flee the house out the back door, where he would have an excellent line of sight, illuminated by the fire of her burning home with her precious deputy. Axel didn't care about the house itself, he wanted to send a message: there was nowhere she could ever consider a home that wasn't with him.

Then for the first moment since he entered the house, he felt a jolt of alarm when he heard the jingle of keys before the front door banged open. He cursed, bolting downstairs at a breakneck speed.

How had she gotten more keys? She couldn't get in the truck. Owen was supposed to be the one to drive it, not her.

"Caitlin, no, stop!" He screamed, tearing through the house after her as

She slammed her hand down on the door lock when he made it to the side of the truck. Pulling his knife from his belt he used the butt of the handle to smash the driver's side window as she started the car, fumbling with the keys.

The glass fractured as the truck roared to life. Knocking the fractured pieces inside, he felt real panic rise in his chest.

"Caitlin, no, it isn't safe, don't," She didn't listen to him, putting the truck in gear and driving through the empty flower beds sending chunks of soil, fresh mulch, bits of flowers and driveway gravel flying.

He couldn't hang onto the truck as she tore down the driveway. With a curse, he ran for his own vehicle. The best he could hope for was to chase her down and force her off the road.

CHAPTER THIRTY-NINE

OWEN

"Fire, Medic 5, Deputy 142: respond to emergency traffic to mile marker 143, Highway 158, reference MVA, a 28-year-old woman pregnant with known injuries. Checking on life flight status now."

Owen's mind was calm as he flipped on his lights and sirens, grateful Caitlin was at home safe with Tyler, bracing himself mentally for whatever he would find when he was on scene. A Toyota Forerunner was parked on the side of the road where a lifted gray pickup was flipped over. When Owen spotted the softball league bumper sticker on the truck, his insides turned to lead. Grabbing his radio he checked in on scene mechanically, stepping from his car with a flashlight in hand.

"Communications: Deputy 142 on scene,"

An unidentified male was on his knees by the truck in a full blown panic.

"Kitty Cat! Caitlin, talk to me!" When the stranger looked up to see Owen the man's face turned from hopeful to enraged.

"Sir, I need you to step back so we can help her," Owen said, not caring who the man was, wanting to get to Caitlin.

The man drew back, giving Owen a moment to see Caitlin's body in the cab, her body at a bizarre angle. The unmistakable metallic smell of blood hit Owen with a sickening lurch. He didn't have time to process that. Her eyes fluttered open, he had a brief moment of relief when the sharp crack of a pistol shot rang through the air as the shot knocked the air out of Owen's lungs and he fell to one side.

"It should have been you!" The man snarled, pointing the gun at Owen's leg and firing again. Owen's scream echoed off the mountains as the sound of sirens came closer.

The man reached down and grabbed Owen's radio from where it had fallen to the ground, turned back and looked at Owen, considering him for a moment. He took the butt of his gun and slammed it into the side of Owen's head.

"WHAT THE FUCK, OWEN." Arion, one of Pinehurst paramedics said.

"Dumbass probably shot himself." Arion's partner Carina said, then turning to the paramedic student, she ordered, "Radio it in."

The paramedic student grabbed their radio and held it up, their mind blanking for a moment.

"Communications, this is Medic 5, um, somebody's been shot," the student finally said over the radio, his hands shaking.

"Medic 5, who's been shot?" The dispatcher asked, an edge of irritation creeping into their voice.

"Um, I don't know," the student said, panicking as the back of the ambulance opened and the experienced medics pulled bags and the monitor off the truck.

"Medic 5, put an adult on the radio," someone else spoke, sounding exasperated.

The medical student hurried to where Arion and Carina were raising Owen on the stretcher.

"Um - they want an adult," the student said.

With a grunt they got Owen loaded while he cursed heavily. As they wheeled by, Owen snatched the radio from the student's hands.

"Communications this is deputy 142, send... everybody. The bastard who shot me took Caitlin."

CHAPTER FORTY

AXEL

$\mathcal{A}$xel moved her as carefully as he could, packing her into his car then he drove like a bat out of hell down the county road. As soon as he passed the county line he pulled over, dialing 911. His hands were slick with blood, her blood, and he dropped the phone, slipping into the floorboard as he fumbled.

"I need help, my mate, there's been an accident. She's pregnant and there's blood everywhere. Somebody's got to help me." He said.

This wasn't what he'd meant to happen. Owen was supposed to be the one driving the truck, coming after Caitlin. The truck would flip and it would slow him down, or hurt the fucker who'd been playing house with *his* mate. This wasn't what was supposed to happen at all.

The life flight crew had them up and transported them to the best trauma center in the region, which, thankfully, was close to Burlington. If she lived he could get her home easier from there anyway. Maybe it would all work out.

CHAPTER FORTY-ONE

OWEN

*W*hen Owen managed to open his eyes, his lip curled back in a snarl at the nurse who was holding a syringe to his IV line. She gave him a reassuring smile and looked largely unperturbed at his aggression.

"Caitlin," Owen's thoughts swam, foggy from the drugs and pain.

Finley was there in his mind, but the pain meds made their connection fuzzy so Owen could only feel impressions of his feelings, none of his thoughts.

"Hey, don't move," Owen jerked at the person's touch on his arm.

"Where's Caitlin? Caitlin. He shot me and he took her," the haze dragged him under again as he fought it, but the blackness swallowed him whole.

"THERE YOU ARE!" A cheerful feminine voice greeted him when he emerged from the darkness. "Welcome back. This is just a little medicine to help your pain."

"No pain meds. I need to go get Caitlin," he said, grunting as his ribs objected, a searing pain ripping through his left leg.

"Hey, buddy. Lay back. Caitlin's at St.Mary's," Brian Lawson's hand was firm on his shoulder.

"He shot me. The guy who was there, on scene. He shot me. Fuck that hurts," Owen said as pain shot up his leg.

"That's why you should let the nice nurse get you some meds," Brian said.

"Owen, can you tell us what happened?" Scott asked, his notepad out.

Owen recounted every detail faithfully, then insisted, "I need to talk to Caitlin."

"She's in surgery."

"The baby?" The room went quiet, Brian and Scott looking at one another.

Scott spoke, meeting Owen's gaze with misery and regret, looking like he wanted to say anything but give Owen the bad news.

"We're still waiting to hear if Caitlin's going to be okay, but..." Scott shook his head, unable to say it.

"What happened?" Owen croaked out.

"Uterine rupture with placental abruption," Brian informed him.

Owen closed his eyes as his world shifted. He looked at the nurse and spoke with quiet resolution.

"DC this line or I'm going to. I've gotta go."

"Owen, she's not taking your IV out. Can you give us a minute?" Brian asked the nurse, giving her a smile that indicated he knew what a pain in the ass Owen was being, and he was trying to handle it.

"He can't get out of bed yet," the nurse said, then left the room with a stern look at Owen before she turned to go.

"Owen, something happened - at your house," Scott said.

"What?" Owen asked, his throat hoarse.

"There was a fire," Scott began.

"What?" Owen asked, his throat constricting further.

"There was a body in the rubble and Tyler's car was out front. Whoever burned it used dragon-fire charms, your house is gone too,"

Scott informed him. "Fire's still working on the house. Caitlin's dog is gone."

Caitlin. Tyler. Her dog. The baby. The house she loved so much.

Owen closed his eyes against the onslaught of tears, clearing his throat.

"Get that nurse back in here. I need to go, and one of you to get me some water. My throat is as dry as sandpaper."

He needed to go, needed to get to Caitlin. He panicked as he reached for his mental link to Finley but couldn't hear him clearly.

"Owen, you can't leave now. You've got broken ribs and-" Brian began, but Owen was struggling to sit up while Scott moved to get him some water.

"Tyler was there because Caitlin thought her ex was sniffing around. He was there to keep her and Jamie safe. Then some guy who called her Kitty Cat shoots me and takes her. Doesn't take a genius to figure out what happened."

"It's a four hour drive to Franklin," Brian said.

Scott got a cup and poured water in it, but Owen waved it away and reached for the pitcher. Gulping down the water that only partially helped his parched throat, Owen felt some dribble down his face, spilling onto the hospital gown.

"Is there any point in trying to get you to stay in bed?" Brian asked.

"She's my mate, and her rapist ex took her. What the fuck do you think Brian?" Owen snapped, "Somebody get me some fucking clothes."

"I've got some in my car that'll fit, I'll go get 'em," Scott said, leaving the room.

"Let them give you one more hit of pain meds, you can sleep it off in the truck. Give you a break while we get to your girl."

"Fine, but I'm not staying a single minute longer than I have to."

"I understand. We'll call Franklin PD to let them know what's going on, and have them send a unit up there."

EMMA MET them in the parking lot of the hospital wearing pajama bottoms, looking sleep-tousled and grim. James leaned against an expensive sports car.

"Hey, I have these." Emma said, handing Owen a small black duffel bag, "They're for you, and Caitlin."

"What are they?"

"Charge pads. You stick them on and they slow-release the charge inside. Don't use more than two pads at a time for Caitlin, and three for you." Emma instructed, "You just peel the backs off and stick them anywhere, but if you can put it on your core it's easier."

"Thank you,"

"Is she doing okay?" Emma asked, eyes full of unshed tears.

"Thank you for this," Owen said, lifting the bag, and pulling her in for a quick hug, not answering her question.

"James," Scott said, holding out his hand in greeting.

The two exchanged keys and Owen looked between them.

"You won't get pulled over in this, and it's fast," James explained, flashing a brief, tight smile. "Red switch by the ignition engages stealth magic. Good luck."

Owen nodded, grimacing as he made his way around the car, lowering himself down with a groan as Scott got behind the wheel of James' car.

"Put one of those patches on. Let's go get your girl," Scott said, putting the car into gear.

CHAPTER FORTY-TWO

CAITLIN

*E*verything hurt and she swore she could smell Axel, so she kept her eyes shut and tried to remember what Olivia had told her. *Picture lemons and spring rain.* She could picture it, but she couldn't shake the smell. She needed a distraction, so she tried to open her eyes.

Her eyelids were so heavy, why were they so heavy? Her stomach hurt so much. Was this early labor? Was this what it was supposed to feel like? In a panic, she tried to call out for Owen, but her mouth was full of cotton and nothing was working right.

"There she is," a nurse said softly as she opened her eyes. "Caitlin, there was an accident, you're in the hospital at St. Mary's."

"Owen, I need Owen," Caitlin said as soon as she could get her mouth to work.

"He's right here," the nurse nodded to her other side.

Caitlin closed her eyes for a moment in relief. Turning her head felt like a monumental effort.

"No," she tried to sit up, but the nurse soothed her. Caitlin started to panic, trying to rise from the bed as pain ripped through her abdomen.

"Feeling upset is perfectly normal, anesthesia and hormones

together are awful. You've got to sit still, though, you just had major surgery. I'll give you more meds to help you."

"Baby, the nurse is here to take care of you," Axel's brown eyes narrowed slightly in warning when the nurse turned away.

Caitlin cried harder, slipping into hysteria. The nurse left and Axel leaned in, placing what looked like a soothing hand on her arm. She was going to be sick; she felt bile rise in her throat, Axel saw and handed her a container. He pulled the hair back from her face as she was sick over and over, but there was nothing inside of her to empty but bile. When she stopped he took the container and leaned in.

"Kitty Cat, I'm here for you. We don't want to alarm the nurses, do we? So, be a good girl and keep quiet, so I don't have to hurt them." The nurse walked back in. "Shh, it's okay. Everything's going to be okay."

"Jamie?" she asked, her hand on her stomach, looking up at Axel because the effort of turning her head was too much.

"The baby didn't make it, Kitty Cat. But if you want to try again we could, when you're ready."

"Try again?" her head swam. She was groggy and nauseous. Her stomach hurt. She put her hand to reassure herself, but it felt - wrong. She was empty, her stomach soft under the thick dressings.

"Shh. Now, don't make a fuss. You're going to be discharged, and you're going to let them send you home with me, your mate. Nicely. That way, I can take you back home to Burlington where you belong. It will be like you never left."

"Owen?" She whispered.

"Your shifter friend didn't make it," Axel said tightly. "I'll take you home and we'll make up. You can have the bakery you always wanted, or you can stay home and we'll make a family."

"Jamie-" her stomach was soft, smaller. Grief ripped through her. Her head spun and she blacked out.

Axel was there when she woke up from one nightmare into another, but this one she wasn't waking up from.

"It's time to go home, Kitty Cat," he informed her.

"I don't think I can move."

She wanted to stay here, where there were people, people who would keep him from hurting her. Plus, she really wasn't sure how much she could move between the pain meds and the wound in her abdomen.

"We're getting out of here, one way or another today."

"Axel, please," she begged, tears spilling over.

"Kitty Cat, shh. I don't want you to worry." He sat on her bed and she shrank away from him. If he noticed, he didn't acknowledge it. "I know things weren't great before, but I'll be better. We can be better. I watched you with him, and I know what you want now. I can give it to you."

"What I want?" She echoed stupidly.

She wanted her baby. She wanted Owen back. She felt foggy and couldn't think clearly, but maybe that was a good thing. If Jamie and Owen were both gone, she didn't want to be here either.

"Yes. You want a nice house and a baby to love. If you want, I'll even let you drive sometimes."

"You'll let me drive?" She repeated.

He was insane, genuinely unhinged. A wave of dizziness and pain made the room spin as she sat up.

"Sh, don't say something that will make me angry, Kitty Cat. I don't want to be angry right now. Just let me take care of you and we'll go home. Things can be just like we always wanted. You can open your bakery."

"I can't leave, I can barely move," she objected as the room spun.

"The best place for you is home, Kitty Cat. I'll take good care of you."

She insisted on dressing herself in the clothes he'd brought for her, some of the things she'd left at the house. The shirt was tight on her, but it was hers, sort of. When he came back out into the room, he'd brought her a wheelchair.

"Here, baby. Put this on," he directed, putting his jacket around her shoulders before she could object. She gagged. It smelled like stale beer and the mechanic shop.

"Come on, I got you." He wheeled her down to the front doors.

She looked at the parking lot, paling at the idea of standing, much less walking to the truck. He engaged the brakes and came to crouch down in front of her, speaking quietly as he zipped his jacket up around her.

"Say anything to anyone and I'll shoot whoever you talk to, like I shot your deputy." He murmured, his face placid.

"Owen," she whispered.

Axel stared at her and she nodded to show her compliance. She didn't want anyone else to get hurt. Placing her arm around herself, feeling the strange soft emptiness of her abdomen. She grimaced at the pain, crying softly as she sat in the wheelchair waiting for him to come back. People came and went.

"You okay, honey?" a kind looking brunette in forest green scrubs asked, looking over her with concern.

"Oh, I'm fine!" Caitlin replied quickly, her voice too loud and falsely cheery.

"You sure?" the woman asked, frowning a little.

"Yup. Totally fine. That's my mate now," she said, nodding to the truck.

"Okay,"

"Thank you!"

They drove to the other side of the parking lot and parked in a quiet corner. Axel pulled out a small black shell case out of the driver's side door.

"You know what kills me? I never said shit about you. You were my everything. When you left, I let you go and never said anything bad about you. You've been telling everyone all over that shitty little town all of these things about me. You know, if people believed you, they could take our baby from me, right? Is that what you wanted? Well don't worry, it wouldn't have worked. I made sure of that with the next baby."

She sat quietly and stared out the window, too terrified and numb to move or try to escape.

"What do you mean?" She asked, confused. How would he make sure of anything?

"Baby, no one would believe you if you said I was the one who raped you. I have proof that you were the one who raped me that first time."

"What do you mean, you have proof?" She asked.

Was she dreaming? She had to be dreaming, that was why nothing made sense.

"You admitted it, apologized for it. You were stupid enough to do it in writing once, in a text message. This is why you need me, baby. I'd never let you do something like that when I was in control of you. You always said you wanted all your freedom taken away, now I'm going to give that to you. I couldn't be what you needed before, but I can now."

She couldn't even try to make sense of what he'd said. She felt like she'd fallen into a world where nothing made sense. Maybe it was the drugs, or maybe she was in shock. How long could being in shock last? She kept looking for little clues that this was a nightmare, something that defied the laws of physics, something that wasn't possibly real, anything that would give her a clue that she was going to wake up any minute in her own bed at home with Owen and Toten beside her.

"I never raped you," she objected.

"I was reluctant, and you pushed me," he said, reciting her own words back to her.

He reads things and decides they're his story. He rewrites things, she reminded herself. She remembered the fight he was talking about. He'd been mad that she didn't want to have sex anymore, she'd been adamant that she didn't trust him because he'd done things she didn't want. To turn the tables on her, he'd accused *her* of raping *him.* Caitlin closed her eyes, fighting a wave of pain and nausea.

"I'm sorry about Jamie," he said, shifting in his seat.

Why wasn't he driving? If this was real, he would be driving, right?

"How did you find me?"

"A friend saw you with that deputy of yours in Red River. He said he worked for Pinehurst, it wasn't hard to find you two after that."

"Please let me go," she pleaded.

Her whole body hurt, or she would consider pinching herself to try to wake herself up. That always seemed like a stupid thing to do, but now she understood. Reasoning that if she woke up from this the pain would all be worth it, she pinched her arm hard enough that she winced and sucked in her breath through her teeth.

"You're my mate," he replied, as if that was the end of the discussion.

He was insane. Really, truly insane. She'd felt their bond dissolve the moment she decided to leave, they weren't mates any longer.

"No I'm not."

"I think our families who were there when we swore the oath to each other would disagree," he said, patting her leg like she was a child throwing a tantrum, one who would be soothed by a nap.

"You lied to me. You said you imprinted on me."

"Which I wouldn't have had to do if you hadn't been so insecure!" He shouted, hitting the steering wheel as his control over his temper slipped. After calming himself down he turned to her and spoke as if the outburst hadn't happened.

Caitlin cringed, shying away toward the door, wincing as the movement tore at her incision and her damaged insides.

"Kitty Cat, I don't want to argue. You're hopped up on pain meds and you're in shock from the loss. You're not thinking clearly."

"Please Axel, let me go. I'll leave and," Axel's barking laugh interrupted her, terrifying her into silence.

"You think I'll let you leave me again? You think being with *him* makes you safe when someone like me can replace two bolts in his steering column with hack-sawed bolts and end his life? Of course, I never meant for you to get hurt, or Jamie, but it's okay. We'll make another baby. You can even pick the name, I know that was always important to you," he assured, as if he really expected that to bring her some comfort.

"Please, let me go. I won't say anything to anybody."

"I know you won't, baby." He reached across the cab of the vehicle to cradle her cheek in his hand. "I'm going to take you home and then we'll just pretend like this never happened."

"Please, Axel, don't," she said as bile rose in her throat.

"Hush, now." He pulled a syringe out of his pocket. She was too terrified to scream, too terrified to move. "Don't fight me, I don't want to hurt you any more. We'll be home soon."

CAITLIN WOKE with a feeling of deja vu. She was in her bed, in her room. Everything was the same as it had always been, but different somehow. It smelled nicer. A candle burned on the bedside table. She tried to move, but couldn't. Panic filled her as she struggled to move. What had happened? Then she felt a twinge in her lower abdomen. The baby. Jamie was gone. Axel. Owen. Tyler.

Images flashed through her mind as she struggled to reconcile what she remembered. He'd kidnapped her, taken her home. By the time she was able to move, she was in a full-blown panic attack. She opened the bedroom door. Axel was standing there with a tray for her.

"Oh good, you're awake," he sounded genuinely pleased, as if they were a normal happy couple and she'd just awoken from a normal nap. "You feel better, Kitty Cat?"

"No. I don't feel good."

"The doctor said you would need some pain meds. Take these."

"I - need a shower."

"You haven't had much time on your feet, and you're weak. I'll make you a bath. When you were gone, I got one of those fancy claw bath tubs you like, and a bigger water heater. That way you can fill it up and soak for as long as you like. I even got those fancy bath bars you like."

She stared at him, the phantom of her nightmares standing before her, talking about bath bars and clawfoot tubs.

"What?" he asked, catching her staring.

"I want to go home," she replied, feeling removed from her body.

This couldn't be her body, this wasn't her life. She was pregnant, she had Owen. She just had to trust Owen - he would protect her, he would keep her safe. He promised he would keep her safe. None of this was real, she just had to wait to wake up.

"We are home, Kitty Cat," Axel's voice sliced through the comfort of her delirium.

"I want to go home to *my* home, in Pinehurst. With Owen and Toten."

"This is your home, Kitty Cat," He said with an edge in his voice that silenced her.

He mastered his temper with some effort before setting the tray down on the bed and reached for her hands, ignoring how she flinched away.

"I know things were...rough before. We will make them better, I'll make them better for you, I promise."

"I don't want to."

"Now, the doctor said to give you four to six weeks before we start..." his eyes raked over her body in a way that made her shiver, "trying again. So for now we won't do any of that. I want you to rest."

He ran water in the claw foot tub, so similar to the one in Owen's house. When she couldn't get in on her own, Axel scooped her up behind the knees and arms to set her down gently.

"When you're feeling better, we could have some fun in here," he suggested, handing her a bubble bar. He was right, it was her favorite. He scooted closer, letting his hand in the bath water.

"Is the water warm enough, Kitty Cat?"

"Yes, thank you,"

I am safe. I'm with Owen, I'm safe here with Owen. Any minute now I'll wake up at home, safe with Owen and Jamie will be fine. This is all just a bad dream. I am safe. This is all a bad dream.

CHAPTER FORTY-THREE

AXEL

*S*he was like a goddess. He'd pictured her in this tub so many times. Now he looked at her naked body, nothing hidden from him, and he was almost unbearably hard.

"Gods, you're so beautiful," he said huskily.

She kept her eyes lowered, nodding meekly. He wondered if he was careful if he could fuck her, just this once. He adjusted his jeans as his erection strained against the fabric painfully.

"I put the TV in the bedroom. I know you usually don't like TV in the bedroom, but I thought while you recover we could hang out in there together. It would be like that time you fell and hurt your leg. Remember? We couldn't have sex then either, but we managed to have a good time."

She nodded again, not saying anything. He was pleased with her. Once she got over the loss of Jamie they would make a new one and she could be happy here, happy like they've always wanted.

CHAPTER FORTY-FOUR

OWEN

"What do you mean, she's gone?" Owen demanded of the nurse, who looked nonplussed.

"She left a few hours ago. She didn't even take her phone." She looked at the men in the hall, all bulky and powerful specimens.

Scott went into her room. The sheets and blankets were mussed, but no personal items remained in the room. He checked the bathroom, but it was empty as well.

"Get stuffed," Owen growled, but his voice cracked.

He saw the note on the mirror and his voice dropped to a dangerous cracked whisper. "Where's my mate?"

"We don't know. There was some man with her."

"Are you all looking for Caitlin?" a pretty nurse asked.

"Danika - did you see her leave?" The other nurse asked.

"Yeah, her mate took her home," Maddie said, looking from face to face. "She was wrecked, understandably. Losing a baby like that… she said she just wanted to go home."

"Her mate?" Owen demanded, taking a step toward Danika.

"Yeah. He kind of gave me the creeps," Danika said.

"What did he look like?"

"About so tall," Danika held her hand up, "Thin blonde hair. He was really nice, barely left her side, and was always right there, taking care of her. She was pretty shattered."

Owen knew the feeling as he looked at Scott, feeling helpless. Scott thanked the nurse and escorted Owen back out of the hospital.

"I don't know what to do," Owen said.

"I have somebody I can call," Scott said, drawing his phone out of his pocket.

"Hey Barrett, sorry it's late," Scott said, cutting his eyes to Owen for a moment. "I need your help. We're over in Franklin and I need help finding somebody, I figured your friend may be able to help us. I wouldn't ask, but it's Owen's mate."

Owen's phone rang and he answered without looking at the name. "Hello?"

"Owen, how's it going?" The chief's voice was tense.

Owen explained how Caitlin had left the hospital with Axel, who had told everyone he was Owen.

"Come back and we'll handle this as a pack," Jason ordered.

"Respectfully, no."

"You're a newly imprinted male with a pregnant missing mate, you're injured and you're not thinking clearly. You and Scott will both need to sleep. Get your asses back here, I expect to see you at the community center when you get into town. That's all, Kessler."

"She's not pregnant anymore," Owen said, swallowing as his grief threatened to consume him. "Jamie... the baby didn't make it."

Jason was silent for several beats, his breath the only sign he was still on the call.

"Come home."

"Yes, chief," Owen said, then hung up, closing his eyes as he fought back tears he didn't have time to shed.

Scott was also ending his phone call.

"I've got somebody working on finding Axel, he's got some guys who are going to help."

"Chief ordered us back to Pinehurst," Owen informed him.

Scott wrinkled his nose, but nodded.

"Barrett will let us know when he has an update," Scott assured.

Barrett was good people, one of their friends from school who had grown up in Pinehurst. Barrett wouldn't let Owen down.

Owen nodded numbly. The pain meds were wearing off, he wished they weren't. The medication made his head fuzzy enough that he couldn't feel so much of the grief threatening to drag him under.

Caitlin. Finley whined through their mental link. *The baby.*

We'll get her back, buddy. Owen reassured woodenly as Scott helped him into the car.

CHAPTER FORTY-FIVE

CAITLIN

She was hazy from the pain meds. All she wanted was the oblivion of sleep where she could forget all of this. Her body sank deeper and deeper into the haze until Axel climbed into the bed behind her.

His warmth seeped into the bed, but instead of feeling comforted she just felt sick, despite the cold. She wondered if he'd left the house cold on purpose so she would want to be near him.

"Remember back when we just heated the house with the wood stove because we were so broke?" He asked in the darkness.

Caitlin closed her eyes, hoping he would believe she was asleep. That hadn't been how it happened. They'd had plenty of money, but he hadn't wanted her to spend it on 'frivolities,' so she'd walked around wearing three pairs of socks and thermals under her clothes, but she could never get warm. When he'd mocked her for it and tried to accuse her of being unattractive on purpose to avoid sex, she'd told him it was his fault for keeping the house so cold and he'd 'accidentally' pushed her down the porch steps.

After that he picked out her outfits and insisted on keeping her physically close to him for warmth, telling her how much money they'd save on the heat this way, and maybe they could use it for a vacation somewhere warm and sunny.

"Remember how we used to cuddle together?" He scooted behind her on the bed.

Despite how much it repulsed her, she didn't move away, terrified of angering him or injuring herself further. Every move made her incision hurt and sent panic-inducing pain through her lower abdominal muscles. She shivered under the thin blanket.

"Aw, come here kitten." With alarm, she felt his erection pressed into her chilly flesh and it occurred to her that there were worse things than setting off his temper.

"Axel, we said we were going to wait," she tried not to sound panicked or afraid, desperate not to activate any instincts he had to subdue or terrify her further.

Her fear drove him crazy, made him do things to push her harder, and she wanted none of that. Then again, she wondered if she'd die if they had sex. She was in a lot of pain, surely that was a sign of something wrong. Maybe she'd moved too much and she was bleeding internally. The thought of dying wasn't unappealing, anything would be better than this, and it would make the pain stop.

"I know, baby, but you're so fucking beautiful and you smell so good." He moved so his hot skin was pressed closer against her back and she felt bile rise in her throat.

"The doctor said," she reminded him, her voice sounding oddly removed to her own ears.

"I know, we won't do it there." His hand moved between them, his fingers going between her cheeks.

"Axel," she pleaded.

"I need this, Kitty Cat," he said urgently, turning from her to reach for the nightstand. "It's been months. Months since you left. You know how many times I had to go out and find some whore to fuck because you left me with nothing?"

There was an anger to him, an undercurrent of violence she recognized all too well. She had a choice. She could fight him and lose or she could let him do it, make it not as bad for herself. She always lost, and besides, no one was coming for her, no one would know where she was. Owen was dead and gods only knew how long it would take Charlotte to notice she was missing. Tyler would have been the first one to notice Owen wasn't texting, and he was gone too.

"Axel, please, I want you," she whispered, barely able to push the words out through her nausea.

"Say it again," he growled, gripping her hips to him as he ground his erection into her.

"I want you in my mouth," she choked on the lie but prayed it would be enough as she closed her eyes, tears streaming down her cheeks.

He gave a contented rumble and urgently moved against her, inhaling the smell of her hair deeply as she forced herself to breathe through her mouth so she wouldn't smell him. Her abdominal muscles screamed in protest as she tensed at the mere idea of him violating her but she could take it easier in her mouth than in other places.

"Aw baby, soon, soon I'll fuck your mouth. But now, I need to be between your legs, to feel you under me."

Her body was slow to respond, but she heard the quiet of something and the sound of lubricant sliding over flesh, his half-groaning sigh as he stroked himself. The squelching sound that continued as he repeated the motion was making her sick. He used one finger to part her folds, sliding up to her other hole.

"Axel, please," one last try, one last final prayer to whatever god was listening that something, anything would save her from this moment, or that it would kill her and be her last so she didn't have to exist in this hell.

"It's either this, or I hurt you for letting another man inside of you, Kitty Cat." She unclenched and let him slide a finger inside of her.

His noise of appreciation made her sick. When he eased another finger inside of her, she shifted.

"That's right, Kitty Cat. It feels good, doesn't it?"

She didn't make a noise, but he didn't need her to.

"Don't worry, Kitty Cat. I know how you like it." He withdrew his fingers.

His tip was pressed at her other hole for a moment before the bedroom door burst open and Axel's weight was knocked off her as something hit him with a loud crack. His body flew sideways, taking her blanket with him and exposing her to the cold air.

Caitlin was frozen. Someone draped something over her. There was shouting and scuffling, but the bedroom was dark so even when Caitlin looked to the side all she could make out were the shapes of bodies moving, two men possibly, and the glint of handcuffs in the dim light of the bedroom.

Were they arresting him? Had someone read him his rights? Was something wrong with her hearing? No one was speaking to Axel once they got the cuffs on him.

"Caitlin Montgomery?"

One of the men dragged Axel away. They must have secured his feet together because whoever they were literally dragged him by... something. A rope, maybe? She lay still, too stunned to move.

"It's Caitlin, right?" The same voice asked.

"Yes?"

"I'm Alec, that was my associate Barrett. We're going to take you home to Owen."

"Owen's dead."

"No ma'am. Owen's alive. He's been looking for you, but we were closer. Have you taken something, medicine, anything?"

"Owen's alive?" Caitlin repeated dumbly, Alec confirmed with a nod.

"Owen's alive," he repeated for her benefit. "I'm going to cast a mage light so I can check to see what we're working with, alright?" He asked calmly.

Caitlin nodded and a green sphere appeared and then grew in the man's palm until it was the size of a bowling ball. He tossed lightly and the sphere hovered in the air. He walked over to the side of the bed and stopped a few feet away.

"Are you hurt?"

"Um," she thought about her stitches, the pain all over her body, and struggled for an answer.

"I know about your accident and the stitches. Do you need medical attention? We can meet Owen at the hospital, or take you back to Pinehurst."

"I want Owen. No hospital." They might sedate her at a hospital, and she couldn't let that happen. The only thing she wanted, the only thing that it was possible for her to have, was Owen. Nothing could bring back her baby and her dog.

"Okay. We should get you up and dressed."

"I don't think I can."

"I can help, if you like." He offered, but Caitlin pulled the blanket they'd draped over her close around her, eying him warily. "Trust me, ma'am, I'm not looking at you like that, but if you're willing I'd like to look at your incision before you're all dressed."

When she nodded he ducked out of the room and came back with a duffel bag, which he set on the bed and unzipped.

"These should fit, they're meant to slide up over the incision," he said, opening a pack of black high-waisted underwear.

"Your core muscles need to rest, so let me lift you, alright? Put your arms around me and I'll help you sit up," he directed.

She let him move her like a lifeless doll. She heard the other man out in the living room, but he didn't appear in the doorway. She tensed and cried out when the movement sent pain searing through her abdomen.

"He won't come in unless he's asked," Alec said without looking up once she was sitting up, her weight resting heavily on her arms.

Alec reached over and pulled a pack of pads out of the duffel, opening one and arranging it in the crotch of the underwear before kneeling down to slip her feet in the leg holes. Her cheeks burned with embarrassment, but Alec made no comment as he proceeded to help her get them on her body before lowering to the bed. If the pain hadn't been so intense, she would have wondered more about who this man was, how he knew her clothing size, and how he'd found her.

"Would you like a bra?" He asked, pulling a comfortable sports bra out of the duffel.

"No, thank you."

"Alright, it's chilly, but I thought this might be comfortable and not restrictive." He pulled out a gray tunic dress made of a soft jersey knit. The fabric reminded her of the dress she'd worn the first time Owen and Tyler had shared her. Grief and guilt clogged her throat, making it hard to breathe.

"Caitlin?" Alec asked.

"I'm fine," she assured, clearing her throat.

He helped her dress, then helped her to the bathroom before he insisted on carrying her out to the car that waited by the side steps.

"I'm sorry, I'm trying to be gentle with you," he said as he lowered her to the ground and she cried out, clutching his shirt in a white-knuckled grip.

"No, it's not you, it's just movement in general," she said with an attempt at a laugh.

"You don't need to do that," Alec said quietly.

When she looked at him in confusion, he clarified.

"You don't need to fake being alright. You have every reason to not be alright." He leaned over her to buckle her in, then pulled a blanket from the seat next to her. Grasping the corners, he unfurled it with a sharp flick of his wrists then draped it back over her lap against the chill.

"Caitlin," he said her name in a familiar way that made her feel like she'd known him all her life, "I have some magic abilities. You've had a traumatic experience. If you like, I can help your mind rest until you get to Owen. You'll be safe."

"Axel gave me painkillers," she said with a frown..

"I understand. Take these-" he drew out a medicine bottle of pills, explaining as he poured a few into his palm, "They're charge capsules."

"That's safe for the baby?" she asked automatically, then she remembered: Jamie was gone, there was no baby. Now that she wasn't scared, there was room for the loss to swell, choking out everything else.

"Caitlin?"

"Never mind, uh, yes please." Whatever it was, she would take it.

"You don't need to apologize to anyone," Alec said sincerely. "You're familiar with Miss Rhodes and her magic?"

"Who?"

"Emma, Ryder's mate?"

"Oh, yeah."

"This will work like her magic, but stronger. Take the bottle with you, these will make you feel numb, just for a bit. Taking more than one will not increase the effects, but it won't hurt you either." He looked at her for a moment and she saw something in his eyes, something foreign like when Finley was looking out of Owen's eyes, their usual blue turned to dark brown. Alec's eyes didn't change color though and she felt like he saw *her*. Not her physical body, but that he saw into her mind, to the depths of her pain as she drowned in the ocean of mingled grief and shock.

She dropped her eyes, unwilling to face the depths of her grief, let alone share it with this stranger. She looked at the bottle and contemplated: how many would it take to make it all end?

"Taking more won't make all of your pain end," he informed her in a conversational tone, the look he leveled on her said he knew what she'd been thinking.

"Thank you."

"Is there anything you need from inside?"

"No." She didn't want anything from that house, it could burn to the ground and she wouldn't have been sad at all.

Soon she would be home, safe with Owen. Their friends would have gotten to the fire in time. Of course, they would need to repair the damage in their bedroom, but they would be fine. Everything would be fine. She could curl up with Toten and- her mind conjured up the last time she'd seen him, her happy sweet dog, tail wagging just before Axel- no. She couldn't relive that, not now. Toten was gone too.

She didn't know what she would do once she was back home, but she could figure that out. One thing at a time, right now she was going home to Owen. Owen wasn't gone.

"Hey. I've got Caitlin, we're on the way to you. Yes, he's in the back," Alec was saying into his cell phone from the passenger seat.

Caitlin looked around her. She was in the backseat and no one was back here with her. Then it dawned on her: the trunk. They'd put Axel in the trunk, like a kidnapping victim.

"Sure thing," Alec said, handing the phone back to Caitlin.

"Owen?"

"No, sorry, this is Ryder. Finley's in charge for the moment, I'm putting you on speaker, okay?" There was a brief pause, and then Ryder's voice came from further away, "Alright, he can hear you."

"Hey, boy," she said, her eyes tearing.

She heard a happy yip and she let out a breath.

"Hey, I'm coming to you, I'm - I'm coming home, okay?" she said, her voice catching.

Finley whined and she started to cry and Ryder cursed, the phone clattering to the ground.

"If you knock it out of my hand, I can't hold it for you to talk to her," Ryder said impatiently.

"Finley, I'm coming home, alright? I'll be home in a little while. I'm-" She started to say that she was safe, but that word no longer held any meaning for her.

Perhaps safety was an illusion, maybe it had never been real, just an idea that people like therapists traded on to make their mortgage payments. In any case, she wasn't ever going to say that she was safe.

"I'm coming home."

She handed the phone back to Alec and he spoke to Ryder, gave them their approximate time of arrival, then said he would share his location with him so everyone would know where they were easily.

CAITLIN LAID down in the back seat, the effort of sitting up too much of a strain on her muscles, but before she could fall asleep she raised her head. Alec looked back over his left shoulder as if he sensed her wanting to ask something.

"Yes?"

"Are you cops?" she asked a little uneasily, "How did you know where to find me?"

"I know Owen, and Barrett knows me," Alec explained.

"You had handcuffs." Caitlin pointed out.

"We wanted to make sure he couldn't hurt you, or anyone else anymore," Alec explained.

"Also, he's a dick," Barrett growled out from the driver's seat.

"How did you find me?" She persisted.

"Magic, and the help of a few cops. You should get some rest. It's a bit of a drive."

Caitlin laid down, sure she wouldn't be relaxed enough to rest, but she took one of the pills Alec had given in the unmarked prescription bottle and soon her mind was quiet. Her emotions were flat, her thoughts emotionless and safe.

"You won't have any dreams," Alec assured her, his eyes soft with compassion, "Sleep."

CHAPTER FORTY-SIX

OWEN

*A*s soon as they'd arrived back in Pinehurst, Finley had asserted himself, barely waiting for Owen to strip before he phased. Not even hearing Caitlin's voice could make him take up their human form. He snarled and snapped whenever anyone approached him until the chief threatened to put him on a tether like an untrained puppy.

"Unfuck yourself, Finley, or I'll unfuck you. I've got a puppy tether in the other room if you don't know how to behave," their Alpha said irritably when Finley snarled at no one in particular from a corner of the chief's kitchen unprovoked.

When Alec had called to let them know they were not too far out from Station Four, the Alpha had ordered Finley to give Owen control again, setting some clothes on the kitchen table.

"Take my truck, go to Station Four, I'll follow shortly."

Finley ceded control with a great deal of reluctance. Owen didn't have to be told twice, dressing in a hurry and heading down to the little outpost beyond the northeast boundaries of town. A nondescript black sedan was parked in the parking lot, and his friend Barrett leaned against the trunk smoking a cigarette. When Owen got out of the truck, Barrett pointed to the passenger side of the car.

"Back seat," Barrett said, making no effort at the small talk Owen didn't care two shits about. All he wanted was his mate.

"Cupcake," Owen said, opening the door of the car.

"Owen, you're hurt!"

He wanted to laugh. He could smell the blood from her incision and the possible beginnings of an infection, and saw the high color of her cheeks where she had a fever starting, she'd lost their baby, and gods only knew what other emotional damage she'd had inflicted on her the last few days, and she was worried about him.

"Psh, I'm fine," he said, looking her over as he crouched down. "You should have seen me at the hospital. Come on, I need you safe inside."

"She's on painkillers and a flat emotional charge. You should probably carry her in," Barrett suggested from behind the open car door.

Owen reached in, unbuckled her like a child, scooped her up without a word, and carried her inside the station, her cries of pain piercing his soul. He carried her straight into the small dorm room with two bunk beds. Someone, probably Reese, the ranger who was often stationed here, had made up the bed with fresh sheets and pillows.

"Did he hurt you, Cupcake?" Owen asked, pausing before he put her down.

"I'm not talking about it."

He shifted his weight, waiting for her to answer.

"I need you to tell me exactly what he did to you. We don't ever have to talk about it again, but I need to know." He needed to know so he could give the man exactly the kind of justice he deserved, which is what he should have done when he found out Caitlin was pregnant, or when Owen learned that she'd been with a rapist.

"He used his fingers," she closed her eyes.

He only had a moment's warning before she started to heave. Owen reached for the trash can he'd placed next to the couch and held her hair back while she retched.

"After you just lost-" he broke off, biting his cheek.

"Not - there. He wanted to, but the doctor said we would have to wait so he was going to in the... other place."

"Oh, Caitlin," he tried to hug her but she winced.

"Please, don't hug me. I just don't want- I need a shower. I need to wash off."

He wanted to tell her that she shouldn't be standing, but he couldn't tell her that she couldn't shower off the evidence of what that man had done to her. He got her into the basic shower where he washed her body with excessive care. She was pale, exhausted and her incision looked terrible.

"I think I need an antibiotic. He made me take a bath, but I'm pretty sure I wasn't supposed to. There was a bath bomb." She recounted, looking up at his face, "You always say patients lie, or they don't tell you things. I don't know if that matters."

"That's perfect. Do you hurt anywhere else?"

"Just where they cut out Jamie." She said, her voice flat as her eyes glazed.

Pain worse than the gunshot sliced through him hearing her talk about their baby. Once she was clean she insisted on getting dressed before being laid down on the bunk bed.

"I'm going to leave, just for a bit. I need to take care of something, then I'll be back. I'll leave somebody here, just outside."

"Then you'll come back?"

"Yes."

"Promise me you won't put yourself at risk," she said, gripping his pant leg.

"I promise."

"Swear it. Swear you're coming back."

"I swear I won't put my life in danger. I'll come home to you safe and sound, and we'll- be together." Owen leaned down and kissed her forehead. "I'll be back."

"Owen?"

"Yeah, baby?"

"Are you going to kill him?"

Owen took a deep breath.

"Yes."

"Make it hurt," she whispered.

WHEN OWEN EMERGED, Scott was in dark civilian clothes, extending his hand to Barrett, standing close to the sedan. A stranger stood at the corner of Base 4, presumably the man who had helped Barrett track down Axel. Owen couldn't be bothered to care, focusing on the one thing he could do for Caitlin.

"Thank you," Scott shook Barrett's hand. "I owe you."

"No you don't. Just because I don't live here anymore doesn't mean I'm not one of you. He's undamaged like you asked." Barrett shook his head, then added with a dark grin, "Well, mostly."

Owen came out of Station 4, pausing for a moment outside the door to close his eyes, running his finger through unkempt hair.

"How's your girl?" Barrett asked.

"She'll be better when this," he gestured to the trunk, "is taken care of."

"Want me to stay? I can stay out here. If I could shift with you, I'd help, but seeing as I can't-" Barrett shrugged. "I can keep her safe."

"Thanks. Yeah."

A white pickup pulled up. The chief got out of the cab. Calen, John, Blake, and Arion piled out of the truck looking grim and determined, if a bit haggard.

"Chief," Barrett said cautiously.

"What are we waiting for?"

"You, Alpha," Owen said tightly.

"Caitlin is your mate. I'll defer to your judgment," Jason said. "I'm just here to see justice is done."

Owen nodded and popped the trunk. The man's shouts muffled by a layer of duct tape echoed into the night.

"Get him up," Owen said.

Strong arms lifted Axel to his feet. Owen pulled a medical auto-injector with a neatly typed label reading PANIC CHARGE in bold letters, and handed it to John, tilting his head toward Axel. John looked at the label, eyebrows widening, but jabbed it into Axel's thigh and depressed the button. Owen came forward, reaching down out of habit for trauma shears that weren't there.

"What was that?" Calen asked, peeking over at the device in John's hand.

"It works like an EpiPen, but instead of injecting medication, it puts the charge directly into the bloodstream. They usually use them in the military, so a medic can help a guy even if he isn't a mage. They're more effective than sedatives and work faster. I've never seen one that wasn't for calming."

"Nice," Calen said.

"I want him to feel what Caitlin felt," Owen explained quietly, Calen and John sobered as the trunk popped open and revealed Axel, dried blood covering his face from a broken nose.

"Here," Barrett said, handing him a knife.

Owen walked around to the man's back, carelessly cutting away the man's clothes, inflicting several deep slices into his skin as he worked. Barrett handed Owen the keys so he could unlock the cuffs.

"She'll never be yours," Axel snarled, lunging for Owen.

Without hesitation, Barrett pulled the pistol off his belt and shot Axel in the side. Everyone there turned to stare at him, Barrett reholstered his weapon and watched Axel dispassionately as he writhed on the ground while Owen began to strip, as did the other bystanders.

"I suggest you start running. You won't be able to phase, but I'll give you a fair head start," Owen spoke in measured tones.

"What are you talking about?" Axel snarled, looking around the group of men. "You can't take me in human form, pussy boy. You can't keep her safe, you couldn't even leave her with someone smart enough to lock the back door when you knew I was around. That stupid fucker was asleep on the couch when I came in. He didn't even move until I slit his-" Barrett barreled forward, a knife held in one hand as he jabbed hard into Axel's abdomen.

When Axel fell to the ground, Owen resumed undressing.

"You have until I'm undressed. I suggest you make use of the time," Owen suggested evenly as he slipped out of his work boots.

"Oh, why's that?" Axel sneered.

"I'm going to make sure that you leave this world how you came into it - screaming and covered in blood," Owen informed him dispassionately.

Everyone else continued to strip out of their clothes, except Barrett, who was wiping the knife on his jeans. Owen raised an eyebrow.

"Tyler was a friend of mine," he explained. "And I don't take kindly to men who hurt females."

Axel made his way clumsily to his feet, standing well clear of Barrett's reach as he cradled the spot below his ribs where he now bled freely.

"Trails are that way," Barrett said with a feral grin and a tilt of his head. "I'd get going, these fuckers are fast and they mean business."

Axel staggered away, stumbling as he made his way up the trail. When the other men were stripped, watching the naked bleeding figure.

"I hope he goes up 156," John said as they watched him, "There's a great overlook he might fall off."

"Nobody touches his face. Everything else is fair game." Owen said as he stripped out of his sweats.

"Why not his face?" John asked.

"I need Caitlin to be able to recognize him when we bring him back," Owen said quietly.

"Son, I don't think that's a good idea," Jason began, "She's had enough trauma-"

"She'll never believe he's gone unless she sees it for herself. She spent *months* with me and Olivia and everyone else telling her she was safe. She had this stupid mantra that she said all the fucking time about how she was safe, how she was with me, then *he* happened to her all over again. Now she's-" Owen broke off, his body vibrating with rage. "If you have a problem with me proving that her abuser can't ever hurt her again then stay behind."

Owen phased and howled, then turned to the Alpha for a moment. Jason nodded, then looked around at his men.

"You heard the man. Let's go run down an animal."

CHAPTER FORTY-SEVEN

CAITLIN

"ey Caitlin! How are you?" A friendly matron asked from the sidewalk in front of the justice center.

Caitlin smiled politely and gestured to the headphones she wore constantly now, even though she never listened to anything. She couldn't remember the last time she'd even charged them. She just wanted to bake. Why couldn't everyone leave her alone and let her bake in peace? Did they think asking her if she was okay would help her miss her baby less?

The sheriff's office was quiet, so she set up a beautiful display on the break room counter that took up six plates, enough scones for an army, or a single shift of hungry men.

She headed over to the EMS base next, where things were not as peaceful. Jason greeted her at the door with a sympathetic smile.

"Morning, Miss Caitlin," he said.

"Morning, chief! I have scones."

"Aw, thanks. How are you holding up?" he asked softly.

"I'll just set these up in the day room," she said with a politely efficient move past him.

Walking away, she set up a similar display to the one in the Sheriff's office with double the number of scones. Patrick Lawson came in, saw her and nodded. Taking a look over the massive display of scones, he seemed to be gathering his thoughts. She was going to chuck a plate of scones at his head if he asked her if she was okay.

"What flavors do we get today?" He asked.

Removing her earbuds, she placed them in her case and responded cautiously, not wanting to discuss anything other than the scones.

"Lime pomegranate, orange vanilla, lemon blueberry, and plain old chocolate chip for the traditionalists." She pointed out each flavor.

He grabbed one, biting into it and chewing thoughtfully, like a sommelier sampling wine.

"How is it?" she asked anxiously.

"It's not your best," he admitted, giving the scone a critical eye then amended with a grin. "Don't get me wrong, I'd eat myself sick on them. But they need some granulated sugar on top or some icing."

"I thought that, not sweet enough, but I've tasted so many that I wasn't sure if it was just me." She said, relieved he wasn't going to try to talk about anything emotional.

"Yeah. They're good. So, scones, huh?" He said, giving her a neutral look.

Since the accident, she'd gotten close to Patrick, mostly because he didn't press her to talk. Everyone else was always asking *how she was,* and she just didn't have an answer to that. Even if she did have a good answer for it, which she didn't, she didn't feel like anyone was ready to hear about the depth of her grief.

"Next week I'm going to work on perfecting my bagel technique. I can't quite figure out how to make them look right on the bottom."

One of the part-time medics walked in, asking "What does it matter what they look like on the bottom if they taste good?"

"It matters," Caitlin and Patrick said in unison in all seriousness.

"Can't see why," the medic said with a shrug as he devoured one of the chocolate chip scones.

"Any half-decent baker can find a recipe online and make something that tastes good. It's art when it looks good *and* tastes like heaven," Caitlin explained.

Another part-timer came in, making small talk over showing off the latest pictures of his newborn on his phone. He showed Patrick, who said the baby was lucky it didn't get its looks from its daddy. The medic grinned, holding his phone up to show Caitlin.

Grief slashed through her, restricting her throat and bringing tears to Caitlin's eyes. A perfect baby boy swaddled in a receiving blanket in his mother's arms.

"Beautiful. Just perfect," Caitlin whispered and the young medic moved on, completely oblivious.

Patrick took another scone, biting into it quietly as Caitlin brushed away two tears that refused to stay unshed.

"These are better. The lime is really strong, I like it."

"It's not too much?" She asked, clearing her throat.

"No. It's delicious." He chewed for a long moment, then said in an offhand, casual way, "What kind of bagels are you baking next week?"

She gave him a grateful smile, then launched into the descriptions of the flavors she was considering. By the time she left the base, she felt a bit better. The hole felt smaller, maybe today she could make it through.

CHAPTER FORTY-EIGHT

OWEN

"Owen," the chief greeted.

"Chief," Owen said, tucking his fingers in his belt.

"I noticed Caitlin's been baking a lot," the chief said.

"Yup," Owen acknowledged.

"How's she holding up, really?" the older man asked.

Owen took a deep breath, his eyes raising to his Alpha's, his tongue working in his cheek.

"I don't know how to answer that question. She won't go to therapy. She bakes, fills orders, oversees the construction of the new house, she functions, and that's about it. She goes through the motions like a robot and I don't know how to do anything besides love her through it."

"Have you thought about having more children?" The chief asked.

"Yeah, but not any time soon. She's still healing. The doctor said it would be a minimum of six months before we could consider it, but even then... nothing would replace Jamie. I don't know that she wants to be pregnant again, and I can't blame her. But yeah," Owen shuffled his feet. "Yeah, I wish we could. I don't see it happening."

"Well, it could, if you wanted. Right now."

"How's that now?" Owen asked.

"There's a baby in the nursery right now, we transported him and the momma last night. The momma didn't make it, and the dad isn't in the picture. His momma was part of the pack, so it's our job to make sure he goes to a family who will love him."

"You're offering me a baby," Owen said, his heart rate increasing.

"I'm offering you and your mate a baby. I know it's a decision you and her will need to make together, but I wanted to talk to you first. I know you're broken and I'm not saying you aren't grieving, but it's different for them, when a female loses a baby like that. I don't think you or I could really understand what it's like to lose something that was only ever a part of us unless we lost our wolves."

"Yeah," Owen agreed, hedging.

"What's your question, son?" The chief asked.

"I know in a perfect world it wouldn't matter, and I wish I could say it didn't, but is he healthy? I know being healthy isn't a guarantee that nothing will happen, but I don't want to bring home a baby just to lose it," Owen asked half-apologetically.

"He's healthy as can be. APGAR scores were perfect, all his tests come back normal, and he pees on the nurse in there every time she changes his diaper. He's going to be ready to go home anytime."

"Alright, let me talk to Caitlin."

CHAPTER FORTY-NINE

CAITLIN

The waiting room in the hospital spun. Caitlin dropped into the chair behind her.

"A baby?" She repeated.

"He doesn't have a name yet, but he's ours if we want him."

"We don't have the things for a baby," she replied, her mind going a million miles an hour.

They could have a baby. Nothing would replace Jamie, of course, but it felt like once she'd made room in her life for a child, it was impossible to fill that space with anything else.

"The chief put Miss Linda on it, we'll have everything we need by the time we get home."

"What happened to his parents?"

"His mom was in a car accident. She and his daddy were both shifters, so although there's no guarantee, he will most likely be one too depending on their genetics. We'll get him tested so we can be prepared."

"They're both... gone?"

"Yeah," Owen said, waiting for her to process.

"Do you want him?" She asked, raising her eyes to his.

"I do, but only if you do. I was thinking, I could take leave from

305

work and come home with you two, help you settle in. That way you can still bake all you want to," he stopped speaking when she looked horrified.

"Owen, I love you, but you can't stand being out of work for more than three days in a row," she laughed for the first time since they lost Jamie, her eyes sparkling. "Thank you for the thought, but no, we'll be just fine. When do we get to meet him?"

"Right now, if you want to," Owen said, standing and offering her his hand.

"We've been calling him Ethan," the nurse explained, "It just seemed to fit."

"Hi, Ethan," Caitlin whispered, brushing her fingers against the back of his hand, watching with joy as they splayed out. She cradled the little one to her chest.

"What was his momma's name?" She asked.

"Hannah," the nurse supplied.

"Owen, take the baby," she said, standing and handing the little bundle carefully to her mate.

She wasn't familiar with the hospital, so she asked a helpful nurse who pointed her in the direction of the hospital's chapel. Caitlin walked there, rehearsing what she would say.

Thankfully, she was alone in the room. She'd never been religious or superstitious, but she lit two candles: one for Hannah, and another for Jamie. On an impulse she lit another for Toten. Maybe it wasn't the custom to light a candle for a dog, but she'd loved him, and she hoped if there was an afterlife for dogs that he was running free somewhere happy.

She knelt on the prayer bench in the front of the room and folded her hands.

"I don't know if you can hear me, or if you're even there," Caitlin closed her eyes, "but my name is Caitlin. I was thinking we could maybe trade for a while. See, my baby Jamie is up there, and I didn't get a chance to love him before he was gone and since your baby is here…I figured maybe I could love him while he's down here and you could love on my boy. I know I'm not you, but I promise to be the best momma I can be for him."

Silence filled the little chapel, but it was a full, loving silence. For the first time since the loss, she felt at peace. It wasn't that little Ethan would replace her boy, but she could love him in service of another mother, and that way both her and the baby could have a chance to get back some of the love they'd missed out on.

"Okay. Thank you. Also, if you're a dog person, maybe you could give my dog a good hug for me too."

Caitlin came back to the waiting room tear-stained and radiant. Something had changed, he didn't know what, but when she reached for the baby and took him with a gentle kiss on the forehead, she looked from Owen to the nurse and asked one question.

"So, when can we take our boy home?"

AFTERWORD

Dearest reader,

Thank you for joining me for Caitlin and Owen's story.

If it pleases you to see this as purely a work of fiction, I hope you found it entertaining.

However if you, like me, relate a little too well with Caitlin and some of the things that happened to her, I wanted to take the time to pull you into a hug, give you a cup of tea and share a little glimpse of my story.

There are too many things I could share to begin to unravel it all here, so I'll just say this: I know what it's like when safety feels like an illusion. I know what it is to give in to a partner because your 'no' won't be enough. I know what it's like to stay until, finally, he hits you and *then* you realize that maybe, just maybe, you're being abused.

I know what it's like to convince yourself that you're safe after trauma, only to have that sacred place violated by a partner who gaslights you and tries to place the blame on you for their actions.

I don't know your story, but I know about those things intimately.

I don't have Alec or Emma's charge magic to make the feelings go away for a while, but please know that you're not the only one walking down the road of healing and recovery. I can't shoulder your pain, but I am walking here too.

Neither one of us is alone.

A fellow survivor,

Christina Mattingly

ACKNOWLEDGMENTS

To that ex who made my art better. If you hadn't made my life a living hell, I wouldn't have been able to write this book.

To Jessica, who helped me see that I was worth standing up for.

To Kea, who moved in and rescued me from my Axel.

To the boys at the Brazilian jiu jitsu gym who grappled with me and helped me overcome the trauma responses left over from my marriage. You all changed my life in so many ways. The way you brought me into the tribe and adopted me, helped me, supported me when I cried and then didn't think less of me when I had panic attacks on the mats. You helped me relearn how strong and capable I am. Thank you for helping me find myself again.

www.ingramcontent.com/pod-product-compliance
Lightning Source LLC
Chambersburg PA
CBHW070917260626
47162CB00007B/2700